RESTLESS
WATERS

JESSICA PARK

MUSIC AND LYRICS BY TROY

OTHER BOOKS BY JESSICA PARK

Flat-Out Love
Flat-Out Matt
Flat-Out Celeste

Left Drowning

Clear

For Troy,
who beautifully and selflessly pours his soul into his music.
It takes bravery to dig deep and share raw emotions,
and he does that with incredible spirit, unfailing determination,
and a voice that will touch even the darkest of hearts.

NOTE FROM THE AUTHOR

THIS BOOK WOULD NOT HAVE COME ABOUT WERE IT NOT FOR THE ferocious loyalty of my readers, many of who have written to share their own stories and experiences after reading *Left Drowning*. The truths you shared, the excruciating realities of life, the strength that it took you to survive…I was left at a loss for how to respond in any way that felt to be enough. So, now, there is this book, in whatever testimonial it is to your survival.

A month after *Left Drowning*'s publication, I started an outline for a second book. I soon realized though that it was too soon to start a second book. I wasn't ready. It takes a certain emotional headspace to be willing to delve into some of this material, and I had to wait for the right time.

I also had fears about following up that story because I knew I couldn't repeat what I had already written. I couldn't write *Left Drowning* again, right? I would need to do something different. So, I refocused. *Restless Waters* is less expansive and narrower in its story, and it was a pleasure to have the chance to hone in on the dynamic between Blythe, Chris, and Sabin.

Troy was gracious enough to let me lift lines from his songs to open every chapter. He writes lyrics in much the same manner that I write books. He writes to explore what it means to experience life and all that comes from feeling everything as powerfully as we can. He experiences, he broods, he intellectualizes, and then he explodes with emotion. In many ways, listening to his music empowered me to continue on with these characters, and I will be forever grateful to him for that.

As Sabin points out, trauma is the gift that keeps on giving. The start of healing that we saw in *Left Drowning* was indeed only the beginning. The characters you followed faced real-world challenges, and no one is done. There are flashbacks, repercussions, endless effects that will haunt. There is, however, survival. And there is bliss.

Recovery is a process, a long one, and I send out love and support to all who are struggling and fighting for survival.

I fight for you. I hope for you. I believe in you.

1
THE SCARS ARE MANY

**I PUT ON A FACE,
FACE IT TILL THE END.
I CANNOT CONTINUE TO PRETEND.
THIS LIFE AIN'T ME.
OH NO, THIS AIN'T LIKE ME.
I DON'T KNOW WHAT WE'RE MOVING TOWARD.**

I KICK MY FEET IN THE COLD OCEAN WATER AND OPEN MY EYES FOR a fraction of a second before the sunlight blinds me, and I shut them again. The glare is still strong and heating my skin, deepening the tan that has built from my hours outside. The dock presses against my back, but the wood is smooth and soft from age, so I meld into it. My hand moves over the slats, and I trace the familiar texture. I will never tire of this dock. So much has happened here, been revealed here.

Pain and truth, yes, but it's also a place where friendship and love have been solidified.

Maine has become my place of healing and stability.

A breeze rushes across my body, and I inhale deeply, taking in the strong salty air. Late August here on Frenchman Bay in Bar Harbor, Maine, has brought ideal weather with sunny days tinged by a crispness that tells me fall will be here soon.

I kick the water harder. For a moment, a sense of melancholy washes over me. Fall means that Chris's brother Eric and their sister, Estelle, will return to Matthews College for their senior year, and my brother, James, will go back to Colorado for his. The twins should have graduated last spring, but both changed majors and had to register for additional required courses. I hate that they're leaving soon because this summer has been a dream. The Shepherd siblings, my brother, and I have been under one roof, all safe, all finding peace.

So, I brush my brief sadness away. I really can't complain about anything.

My calm reflections on peace, however, are short-lived when I am suddenly doused in icy water.

"Sabin!" I scream, throwing my hands in front of my face way too late to stop the deluge of water that soaks me. When I wipe my eyes enough to see, I sit and look up. "You're a prick!"

But I can't help laughing, even while shivering from the shock of the chill. Also, the swim trunks he's wearing are covered in sock-monkey prints, and that does nothing to lessen my laughter.

"You're a prick!" I scream again.

"But you love me anyway." Setting down a large plastic bucket, Sabin smiles broadly with a bit more pride at his stealthy attack than I'd like to see.

I do my best to glare at him.

"Say you love me anyway!" he demands. "Say it!"

I stick out my tongue and reach for my nearby towel.

Sabin gets to it before I do and holds it above his head. "Lady Blythe McGuire," he says all too seriously, "I suggest you say that you love me anyway, or this towel is going to sleep with the fishes!" He waves it around in the air. "Like a tragic victim of a mafioso vendetta!"

I stand and start to jump up and down in a desperate attempt to grab it, but I'm no match for Sabin's height or his incessant giggling. "Fine. I give up. I cave! I'll say it! I love you anyway."

He cups a hand to his ear. "I'm sorry. What? Once more—with feeling."

"Sabin! I'm freezing!" I say, laughing. "I love you anyway! Sincerely! With as much feeling as a very cold person can muster!"

"Victory!" he hollers, lowering the towel.

I go to take hold of it, but he lands it on my head, covering my face, and then he wraps a big arm around me so that I can't move. I feel him furiously rubbing the top of my head while I giggle and try to squirm free.

"I'm going to kill you," I mutter through my laughter.

"You poor thing," he says. "Sopping wet! Bitterly cold! Your moment of sunny solitude interrupted so callously! Who would do such a thing? Let's dry you off."

He starts rubbing the towel over my face and then drops it to my back so that I'm pinned between it and him as he wildly yanks it back and forth, spinning me from side to side. These days, he's much too strong for me to even think about getting free, so I accept that I'm basically putty in his hands until he's had his fill of goofiness.

Finally, he stops, and I dizzily look at him.

"Sabin?"

"Yes, my lady?"

"I see two of you."

"Lucky girl!" He leans his forehead down against mine. "Oh, whatever shall you do with two Sabins?"

"I can barely handle one."

Sabin wipes the towel over my cheek. "Missed a spot."

I shiver, and he pulls me into his hold. A Sabin hug is always a good place to be. Today, his chest is hot from the sun, and it helps warm me.

He's lost a lot of weight over the past year, and I notice that I'm more fully against him than I used to be when he'd hug me. For a moment, I miss his big belly. Of course, he looks a lot better, but the absence of his soft extra weight is undeniable.

About once a month, he'll agree to go on a run, but he bitches and moans most of the way. Running a section of the Boston Marathon with me last spring was not, it seems, a catalyst for taking up regular routes. Yet I can feel that he's getting more muscular and less flabby, thanks to the lifting that Chris has been pushing him to do and the work he's been doing with James on the house all summer. My architect-to-be brother redesigned one of the bathrooms, and Sabin was totally on board with smashing tile, hauling out the old tub, and lugging materials up and down the second floor.

I touch a hand to Sabin's bicep and squeeze. "You're getting all beefy, Sabe."

"I'm quite sexy, you know. It's sickening how ripped I am. I don't know how any other dudes can stand to be around me because my macho manliness is too much to bear." He steps back and begins striking a series of clichéd poses in which he flexes his muscles.

3

I shake my head in amusement, but the truth is that he does look good. His black hair flops around his face as he moves, and his green eyes twinkle. While he's not exactly ready for underwear modeling, the change in his physique is obvious. He looks healthy, and even his face has slimmed down a bit. It turns out that Sabin had cheekbones under the fullness.

After he finishes the umpteenth muscle stance, I step closer and touch a hand to his cheek, rubbing the scruff. "Are you ever going to shave this off, so we can see your pretty face?"

"That would be too much hotness to handle. I need my scruffiness to minimize the impact." He shakes his face against my palm and grins.

I suppose the big sideburns and perpetual five o'clock shadow suit him.

"You shouldn't make jokes, Sabe. I'm really proud of you." Now, it's my turn to embrace him, and I slip my arms around his stomach. "I'm so glad you're staying with us. I couldn't stand to lose the twins, James, and you." I squeeze him hard.

He is such a source of solace and stability for me. Of that, I am constantly aware and constantly appreciative. I feel like I can't explain that wholly to him, but I try to remind him of it as much as possible. It just never feels like enough.

There aren't the right words or right phrases to encapsulate how powerfully he's become part of my being, how to convey how I worry about him, how I celebrate him, how I mentally fuss over every hour he is awake. Maybe it should feel creepy, but Sabin's mother died years ago, and he doesn't have a girlfriend or other close friends. He's a young guy still, and I cannot help but feel that someone should watch over him, that someone should love and adore and hover.

But I say what I can—for now. "You're my best friend, Sabin. I feel like you always have been, even before I knew you."

He pauses for a moment and then rests his chin on top of my head. "And you're my best friend. Of course you are."

I rub his back and move to his side. He actually has a waist, and I'm almost entranced by the way he's changed. "You've done so much since rehab—"

"Oh God, don't call it rehab. That's such a hideous word. Let's just say, I was at a spa getaway, suffering from exhaustion, like a celebrity."

"Stop. There's nothing wrong with rehab."

"It wasn't really rehab. It was excruciating intensive therapy."

"Well, you haven't had a drink since you left. That's sort of rehab*ish*."

"Alcohol wasn't really my problem, sweetheart. That was a poorly thought-out coping mechanism, I'm told. A replacement for actual self-analysis and change. Boring psychobabble." He pauses for a bit too long. "And can we not do this? I did what I had to do, and now, it's done. It's handled."

I didn't mean to stumble into this conversation. Talking about his past, everyone's past…it's a bit of an unspoken rule that we don't go there. There are details that he cannot bring himself to share with me, and I get that. I want him to have privacy and containment, if that's what's helpful.

I know that Sabin feels ashamed, and I've learned not to dig too much with him. Whatever he's been doing to free himself from his childhood trauma seems to be working, so I give him space. But I also want him to know that I acknowledge what he's pushed through, and I'm proud of him.

"Sorry. I just meant to tell you how much I love you, and I'm glad you moved in here."

We stay quiet and listen to the gentle splash of waves as the tide finishes coming in.

"This fall, we can go apple-picking and jump in leaf piles and…and…do things with pumpkins."

"Do things with pumpkins?" he asks with a small laugh.

"You know, carve them, make pumpkin bread, smash 'em up. Whatever you like."

"Okay." He kisses the top of my head.

"And, you know, you'll perhaps disappear for the night with another tourist and crawl home in the morning. Then, I'll make you pancakes while I avoid hearing lurid details and lecture you on how stupid one-night stands are."

"And I'll tell you how sexy and awesome they are and how I'm just adding to my glowing reviews on Yelp."

"Shut up. You're worth more than a Yelp review. You're more like Zagat's." I hold his waist in my hands and squeeze. "Seriously, look how lean you're getting." Then, I put my palms on his chest. "And these pecs!" I throw my arms around his neck and tightly hold him. "God, my best friend is gorgeous."

"Blythe...stop..." Sabin starts. It's unlike him to look embarrassed, but he does now.

"Mmm?"

"Blythe, don't..." He sets his hands under my arms and eases me back. "It's just...you can't..."

I look up and see that his face has a more serious expression now. "What? What is it?"

He half-smiles and tucks a stray hair behind my ear, but he doesn't say anything.

"Sabe, what is it?"

Suddenly, he twirls me around and then yells, "You can't stop me from doing a cannonball!" Then, he lets me go and leaps from the end of the dock, tucking his knees into his chest, before pounding into the water.

Just because he's dropped some pounds doesn't mean that he's a small guy by any means, and the splash he makes when he crashes through the water's surface soaks me again.

My dog, Jonah, barks sharply, and I turn to see him running, soon passing me, before flying off the dock to reach Sabin.

Even though I'm not a fan of the freezing water, I still do laps every few days. Jonah though has logged more hours swimming than I have. That's mostly because Sabin spends at least an hour a day playing with him, throwing a tennis ball into the water over and over for Jonah to retrieve. There's nothing my German shepherd loves more than swimming with Sabin, and it tires Jonah out almost as much as going with me on my runs.

I hold a hand up to my eyes and watch as Jonah paddles to reach Sabin, who is now floating on his back while lazily kicking his feet and sweeping his hands through the water, letting the gentle current determine his drift.

A voice carries my way. "With a little imagination, that white bathing suit is practically see-through."

I laugh. "It is not." I pivot on my feet and try not to look as stupidly in love as I feel. I'm sure I'm failing, but I'm all right with that.

Chris walks slowly down the steps from the house to the beach area. Part of me wants to rush to meet him, and the other part wants to just watch him. It doesn't matter that we live together, that I'm with him every single day. I have the same strong reaction, the same unyielding surge of love that rips through me, every time I see him.

I don't feel the cold on my skin that should be amplified by the breeze. All I can feel now is that Christopher Shepherd is my home and my heart.

The late-afternoon sun hits his face, and even the sound of Jonah's barking and Sabin's whooping can't distract me. Chris is even tanner than Sabin, and the loose white button-down he's wearing with jeans is damn hot. His hands are tucked into his pockets as he looks at me almost shyly.

Most of the time, he exudes nothing but confidence. Chris is entitled to any self-assuredness and sense of capability he has. I adore that about him, and I rely on it. Still, even after all our time together, Chris has moments where his stance when he's around me is almost nervous, hesitant. There's a questioning air in his approach, as if he needs to check that I'm still completely engulfed in him.

The answer is always yes.

The few seconds of insecurity he can't control are not really about me. They're flashes of his history, which did nothing to breed trust. In Chris's blip of tentativeness, I see a little boy who is alone, who has made himself responsible for shielding his siblings from a sickly abusive father, and who is desperately frightened that he might fail. A boy who fears he might not be accepted and loved because he is not worthy of anything but savage outrage and psychotic delusions.

I am still trying to glue together the broken pieces of this person I love. He manages his tortured side with remarkable skill, but even Chris, with his endless supply of strength and clarity, could not survive all that he did without scars.

And the scars are many, and they are deep.

Together though, we are overcoming both his past and mine.

When he is a few yards away from me, I cannot stop myself from walking quickly into his arms. I put my hands on his face, run a finger over his lips, and study him as though we'd been apart for months, not hours.

He smiles at me with curiosity. "You okay?"

I nod slowly and don't take my eyes from his. I am flooded again with the rush of what the entirety of *us* feels like, what it means for us to be together. "We're doing it, aren't we?"

Because he understands me more intuitively than anyone else could, he nods back. "Yes, Blythe, we're kicking heartbreak's ass."

The power in this truth brings my lips to his, and I kiss the love of my life with more meaning and connectedness than I was ready for. My eyes sting a bit, and my chest tightens with emotion. The taste of his mouth and the feel of his hold as he keeps me close will, without fail, shut down the rest of the world, so I let myself disappear into him.

Then, Chris slows our kiss, dipping me in his arms until my head is hanging upside down.

He strokes a hand down my front and smiles. "Like I said, practically see-through…"

I laugh and grab his hand to pull myself up. He turns my back into his chest, and I catch sight of Sabin in the water. I like how he is drifting, seeming to be without worry, without abandon.

"Our boy taught himself how to float, didn't he?" I say. "You can't drown when you know how to float."

Chris says nothing for a few minutes. "Maybe. But the water is pretty calm today. There could always be a storm." He rubs my shoulders. He breathes against me. He waits. "It's hard to float in a storm."

He's right, but it's not the optimistic attitude I was hoping for. I lift my chin and look back at him. "Let's just enjoy the moment, okay?"

Chris laughs softly. "Okay."

When I turn back to Sabin, I notice that I'm relieved I can still see him, as though I were worried he had drowned when I looked away. Even at this distance, I can see that he's watching Chris and me. I wave lightly, and he waves back before paddling himself in the opposite direction.

The necklace that I wear every day now burns against my chest in the sun. My fingers fumble through the letter charms for Christopher, Estelle, Eric, and me until I find the *S* for Sabin. The silver shape feels the same that it always does, but I rub it between my fingers to be sure of its presence.

It's still here, and Sabin is still here.

Jonah swims to shore, shakes himself off, and comes to stand with Chris and me.

We all watch Sabin, now alone in the vast ocean.

2
LOBSTERS AND ABSENCE

ALL THE WEIGHT I FOUND,
IN MY HOME THIS TIME AROUND.

AFTER I'VE SHOWERED AND DRESSED FOR DINNER, I PAUSE AT THE top of the stairs and listen to the beautiful sounds echoing up to the second floor. It's the sounds of my family—Estelle's riotous laughter, Chris clanging pots as he sets them on the stove, James doing his best Prince imitation along with the music.

The floorboards behind me creak, and Eric emerges from his room. His dark hair has been freshly buzzed, showing off the stunning angled bone structure all the siblings have, and I reach out and rub the top of his head the way I do each time he cuts it this short.

He grins. "Hey, Blythe."

"You ready to head back to school tomorrow?" I'm trying to feign excitement for him, but it's not easy. I can already feel the silence that will envelop the house.

Eric nods. "I am. It's going to be a tough year of work, but changing to a history major feels right."

I raise an eyebrow. "Academics is the only draw to return then?"

He blushes slightly. "Obviously, there's Zach. I'm glad he's staying near school this year."

I manage to keep from clapping my hands together. "So, things are still good?"

"You don't have to keep checking," he says gently. "We're really good."

"Sorry that I've been hovering." I shrug. "Can't help it."

"Well, you're pretty much my sister, so I won't fault you."

Eric and Zach have been back together for more than six months. I know how much they love each other, but Eric is one to lay low and not gush about his love life, so the occasional prod seems reasonable.

Estelle's voice screeches up to us, "Fifty bucks on Alexander! He's a motherfucking winner, if ever there were one! Check out my badass boy!"

"Uh, who is Alexander?" Eric asks.

I shake my head. "Absolutely no idea."

"Oh, yeah? Fifty on Moses!" James hollers.

Eric and I head down the wide wooden staircase that wraps around and lands us in the grand living room, and we both walk cautiously through the dining room and into the kitchen.

I'm still somewhat stupefied at the size of the kitchen. This house must have been a bed-and-breakfast at some point because the oversize stainless steel appliances and matching stainless counters are far too much for a traditional house. The Shepherds, James, and I, however, are far from traditional, so we make good use of it.

I can't begin to imagine what my parents were thinking when they bought this house for just themselves and James and me. Because they never got to move in and spend summers here, I am doing what I can to fill it with family and love for as much of the year as possible.

Cheering and clapping greet us when we enter. Chris is standing on a chair with a whistle in his mouth and his hands up in the air. He glances at me, winks, and simultaneously blows the whistle as he throws his arms down. Estelle and James each set a lobster on the kitchen floor and go wild. Masking tape marks off a racecourse, and about fifteen feet from the twins are two orange traffic cones with rainbow flags stuck in them. This is presumably the finish line.

I roll my eyes but laugh.

"Blythe, get over here on the girls' side and cheer for Alexander the Red with me. James is going down like a little bitch!" Estelle has on a red flippy mini skirt, white tank, and white sneakers, and she's drawn a small megaphone outline on her cheek with what I presume is eyeliner. She's let her black hair grow a bit longer than usual so that it covers her ears and hits the back of her neck. For the first time in ages, she's left it solid black without any sort of neon streak running through it.

"You're seriously racing lobsters?" I ask.

"It's our last night in Maine. Seems fitting," James answers for her before screaming at his lobster, "Moses! C'mon, dude! Stop walking in circles, you moron!"

My brother's cheeks are flushed, and I'm not sure if it's from the apparent excitement over this lobster race or because Estelle is jumping up and down, flashing her black lace panties at him.

I go to Estelle's side and try to copy her rather elaborate cheerleader moves. Given how slowly these lobsters are moving, I think I might have time to perfect this routine.

"Estelle, one more blatant leg kick like that, and I'm going to disqualify you," Chris warns her.

She sticks out her tongue at him. "Fuck you! All is fair in lobsters and war!" Then, she turns her back to James and bends over, briefly flipping up her skirt.

"Estelle! God!" Eric groans, covering his eyes.

I'm about to ask where Sabin is, but just then, a skateboard appears from under Chris's chair, and Sabin pops out from behind him.

"I will conquer you all!" he roars, gesturing to the lobster atop the skateboard rolling across the tile.

His contestant easily passes the other two lobsters that have thus far done nothing but veer off course. Estelle and James scream in protest, but Sabin is already bounding after his lobster that has soared through the finish line and continued into the dining room.

"No way! Chris, tell him that's cheating!" James demands.

Chris jumps down from the chair and throws up his hands. "Estelle said it. It seems, all is fair in lobsters and war. We never actually said skateboards weren't allowed." He walks toward Sabin and high-fives him, entwining their fingers, before giving him a hug and patting his back.

Sabin makes a crazy swoon face as he grabs Chris by the waist and lifts him up, causing the two of them to stumble across the floor. "Older brothers are the bestest ever," he singsongs.

"No, older brothers suck!" Estelle stomps her foot and rescues her lobster from the potential Chris-Sabin stampede. "For failing me," she informs Alexander, "you will be steamed and eaten by the enemy." She turns to Sabin, offering him her losing contestant. "He's all yours."

"Gladly, my darling sister." Sabin sets Chris back on the floor and makes lobster claws with his hands, pinching his way toward Estelle.

James strides to Estelle with Moses in one hand and the other beckoning her. "Come here, missy. I think Moses belongs to you then, tail meat and all."

She crosses her arms but steps into him and takes the lobster. "Given that you are not one of my nasty brothers, I accept. Besides," she says as she walks to the stove, "I always did like your tail."

The rest of the boys let out a raucous, "Oh!" as James grabs Alexander and Sabin's lobster and meets Estelle by the boiling pots.

Eric catches my eye, and I smile. There might be hope for James and Estelle after all.

As far as I know, they haven't touched each other all summer. Not that I want lurid details, but I've been hoping that they'd find their way back together. I never thought Estelle would voluntarily retile a bathroom either, so stranger things have happened for sure.

I watch her and James for a moment, and I bite my lip when he slips an arm around her waist. I know that she went to therapy last year, but the conversation she and I had about it involved her narrowing her eyes and speaking in an Austrian accent.

"And how has your hideous childhood impacted your psychological and sexual functioning?"

That was followed by oversharing in a typical Estelle fashion.

"I haven't had sex since I nailed your brother in the hammock last summer. So, how do you think I'm doing? I mean, I'm not getting rope burns in weird places, but I am buying stock in batteries, okay? An abstinent woman cannot have enough vibrators, right?"

I'm not sure how long the self-imposed abstinence will continue, but the truth is, it's good for her. She spiraled into such a weird dysfunctional place with men and then started to pull my brother into it. It seems very unlike her not to be getting laid every chance she gets, but James seems willing to wait. I haven't heard him mention any girls from college, so his tie to Estelle must run deeper than I know. For that, I'm glad.

"B, where's my potato salad? And my coleslaw? And my corn on the cob?" Sabin's voice booms through the kitchen as he exaggeratedly rubs his hands over his stomach. "Sabin be hungry! Sabin need eats!"

I grab his hand and drag him to the fridge. "Hold out your hands. You can carry the salads to the table, and I'll wrap the corn in foil for the grill, okay?"

Sabin diligently takes the oversize containers and grunts. "Is good, Blythe. Sabin like woman feed me. More dead animal, less vegetable."

"Okay, caveman. There's steak, too."

On cue, Chris passes us with a platter of marinated steaks, and he delivers his own grunt. "We grill animal, yes?"

"Argh, yes. Animal." Sabin lumbers like a Neanderthal, following Chris out of the kitchen.

"If you'd like some help from someone less caveman*ish*, I'm yours," Eric offers. "I suppose I could go club a wild boar or something for you, but I'm also very good at setting tables."

"Ah, the voice of sanity," I say with a smile. "I would love help."

Eric and I are silent as we lay out plates and silverware. Both of us are hyperaware that it could be a long time before we all have dinner together in this house.

Next summer, the twins and James will have graduated. It would be perfectly normal for them to go off and get jobs outside of this small tourist area in Maine. I expect it. I don't like it maybe, but I expect it. I want everyone to explore and flourish and be wonderful. But I also want to keep this group close to Chris and me.

"Please don't look so sad," Eric finally says. "We'll see you again. A lot."

"Okay." I can't look at him.

This summer has been idyllic with hours on the beach, poorly played volleyball in the yard, canoeing, hiking through Acadia National Park, and digging for clams. More than that, it's the unification of this group of formerly lost souls. It's been a syrupy lovefest for the past three months, and I wish it could last forever.

I think about that stupid fucking saying, *Absence makes the heart grow fonder*, and I want to barf. I'm already beyond fond of everyone, so I'm all set.

I mentally shake my head. I'm not going to feel sad. We are all lucky to have this summer and to have each other. Every one of us is in a far better place than we were before, so I try to focus on that and not on the fact that this magical summer can't last forever.

Besides, I remind myself, *Sabin is staying, and that's huge.*

If he puts his mind to it, he can make as much noise as all of us combined, so it'll hardly be quiet around here.

I wince as Estelle lets out a slew of profanity, and she comes running from the kitchen, screaming and laughing, as James chases after her. They both tear out onto the deck, and I hear them running down the steps.

"Hey! Don't go far! Dinner is soon!" I call after them.

Two hours later, when our long farm table is cluttered with empty lobster, clam, and mussel shells and we're all a bit drunk on flavor, James stands and raises his glass. "A toast!"

"A toast!" we all call back.

"To Chris and Blythe, for letting us invade their house and run amok like the unruly brats that we are!"

"Hear, hear!" echoes around us.

Chris and I both shake our heads in protest.

"We wouldn't have it any other way." Chris fiddles with the place mat.

"He's right," I say. "This is your home. Always."

"Good. Because we don't have anywhere else to go, so you're stuck with us." Estelle stretches her arms above her head. "I have to finish packing. Early flight."

James is out of his chair like lightning. "I'll help."

"I've still got laundry to do," Eric says. "And, well, I want to call Zach. But we'll help clean up first."

I wave him away. "It's your last night. Send-off dinner and all. Go do what you need to do."

"Thanks, Blythe," he says. "We're all going to miss you. But we'll call and text all the time."

"Promise?" I ask.

"Promise!" Eric, Estelle, and James all shout before heading upstairs.

Sabin rises from his seat. "I'll do all the grunt work, kids."

"You'll do no such thing." I move to lift the bowl of shells in front of me.

Sabin snatches it away. "Relax, B. I got this."

Chris's arm goes over my shoulder. "Does this mean I get a minute alone with you?" He leans over and lightly kisses my neck.

"Apparently." I sigh with pleasure when his tongue touches my skin, and he growls.

"Dance with me," he whispers.

"What?"

Chris stands and pulls me up before walking us toward the French doors that lead out to the deck. I barely noticed the music earlier with all the dinner banter, but now, I hear it.

He slips one hand around my waist and takes my hand in his free one, lifting it up. Then, he starts to slowly rock us. It takes a full song for us to turn in a complete circle. The sound of the music and the feel of him against me are intoxicating, and it makes it hard for me to pay attention to much else. He's as mesmerizing as the day I met him.

His cheek goes against mine. "Do you remember this song?"

"Of course."

It was on the first playlist that Chris ever made me, the one that helped me run through the pain. I know every second of this song, every layer of its sound.

"We've loved each other forever," he says softly.

"On the day I was on the dock and you were on the shore, I fell in love with you. I didn't know it, but I did."

"Before that." He tightens his fingers around my side. "Forever."

I don't care that it's not possible, that what he's saying doesn't make logical sense, or that it doesn't sound like him. Christopher Shepherd is not a dreamer, not prone to magical thinking. But he is, I'm learning, changing. He's believing and hoping, and the edges of his black-and-white world are blurring.

"Forever," I agree. I say this not to feed his romantic side, but because I know it to be true.

The sunset casts fierce orange and pink light into the room, and I lean against Chris while we dance. Slowly, we keep turning until I can no longer see the sparkle of the ocean or the tiers of color in the sky.

Now, I see Sabin, leaning against the doorframe to the kitchen, with a dishcloth in one hand and a glass in the other.

I smile at him, and he smiles back—or I think he does. Maybe it's a sad smile. Maybe it's just the way the setting sun hits his face. I lock my eyes on his and try to figure out what he's thinking, but I can't.

So, I shift my gaze, but in my peripheral vision, I can see that he's still watching Chris and me.

Something is brewing with Sabin, but I don't know what it is.

3
WE AIN'T RUNNING

AND WE AIN'T RUNNING, NO.
WE'RE JUST STAYING ALIVE.

CHRIS, SABIN, AND I FINISH THE DISHES, AND I GO UPSTAIRS TO check on the others. I'm about to take a step that I know will creak when I hear James's voice.

"I miss you, Estelle. I care about you so much."

"James, I'm impossible. You know that. I'm fucking crazy and hopeless." Her words say one thing, but the lack of conviction tells me that James has worn her down.

"You're wonderfully crazy, and you give me nothing but hope."

I smile. My brother's a charmer.

"Stay with me tonight," he continues.

"I can't. I'm not ready. I told myself—"

"Just to sleep. Please stay with me."

When he pauses, I try to figure out how to go back down the stairs without them hearing me.

"I want to spend the night with you and keep you in my arms. I want to feel when you roll into me and listen to you snore and talk in your sleep. I even miss when you clock me in the face by mistake."

She laughs.

"And I want to hold you when you have bad dreams, when you shake and sweat and run from things."

I drop my head. Chris isn't the only one.

"Please, Estelle. Do you want to? Do you miss me the way I miss you?"

There's another pause. I shouldn't be eavesdropping, but I can't get myself to leave now because I'm desperate to know what she'll say.

Finally, I hear her say, "How are you this sweet?"

"Because I love you."

"James…"

"I do love you, Estelle. You don't have to say anything. Just let me love you, okay?"

I think I might scream if she doesn't answer him. I count to eighteen before she does.

"Okay. God, you're such a fucking asshole. But okay."

I know she's smiling.

When I'm pretty sure that there's kissing and whatever else is going on that I don't want to imagine my brother doing—and when I'm also sure that they wouldn't hear me if I banged cymbals outside the room—I slip back down the stairs.

Eric is on the phone, presumably talking to Zach, when he passes me on the landing where he touches my shoulder before mouthing, *Good night.*

It is getting late, and the van that will shuttle them to the Bangor Airport will be here at six forty-five tomorrow morning.

It seems rather over-the-top that they're getting picked up, but that's pretty much how Chris does things. He remains a minimalist when it comes to his own needs, but he routinely spends money on everyone else. He has the same truck he had in college, but he insisted that I needed a new SUV to navigate the Maine winter terrain. The money the Shepherds inherited when their father died is substantial, and as the executor of the trust, Chris makes sure that everyone around him is more than taken care of.

At my insistence, I use my own inheritance and the insurance money that James and I got from the fire that killed our parents to pay for James's college expenses and most of the repairs and remodeling this old house needs. It's hard to stop Christopher from jumping in to do everything.

From the writing I do for a New England–based magazine, I don't make nearly as much as he does. His job with Acadia National Park has expanded, and he's become deeply involved in his position as the head information management specialist. There's lots of talk about computers, networks, and such that I don't always follow, but he loves his work.

I stop in the living room when Chris comes out. He nods toward the deck, and I listen. Sabin is playing his guitar, slow notes trickling out here and there, wafting a melancholy tune our way. Chris takes my hand, and we walk out to join Sabin.

When he sees us, he picks up his strumming and stomps his feet. "Hello, young lovers!"

Sabin has on his cowboy hat, and I'm reminded of the first time we met in the student union at Matthews College.

In between chords, he taps the brim up a bit and winks at me.

Chris and I curl up on the extra-wide wicker lounge chair. Sitting between his legs, I lazily rest my head on his chest while we listen to Sabin play.

When the last note plays out, he sets down the guitar and holds out a hand. "Tips are appreciated. You know how it is for us starving artists."

"You had two lobsters and a flat-iron steak for dinner. You're hardly starving," Chris points out.

Sabin fake-pouts. "Allow me my artistic angst."

"Speaking of artistic," I say, "I saw in the paper that auditions for the playhouse in Bangor are coming up. They're doing *Othello*. Or *Hamlet*. Or some other one word–titled play I can't remember. You should try out. Don't you miss acting? It's been so long since you were in anything."

He leans back in his chair. "Well, here's the thing, kids—"

"Or," Chris cuts him off, "you could take the job I'm about to offer you."

Sabin wrinkles his forehead. "What job?"

"Come work with me at the park. They need someone to help out in building maintenance."

"Oh God, you're fucking kidding, right? I'd rather get chewed up by a local grizzly than clean toilets."

Chris sighs. "It's not cleaning toilets, Sabin. You know, you've been doing all sorts of work on this house, and you'd be great at overseeing park properties. It's a job, and it pays. I thought maybe you'd be ready for that. You know, have some structure to your day."

"Well, here's the thing," Sabin says with a smile. "First off, I'd like to congratulate you both on your attempt at acting like parents. Really, nicely done. But the good thing here is that none of us have parents, right? They're all dead and gone, so we have no one to answer to. So, you know, yay for us."

I can feel Chris tensing behind me.

"What the fuck, Sabin?" he says.

"Well, it's true, right? It's not exactly a secret. I'm not trying to be an asshole, but let's call a spade a spade. You don't have to feel any obligation to watch over me. I'm twenty-three, so I'm a big boy now. Really." His face softens, and he looks apologetically at both of us. "Okay, sorry, sorry. That was shitty of me. I'm...okay, I'm going to tell you something, and I don't want you to freak out or make a big deal of it. I actually wasn't going to tell you until tomorrow."

My stomach tightens because he's acting strange, and I don't think he's about to deliver whoppingly wonderful news.

He rubs his legs and looks to the side.

"Sabe, what is it?" I ask.

Sabin stands up and looks out at the moonlit water. I slide my hands into Christopher's as we wait.

Eventually, Sabin turns around and flashes us his best smile. "I'm going to San Diego tomorrow," he announces with contained excitement.

"Okay..." I start. "For a trip? A vacation?"

He shakes his head, and his eyes crinkle sweetly when he looks at me. "No, love."

I freeze and continue to stare at him with confusion. My heart sinks as I begin to understand. "You're moving there?"

He nods.

"Why...across the country? I mean..." I don't know what to say to him.

Chris squeezes my hands. "When did you decide this?"

"A while ago. Earlier this summer." He paces, seemingly energized by having finally told us. "You guys! California! Sunshine and beaches! Look, I can't stay in this tiny Maine town. You know how it'll be in the winter—cold, miserable, no hot tourists. San Diego is going to be amazing!" He does some kind of crazy spin and cannot stop smiling.

"Do you have a place to live? A job? This doesn't make any sense." I'm not happy in the least.

"Ah, B, where's your sense of adventure? I don't want plans. I'm going to set off and see what happens. I always land on my feet. Don't you know that? I'll find an awesome apartment, maybe on the beach. I'll get a job collecting seashells or something."

"That's not a job," I say with more annoyance than I intended.

He faces us and tries to look reassuring. "I'm not *really* going to collect seashells. I will get a real job. It's a great big city full of opportunities for a creative soul like me." Sabin throws his arms out and beams. "I could go windsurfing! Or become a chef! Or discover a new fish! Or…anything! Right? Come on, please be on board with this. Oh! Boards. I could get a surfboard, dude! I don't belong in Maine. You know that."

I'm about to explode with a list of reasons this is an idiotic, half-assed idea, but Chris begins softly moving his hands up and down my arms, soothing me and letting me know that exploding is not a good idea. He's right, I know that, and Sabin has quite clearly made up his mind.

"If this is what you want," Chris says, "if this makes you happy, then I'm really glad. You do know that you can stay with us for as long as you want though, right? This is your home, too."

He dismissively waves a hand. "Look, you guys have been great, but it's time. I gotta go."

"Why didn't you tell us earlier?" There is panic in my voice. "You're just taking off tomorrow with no warning?"

Now, he kneels down next to the lounge chair. "If I'd told you, you would have thrown some outrageous going-away party with strippers and a live band and a pig roast. I know how you are." He throws a hand to his chest and speaks with such animation that I can't help but crack a smile, "I couldn't let you nutjobs make such a fuss over little ole me, now could I? And there would have been endless days of clutching and sobbing and prolonged pleading. It would have ruined the summer."

Chris laughs. "Man, we're going to miss you, but this could actually be a really cool idea. Fresh start, a chance to sort of carve your own path." I feel him shrug. "I think it's brave."

"Thanks, man. Since you're being all awesome about this, how about you fish out a few more suitcases from the attic for me? Sabin doesn't do spiderwebs and bats." He shivers and pretends to brush off cobwebs from his face.

"You got it. I'll toss them in your room." Chris kisses me on the cheek and maneuvers out from behind me. "I'm going to hop in the shower. I'll see you upstairs later." He knows I'm shell-shocked and that I need a few minutes alone with Sabin.

Before Chris is even halfway into the house, Sabin stands and begins talking at top speed about the cool restaurant scene in San Diego, the endless perfect weather, the many hot beach babes. "Picture me, surrounded by bikini-clad lovelies, strutting over the hot sand toward a soon-to-be-purchased Jeep Wrangler parked where it's overlooking the ocean."

"Sabin—"

"Late nights cavorting around town, dropping into trendy establishments, eating…well, whatever it is San Diegans eat. Is that what they're called? What I'll be called? Or maybe just Sandies? How's that? Cute, right? I'm a Sandy now. Check me out, being a sexy Sandy and shit." He puts his hands on the back of his head and stretches. "Cool beans, I say."

"Cool beans?" I'm too dumbstruck to respond to anything else.

"Cool beans," he says, nodding. "I'm bringing it back."

"Fine. You and your cool fucking beans can just take off tomorrow like it's no big deal."

"Fucking beans? Is that like jumping beans?"

I snarl at him.

He throws himself into his chair and grabs his guitar before scooting closer to me. "Are you sulking, Lady Blythe McGuire?"

"Maybe."

"I suppose I kinda like that. It means you're going to miss me."

He grins and tousles my hair until it's all in my face, and I can't see.

I push him away. "Knock it off."

"Blythe—"

"What?" I snap.

"Please be happy for me."

"I am."

"Please be sincerely happy for me."

I inhale and exhale deeply a few times, and while I can feel my body relaxing, I can also feel the grip beginning to take hold on my throat and the tears threatening to fill my eyes. "I am. But you're going so far away."

"And I'll constantly call you. And we'll text. And do creepy little video chat thingies and all that newfangled shit you kids are into."

I manage to smile again. "Play me a song."

"Whatever you like, my fairest princess of duchesses of the queendom."

"That doesn't make any sense."

He raises an eyebrow. "Have we met?"

I cannot believe he's leaving tomorrow. It's too much to process. I like him here, where I know that he's safe and loved. Of course he's tough as shit, but he's equally fragile. We're *all* fragile. But I can't force him to stay. And maybe he's right that it's time for him to go. Maybe that's what will make him less fragile.

"Play me a song," I say again.

So, he takes his guitar and straddles the footrest end of my lounge chair, facing me, as he randomly plucks the chords and expectantly looks at me. "Whatcha wanna hear?"

"The song you were playing earlier, before Chris and I came out."

"Ah, that one. Well, okay, I guess. It's just something I've been working on."

He looks down at his fingers even though I know he doesn't need to. He doesn't want to see how sad I'm going to look when I study his face, his movements, listen to the sound of his raspy voice.

"It goes a little somethin' like this…" Sabin makes a little smile for my benefit.

AGED LIKE WINE, YOU OWN MY TIME.
HEY, YOU SORTED OUT MY OWN HEAD.
YOU CALLED IT TIME FOR A WOMAN.
YOU STARTED TO KNOW, KNOW ME.

I STARTED TO
KNOW YOU, KNOW YOU.
YOU SHUDDERED MY BONES,
HOLDING ON TO MY HAND.

HERE WE GO AGAIN. I'M NOT THE LUCKY ONE
YOU NEED.
HERE WE GO AGAIN, LOVE.
HERE WE GO AGAIN, NOT THE LUCKY ONE
YOU NEED.
HERE WE GO AGAIN, LOVE.

WAS IT ALL IN MY HEAD?
YOU FELL INTO MY CELL PHONE AND MY BED.
MY THOUGHTS ARE STILL SILENT WITH
MY HEAD ON LOCK.
I WANNA FOLLOW YOU AND SEW MY TEARS.
FELL INTO MY HEAD, GIRL, MY MIND.
I WANNA FIND A LOVE THAT'S ALL MINE.
SO, SO…

Something in me aches, so deeply and so profoundly. Sabin's voice has always been able to reach into my gut and destroy me in the most utterly beautiful way. Tonight, this moment, feels like a painful transition for both of us. It must be one that he needs.

HERE WE GO AGAIN, NOT THE LUCKY ONE
YOU NEED.
HERE WE GO AGAIN, LOVE.
HERE WE GO AGAIN, NOT THE LUCKY ONE
YOU NEED.
HERE WE GO AGAIN, LOVE.

AND WE LET IT FALL,
AND WE LET IT FALL.
AND WE LET IT BURN,
AND WE LET IT BURN.

YOU WILL LOVE ME ALL,
OR YOU WON'T LOVE ME AT ALL.
I WILL NOT BE PIECES OF YOUR FAVORITE SONG.

RESTLESS
WATERS

HERE WE GO AGAIN, NOT THE LUCKY ONE
YOU NEED.
HERE WE GO AGAIN, LOVE.
HERE WE GO AGAIN, NOT THE LUCKY ONE
YOU NEED.
HERE WE GO AGAIN, LOVE.

Even when the lyrics end, Sabin keeps playing, as if stopping would mean a larger end. But I let him delay because it's giving me time to think.

I shiver from the chill of the night, possibly more.

"Cold?" he asks over his strumming.

I nod.

He moves to get up and sit next to me, but I stop him. "Sabin?"

"Yeah, love?"

"You didn't plan this San Diego move weeks ago, did you?"

"Of course I did! I can keep a secret. Didn't know that about me, did ya?" He continues playing the guitar, the same song that I'm finding so beautiful yet so hauntingly sad.

"No, you didn't. Three days ago, you told me that you'd take my car into town for an oil change. And, yesterday, you ordered a down parka with a hideous zebra-print lining for the winter. You said that, while I might find it grotesque, chicks dig zebra print, and you were going to make it ferociously chic."

"All part of my plan," he says, tapping the side of his head in between notes.

"You told Estelle, Eric, and James that you'd take nighttime pictures of the boats in the harbor on Labor Day when the fireworks were exploding over them and lighting up the sky because I'd told you how awesome it was. You were looking forward to going to that street festival with Chris and me. So, I think that you just decided to leave—maybe today, maybe yesterday. But this was not some long-term plan that you just dropped on us tonight."

Because he won't look at me, because he starts singing again, I know I'm right. "Did something happen?"

I wait him out. I wait until he's ready.

Eventually, his music slows bit by bit, finally coming to a stop. He blows out a breath and puts down the guitar. "What I said before is true. It's just time. It became very clear to me that I needed to find something of my own and quit leeching off of you and Chris." He

27

stops me before I can protest. "I am. I know you guys love me and shit, but it's too hard for me to stay."

He's just making me more lost and confused.

"I don't understand."

"You don't have to. You just have to trust that I know what I want and"—he tips his head to the side and lifts my chin with his strong hand—"what's best for me. For us."

"What do you mean, for us?"

"Look, you have a life here with Chris. You guys are practically married, and you don't need me interrupting what you have."

"Fuck you for saying that. You're not interrupting anything. We're not married, and we're not *getting* married. That's not how we work. We both have more than enough room for you, and I don't mean because this house has a million bedrooms."

"I'm not explaining this well." He blows out a breath in frustration. "I know you want me here. I really do."

I stare at him for a minute. "But you don't want to be here."

He takes my hands in his. "Not right now, no."

"Why? What's changed?"

"Blythe…" Sabin is clearly struggling with how to answer this. He starts and stops a few times before he just shakes his head.

"You just need me to accept that this is what's happening. That moving to the fabulous city of San Diego and breaking my heart in the process is the perfect thing for you to do."

He lifts my hand and makes me wipe the tear washing down my cheek. "Yes."

"Okay."

"Thank you. Thank you for pretending to understand." He smiles. "It's late. You should get some sleep. You have to get up early to say good-bye."

"I don't want to."

"Then, you don't have to get up, sweetness. You don't want some dramatic good-bye scene anyway. So boring and overdone, right? Oh, I know why. You didn't have time to prepare the rhyming good-bye poem done in the style of Dr. Seuss? *I do not like to basket weave. / I do not like when Sabin leaves. / I do not like—*"

Now, I actually laugh. "No! I just mean, I don't want to get up in the morning to say good-bye because I don't want to go to sleep."

His eyes brighten. "You want to stay up all night?"

"I do."

"And make mischief and mayhem?"

"Yes."

"And watch me wait until the very last minute to pack and then giggle unhelpfully while I throw some random shit into a suitcase and leave behind necessities, like underwear and pornographic coloring books?"

"Exactly."

"We can do that."

So, that's what we do.

In the morning, the shuttle arrives to take away the people I love most in this world. I will miss the hell out of James, Estelle, and Eric, but I will especially ache for Sabin.

4
COME HOME TO ME

**I JUST SIT BACK AND WATCH YOU GO.
FALL AGAINST ME NOW.**

FALL ON FRENCHMAN BAY IS PERMEATED BY SILENCE. THE LACK OF sibling chaos is not unbearable, but it is noticed very sharply by Chris and me. The everyday logistics remind us of everyone's absence, like when I first went grocery shopping after the crew's departure. I returned home with so much food that I had to turn all the extra meat and produce into a stew and freeze batches. I don't have to wait in line to take a shower or deal with heaps of laundry. I'm not interrupted by shrieking laughter or screaming or giggling or racing footsteps tearing through the house at all hours.

Nearly three months with a full house created a new normal, and returning to just the two of us has been a relief and a shock to the system. Even Jonah has seemed restless and out of sorts since the first week, continually running to the door or checking bedrooms for his friends.

The late September air has a chill this evening, and it's perfect for running. I retie my laces and lift myself up on my toes a few times to make sure my sneakers feel right. I'm fussy about how much wiggle room I have. Too loose or too tight, and I'll be distracted throughout the entire run. I require perfection.

With my eyes closed, I inhale and raise my arms above my head, and then I exhale and drop them down. My usual stretches pass by in a blur because I'm so focused on the run ahead of me. I'm antsy and edgy, and I'm hoping that this workout will expel some of my mood and some of the emptiness plaguing me.

Music blasts into my earbuds, and I begin. Running over the hilly and often rocky terrain in this area has taken quite a bit of getting used to, and the side roads around here are not exactly paved to perfection. The slope on the main roads makes my legs burn and my lungs raw, but I like that. I have to run harder and stay stronger.

Running is part of how I saved myself, and even now that I am not the fragile mess I was a few years ago, I know that I will never stop. While running is a solitary sport, it's not lonely for me. It never has been. It forces me to think, to examine, while it's just me and the music and the road.

I leave the dusty dirt road and hit one of the main roads where there is actual concrete with painted lines, and I hold my pace while "Tennessee Whiskey" by Chris Stapleton starts in my ear. I smile. Chris made me a new playlist.

No one else in the world understands how I can run to such slow rhythms and melodies, but he knows that I run in contrast to what I'm hearing. The mood or lyrics or tone of a slower song propel me much more than pop or dance tracks ever could. He intrinsically knew this about me before I knew it about myself. The music he sends me is always right.

As I begin to work my way through this new song list and through my seven-mile goal, I'm already feeling more settled. Chris is at home right now, starting on dinner, and I'm looking forward to spending the evening with him. Of course, I feel this every day. I never tire of him, of us.

He is my home. The two of us together are peace and love after too much uncertainty and fearful instability.

The truth is, I like the quiet. After the fire that killed my parents and nearly destroyed James and me and even after the healing from that, I seek serenity. I like the cleanness and simplicity in my days—writing for the magazine from home, conducting interviews often by phone and the occasional outing to meet someone for a local piece, shopping in town, near daily runs, cooking in the evenings, weekends on Acadia's trails or curled up at home. Together, Chris and I have created safety for ourselves, and we fall more deeply in love each day. To some, the idea of reliability and safety might sound boring. For us, they bring joy.

Yet it seems my heart will eternally engage in a tug-of-war struggle between my need for calm and my fervent desire to be surrounded by those who disrupt one sort of calm to bring another. Because there *is* calm among the chaos. There is a completion that comes when I am with an entire group and inundated by noise and constant talk and wild energy. This is not to say that, on his own, Chris doesn't fulfill me more than I could have imagined, but he is one person, not a crowd.

I think Chris feels this as well. He's spent his entire life watching over his siblings, first doing everything in his power to shield them from their father and later fighting to keep the aftermath from swallowing them up whole. He roots for each of them, and he celebrates their successes, but he stays on guard. I know he is always watching, waiting. There is no relaxing, no chance that this particular tension will ever leave his body or mind. I'm not sure he'll ever escape his sense of responsibility. He lives in measured anxiety and fear.

But as much as he wants to keep incessant tabs on his brothers and sister, it's probably good for him to be separated from them. He has to learn to trust in their abilities to function and succeed on their own. Each sibling hides their traumas differently—Chris perhaps better than the others—but I see he is trying to clear out pieces of the wreckage, and he's getting there.

Music pounds through me on this run—and emotion as well. Sometimes, I clear my thoughts and collect my miles in a near trance. Then, there are days like this where I dig my way through feelings. Because I blocked out life for so many years, I'm phobic about missing something. It's why I push myself toward introspection, toward clear thinking. I've missed so much, and I'm afraid I'll miss more—in myself, in James. I failed him massively before, and I refuse to let that happen again. So, I keep myself in check to protect him and to protect everyone I love.

Oh. So, I guess I have that in common with Chris.

That's another thing that ties us—fear that we'll fail those we love.

I run harder because I miss them all and because I need space. It's an impossible fact of life that I might never resolve because we cannot collect our siblings and lock them in the house with us forever while also allowing each of us to define who we are outside of the others. We all need to tolerate distance and find the good that can come with that.

Sabin calls and texts me a few times a week. He hasn't found a job, but he has seemingly found the beach because I have about six hundred pictures of waves. The cheap motel where he's staying doesn't thrill me, particularly because the Yelp reviews I've read universally address a rather severe bedbug issue, but Sabin claims to find something humbling about slumming it.

"One does not stay at the Ritz when one is looking for an entry-level job, my fair lady!"

The song in my ears fades away, and I wait to see what the next track is. Instead, I hear Christopher's voice, and I nearly trip over my own feet. I'm almost embarrassed at the slight shiver that runs through me, and I mentally shake my head at my physical reaction. After all these months together, this boy still gives me butterflies. I regain my stride and listen to what he's recorded.

"If I timed this right," I hear him say, "you'll have another few miles before you're home. *Home*. It's such a stupidly simple word, but it carries so much weight."

There's a long silence now. So, I run. I can pass the time. Because I know what it is to feel Chris even in these moments of silence. It means he's thinking and processing. He's controlled in what he says, and he doesn't waste words.

I round a steep curve in the road. It's one I'm familiar with and one that makes me push myself. The hill hurts every time I run it. My calves ache, my quads ache, but I take this one on because of the hurt and because I know I'll be stronger after fighting to conquer it. So, I take what's in front of me.

"*Home*," Chris says, "used to be a terrifying place. It's not anymore. And you did that, Blythe. You gave that to me, to all of us. I haven't forgotten it for a minute."

It's unlike Chris to even mention his past without my asking, and I can see that he's doing it in a way that's contained for him, having recorded this for me to hear. It guarantees a safety, a way to separate himself from addressing this in a style that's too straightforward. He doesn't have to face me. I can't respond or react. He's pouring out what he can in a way that is tolerable for him. I want to be there for him, I want to let him shed this pain in person, but that is and will always be a lot to hope for.

34

Still, in this audio, he's telling me something difficult. He's putting out so much of his history and himself, even in just a few words, and that makes me even prouder of who he is.

"So, come home to me, Blythe. I know it's been a little rough for both of us. The loss of the summer isn't easy, and we haven't been in our usual groove. We're going to change that. I miss your body and your taste. I miss the way we move together, the way we come together. We need to get back to us and the indescribable way we connect. Your body is part of me. I need you."

Chris and I are not by any means all about sex. We never have been. Yet I can easily admit that it's a near constant with us. A palpable draw constantly lures me to him. Everything we feel and do on a physical level is a reflection of our emotional tie, so I never once feel guilty, nor do I question that bond. The heat we share is there for a reason.

With that said, not much throws off our sexual connection, but this last month of adjusting to our family leaving has slowed even us down. Melancholy does not breed sexual appetite, we've discovered, and we've gone longer than ever without making love. I miss him, and I miss us.

"Come home to me," he says again. "We both feel the difference between a full house and the two of us alone, but I want to remind you that there are benefits to having privacy." The tone of his voice changes here to one that I remember easily. Chris can go from serious and heartfelt to heated and sexually clear the next. "With no one else around, we can make all the noise we want. We can fuck anywhere we want…"

In an instant, I am undeniably glued to his voice, to the essence of Christopher and his desire.

"When I go down on you, when my tongue is moving against your clit, you can get loud. I know how you are. You start with a certain strain in your sounds, a whimper that drives me crazy. I love making you feel that good." Chris pauses, and I can feel he's making that coy smile he gets when he's flirtatious and teasing. "Later, I get to listen to so much more. There's nothing better than when I hear that purr from your throat, the sound of your heat, the way you manage to push out my name when that first wave of your orgasm hits."

There's the Chris I know. It's tempting to pick up my running pace even more, but I have an appreciation for foreplay, so I continue to run evenly.

We got used to stifling our tendency to get loud, to fuck anywhere in the house we liked, to let ourselves get carried into lovemaking in the middle of the day. It used to be easier to ignore the fact that our siblings were always within earshot, but at some point, we started to feel a certain responsibility to control ourselves.

I can't exactly complain about all the times Chris whispered in my ear, trying to keep me quiet, while grinding against me. Like the night he nearly made me lose my mind because we fucked so slowly and endlessly that when he finally picked up his pace, I couldn't help myself from screaming out.

Thinking about that night now makes me wet.

"Shh, baby," he told me as I got close to coming. "I feel how tight you are, how you're on the edge. Breathe, Blythe. Breathe for me. Don't make a sound."

In a haze, I told him I couldn't, that he was too good, that it was all too much. I wouldn't be able to keep silent.

"Of course you can. Because if you make any noise," he said, "I'm going to stop fucking you. You don't want that. I don't want that."

So, I dug my fingers into his back, and he kissed me while I lifted against him over and over, his tongue against mine, until my climax subsided.

"Good girl," he said softly. "Good girl."

Chris has always had control that I can't seem to find without his help. He's teaching me though.

So, as I run now, I turn up the volume while his recording continues, and I don't want to miss a thing. A mix of sweetness and sensuality in his voice compels me to run harder.

"Come home to me, Blythe. Meet me at the first place we reconnected."

The outdoor shower. I remember that very well.

I make that last mile at record speed, but I take the walk on the dirt road to the house more slowly. I have to catch my breath before Chris takes it away again. The last song on his playlist has rhythm and build and lust, and the thought of stripping down in that shower with Chris pushes away any leftover sadness about the lonely house.

The light from the sun is fighting over whether or not to set, casting a nearly electric glow over the house. Near the house, I walk down the steps leading to the level land below, and I can see steam from the shower wafting upward. My earbuds come out, but they're the only things I bother to take off before I step into the large wooden enclosure where Chris is naked and slick with water.

His back is to me, but immediately, he turns and takes me in his arms, my mouth seeking his because I cannot kiss him fast enough. Water pours over us, drenching my running clothes and sneakers, but I feel lighter than I have during the past few weeks. My hands move through his thick hair, pushing on the back of his head to press his mouth harder against mine, to get his tongue deeper into me.

Chris comes up for air and undoes the wide hook on my running bra. "How was your route?" he asks with a smile.

I move my hand between us and stroke his cock. "Fabulous."

For a second, his eyes close, and he inhales sharply. Then, he looks at me and pulls my sopping running bra over my head. Chris kneels in front of me, and I step on the heels of my sneakers to get them off. The water flows over me while he peels off my leggings and underwear, and then he kisses my stomach and my thighs, swiping his tongue between my legs for a heartbeat.

Fluidly, he turns me around, and I lean forward, bracing my hands against the wall, while he glides his mouth up the back of my leg until his lips are on my ass where he lingers for a while. He stands behind me, holding me, while his touch wanders over my stomach and my breasts. He's gentle, caressing my skin and igniting every part of me. I take my hands from the wall and stand fully, leaning into him and dropping my head back onto his shoulder. He cups my breasts, massaging his fingers over me, and then he takes each nipple and squeezes just enough to jolt me with arousal.

"I adore you, Blythe," he says without whispering. "I absolutely adore you."

I reach up to set my hand on his face. "And I absolutely adore you, Chris."

He smiles into the palm of my hand. "You ready to get loud?"

I nod and set my foot on the shower bench, effectively spreading myself open for him. "Absolutely."

So, we get loud.

Chris is behind me with one hand under my ass, lifting me just enough, while the other one is between my legs, his pressured touch on my clit. I keep my eyes open, letting my vision blur, as my pleasure escalates. When my fingers start pressing harder against the wall and when my panting and noises tell Chris that I'm nearly there, he scoops his arm from my ass to move around the top of my rib cage and brusquely pull me back against him, his fingers moving between my legs with more pressure now. I'm breathing so hard, and every time I exhale, the sound of my pleasure is pushed out from deep within my core.

"That's right," he says. "Let me hear you."

His palm pushes up over my breast, his fingers dragging across my skin to the top of my chest. I'm trying to keep my eyes open, so I can stay totally in the moment, but it's not easy. My head nestles into him, and his hand moves higher, settling just below my throat. I follow his grip, inching it higher, wanting him to have more of a hold over me than he already does.

There is something distinctly erotic about this move of his. It's unexpected and deeply arousing. Having his touch around my throat isn't scary or creepily controlling. It's the opposite. The level of trust and understanding between us allows this. I get to enjoy boundaries being pushed because I'm in the safety of our relationship, in the context of something meaningful and based on love.

Because of that, because I like what he's introduced, I tighten my hand over his. I want more, but he keeps the arc of his fingers firm, not letting me break the shape or position of his hand. He knows more than I do what is smart and what isn't. What he's doing is showing me how much he wants me to be his—to drop any extraneous thoughts, to just commit to the moment, to do nothing but focus on my own pleasure.

That, I've learned to accept, is of the utmost importance to him.

Oh God, I can't last any longer. "Chris…"

"Come home to me, Blythe. Come home to me," he says over and over.

My orgasm rocks through me, and the hand Chris has between my legs cups me hard, both to finish me and to keep me standing. When I slow down, I take my foot from the bench and bend to rest my hands on the edge. I don't filter the cry that comes out when he enters me, partially because he likes hearing it and partially because I do. I lift up on my toes a bit so that I can move with Chris and get his cock as far inside me as possible.

We fuck steadily, letting ourselves groan and call out each other's name.

"Come on, Chris," I whimper out through the erotic fog I'm in. "It's been so long. Baby, it's been so long. You can fuck me harder than that, can't you? Fuck me like you mean it."

Romantic? Maybe not. But we're not after romance right now. We're after screaming and intensity and fast, hard fucking. The benefit of being so in love is that we get to do this with meaning.

Chris's hand slaps against my ass as he grabs on to pull me closer against him, and he rakes his other hand down my back.

"Jesus, Blythe," he growls through a moan when he comes.

There's nothing like a shower with Chris.

When we're both satiated—for now—I lather him up. I figure we have another five minutes before the hot water is gone. The automatic outdoor lights have come on, and I admire how strikingly gorgeous Chris is. When his hair is dry, it always hangs in soft waves around his face, so I push it back under the shower spray and gaze up at him. That hard jawline, those green eyes, the perfect shape of his mouth…

He smiles down at me. "Hi."

"Hi, back."

"I didn't make dinner," he confesses. "I was too hot for you to focus on boring cooking."

"It's okay. Because, while you're a great cook, you're an even better lover."

I kiss his chest and let my hands roam over his back. He doesn't flinch anymore when I trace the many scars, even when I touch his back. I know exactly how to rest my arm against him so that the scar on my forearm fills the break in the line of the significant one that crosses from his shoulder to his lower back. Chris holds me tight as I do it this time. It's become an unspoken symbol to us, a connection too uncanny and powerful to speak about often.

We just let it be.

I move my arm and continue touching his skin. While the scar that connects us is the biggest, it is not the only one he has. Courtesy of his father, there are more—a few I know the stories behind, a few I don't. Certain ones, he won't talk about. Christopher's father was sick but smart, I suspect. He was careful that the result of his abuse would be easy to hide under clothing.

This shower feels like a reunion of some sort, so I take my time now to explore his body again, the entire shape of Chris. I work my hands over every inch of his skin. He holds still while I lower myself to slowly trace the line from his ankles to his waist, to slide my hand between his legs, and to reach back further and stroke a finger over him. I continue to move over his form, relishing every curve. My mouth tastes the water running over his hip bone, over his lower back, over his ass. This man has a gorgeous ass, so I take my time.

I entwine my fingers with his when I later move up and stand on my tiptoes to kiss his shoulder and his neck. I touch the solid strength in his lean chest and arms. I could do this for hours.

It can be difficult to get Chris to relax fully, but I feel him ease into my touch as his muscles drop their tension. He watches me with interest, as though slightly amused or curious that I still find him and his body as exciting as I always have. He should understand though, given the care and thoroughness with which he makes love to me so often.

His expression changes when my hands move from his waist to the top of his torso and then to just under his armpits. It's a subtle change—a flicker of fear in his eyes. It's only because I know him so well that I catch it.

My heart sinks because I know this look, and I know what's coming.

I hold my touch where it is. "It's all right, Chris. Don't be scared."

He nods.

"Left side or right?" I ask.

"My right," he says evenly.

I inch my left hand up and feel for it. It takes my force of will for me to stay calm. As many times as I've seen Chris naked and as well as I know his body, I've just found another scar. It's not exactly in a highly visible place, not somewhere I often have my hands, so I failed to notice this one. Or maybe I didn't want to acknowledge it. Chris has enough nightmare stories as it is.

But because it's important, because *truth* is important, and because I want him to keep releasing secrets, I very softly rub my fingers until I find texture changes. This scar is about two inches long and an inch wide. I could fucking kill myself for never feeling this before. The skin here is so tender, and I feel sick over the pain Chris must have felt when this was inflicted on him.

He looks away while I touch him, but he doesn't stop me.

"Do you want to tell me about this one?"

Christopher takes a deep breath and forces a smile. Finally, he makes eye contact and shrugs. "I was egging him on, mouthing off. He retaliated."

He isn't telling me the truth. He wouldn't have prodded his father. Chris has always done what he can to facilitate peace, not ignite war.

"You don't want to tell me about it?"

He thinks for a moment. "I don't."

My fingers keep moving. "It's a burn?"

"It's a burn."

"It must have been…" I refuse to choke on my words. "It must have been very painful."

"Yes." Chris shuts off the water and kisses the top of my head. His arms fall over my shoulders, and he pulls me in so that our naked bodies are pressed close together.

The rise and fall of his chest reassures me. There *is* life after hell. There is breathing and life and profound love after hell. He holds me like this for a while, and together, we just breathe.

"I'm so glad he's dead," Chris says calmly. "I don't care how that sounds to anyone else but you because you understand. Maybe I'm supposed to forgive him. Maybe it helps other people to do that. But I'm just glad that son of a bitch is dead. Do you understand that?"

"I understand." I've never told Chris that I came close to murdering his father myself. That the only reason I didn't was because Zach stopped me. "I'm glad he's dead, too."

I wonder how many more of these moments we're going to have. How many more incidents and injuries and traumas I will hear about. How many more times I will wish that I had followed through and beaten the life out of Christopher's father. It's what that man deserved. It would have been justice.

Or maybe not. Maybe there is no justice for his atrocities, and I would have done something that I wouldn't have been able to live with.

There really is no way to pay back the torture and terror he inflicted on his children.

"Hey?" Chris grabs a towel from the hook and wraps it around my back, pulling me in.

I notice it's just the same way that Sabin did with me a few weeks ago on the dock, except that Chris refrains from shaking me around like crazy.

Chris smiles. "Please don't look like that. Remember what I always tell you?"

"That you're okay now. That it's over."

"Yes. I *am* okay now, and it *is* over."

"But you still have nightmares."

"I'll probably always have nightmares." He smiles again, trying to comfort me.

He knows that my love for him makes his history belong to me to a degree. He knows that, when you love someone, you take on that person's pain. So, I feel his pain, and in part, it becomes my own.

"But I am *still* okay, and it is *still* over. Those are truths that I hold on to more tightly than I hold on to even you, so you need to believe me."

"I do."

"Good. Now, let's go to dinner and drink too much, and then we'll come home and fuck too much."

I kiss him and whisper into his mouth, "There is no *too much*."

"That's my girl."

We refuse to let the past wreck our today. That's why we're the team that we are.

We dry off and head back up to the house. I check my phone and see a voice mail from Sabin. I listen to it twice and then put it on speaker for the third time.

Sabin's voice booms through. "Blythe! Blythe! I found permanent and bedbug-free housing!" he shouts with somewhat alarming glee. "It is *not* in a pineapple under the sea for the simple reason that I am not SpongeBob. Thus, the pineapple-under-the-sea housing board fucking denied my application. Fucking bastards! However, I found something better. You ready for it, B? I live in a tree house! Like a goddamn cookie-baking fucking elf! Call me back!"

I look at Chris with disbelief. "Did he really say that he lives in a tree house?"

Chris grins. "Where else would Sabin live?"

5
CRASH MY PARTY

ALL I WANT,
ALL I NEED,
ALL I WANT.
I'M IN LOVE WITH YOU.

NOVEMBER BRINGS TEMPERATURES IN THE FORTIES, OVERCAST skies, and a quiet town. While there are a handful of cross-country skiing fanatics who might come to the Acadia area, by and large, we are in full winter mode with many restaurants and stores shut down for the season.

After struggling to acclimate when our respective siblings left, Chris and I are now back in our comfortable routine. I suppose we're not like most people in their early twenties who would probably find the idea of semi-isolation totally unappealing. Maybe our troubled histories have influenced us in this way, but neither of us craves bars or crowds or packed social lives. Neither of us is on any social networking sites, which presumably puts us in a minuscule percentage.

Holing up for the winter limits chaos and brings a kind of simplicity and clarity that is settling. It's not as though we don't have friends. Granted, working from home as I do doesn't lend itself to meeting new people, but I still talk to my friend Nichole regularly. Chris has become friendly with some people from work, and we occasionally get together with them for small dinner parties or hikes.

But very often, we're alone, not in a pathological or dysfunctional way. It's just because that's what we prefer—for now at least. Maybe one day, we'll both have calendars booked with plans but not now.

So, it's the two of us for tomorrow's Thanksgiving, and I'm perfectly okay with it—well, mostly okay with it. Flying everyone out here for such a short time really didn't make much sense, and we'll all be together over Christmas and New Year's, so I'll wait for the big family gathering and find plenty to be grateful for with Chris.

Even though it's just us, we're going all out with tomorrow's meal, and the kitchen is a bit of a disaster area.

"Do you remember the first time we cooked for Thanksgiving together?" Chris asks.

I look up from the apple that I'm peeling for the pie. "Like it was yesterday."

"Our cooking skills have gotten better. That's for sure."

"I think Eric shamed us into devoting more attention to the importance of a well-cooked holiday dinner."

He doesn't look up from kneading bread dough. "You looked beautiful in that messy dorm kitchen, sitting on the counter, all covered in flour."

I look back down at the apple and smile as I start peeling again. "And you looked incredibly hot when you asked me to ignore the cooking and dance with you."

"And you made me so fucking horny when you did dance with me."

I laugh. "I did not. You didn't try anything."

"Doesn't mean that I wasn't thinking about it."

I smile again. "Good."

It was a wonderful Thanksgiving. The best, really. When I felt so alone, Chris told me that I had family. More than that, he showed me.

"Are you sad that everyone isn't here with us?" he asks.

I set down the knife and round the counter to hug Chris from behind. "It's hard to be sad when I'm focusing on all that I have to be thankful for." My hands slip under the back of his shirt and cross slowly to his stomach.

When I inch my fingers below his waistline, he laughs. "I'm kind of covered in bread dough here."

I duck under his arm and slip between him and the counter.

He smiles down at me. "You're about to get your hot self covered in flour again."

I quickly kiss him. "Keep kneading."

Chris rubs his nose against mine and then continues with the bread, his body rocking into me as he works.

"I have to say that I admire your technique," I say as I put my hands on his hips. "Such steady rhythm. And really throwing your weight into it."

"You are trouble, young lady." Chris firmly pushes his body against mine and grinds into me while he buries his mouth against my neck.

"This is going to be the best bread ever," I say through my giggling.

Just as I lift my hands into his hair, my phone rings. I pull back and reach for it. "That's Sabin's ring! I have to get it."

Sabin's calls and texts have been sporadic over the past few weeks. I've been trying to give him space because I know how busy he's been.

"Hey, easy there," Chris jokes. "Wrong brother to be getting so excited about."

I lightly slap him on the arm. "It's just that I haven't talked to him in—"

"Just kidding. I know. Grab the call."

Chris steps back, and I catch the phone before it goes to voice mail.

"Sabin!"

"Whatcha up to on this fine holiday eve, oh Mistress of Maine?" His gritty voice booms through the phone.

I have missed him.

"Just being thankful and shit," I say.

Chris leans in toward my phone. "Tell him I am *not* thankful for his timing." But he blows me a kiss and starts to shape the dough into a loaf.

"Oh, horrors!" Sabin says dramatically. "Have I interrupted some sort of disgusting and unnatural sexual interaction?"

"Sabe!" I yell.

"Ah, I have. Well, I have no idea what that might entail as it's been a hundred years since I've gotten laid."

"It's the season to be grateful, not pissy."

"I'm grateful that I haven't fucked anyone and been vulnerable to a hideous venereal disease. How's that?"

47

I frown. "Are you okay? This is hardly the attitude of someone who ran off to San Diego and fell into the most unusual life ever."

Sabin wasn't kidding when he said that he lived in a tree house. He really does. An actual fucking tree house. In perfect Sabin fashion, he got a job with a company that builds rather luxurious accommodations for those who wish to live in unusual habitats. The owner of the business, Pearce, offered Sabin the tree house on his own property for minimal rent. Aside from a bedroom and living area, it even has a small kitchen. Not to mention, it has working electricity and plumbing.

Chris nods at the sound system we keep high on a shelf, away from kitchen accidents. I hit the On button, and he waves for me to step out of the kitchen if I want. Music blares from the speakers, and I cover the mouthpiece on my phone.

"I'm not done with you," I warn Chris.

"Better not be."

I find quiet in the living room and lie on the couch. "Now, tell me, how's tree-house life?"

"Lofty," Sabin says.

"Funny. Say more."

"It's pretty awesome."

"When are you going to send me pictures? You keep saying you will, and you haven't. How am I supposed to relax when I can't picture you in your surroundings?"

"I told you. I'm still fixing it up. It was sort of half done when I moved in. I mean, it was all there structurally, but it didn't have much style going on. I added on a wraparound porch. Did I tell you that?"

"How the hell did you know how to do that?" I ask.

"Pearce helped me. He got me extra lumber from jobs they'd finished."

"You must be learning a ton. This guy Pearce sounds really cool, huh?"

Sabin pauses. "Yeah, I guess. I mean, now, I'm roped into having Thanksgiving dinner with him, his kid, and a whole crew of people I don't know. I'm supposed to make a side dish, but I haven't really figured that out quite yet."

"Um, you'd better get moving. It's, what? Almost six there? The markets are going to close."

"I don't know if I'm even going to go. It's gonna be dumb."

"If you were invited and you accepted, then you're going. And this guy has been very good to you. He gave you a job and a place to live, so go be grateful."

"Fine," he says grouchily.

"Hey, are you okay?" I ask.

Sabin has a social drive that I don't, so I'm surprised he's not more enthusiastic.

"Of course I'm okay. Why wouldn't I be? I have sunshine and surf, missy." His voice lifts, and I feel slightly better. "Just tired. We were doing a job two hours away. Lots of driving on congested freeways, plus the whole hauling lumber and raising it up a story. Oh, but get this! So, the guy we built that tree house for? He had us put in a zip line that goes from his main house to the landing by the tree-house's front door and then a slide that loops out, like, three times from the bedroom to the ground. It's fucking awesome."

"That's so cool! And you like everyone you work with?"

"Yeah, those guys are nice. Real friendly. We hang out after work, grab a drink, and stuff."

I don't say anything about this because I'm not sure what he means by *drink*, so there's a stretch of silence between us.

"Blythe?"

"Yeah?"

"I know you're worrying now, and please don't."

"Okay."

"Like I told you, alcohol isn't really my problem."

"Okay."

"I know you're still worrying, so stop it. It's awesome here. I'm building tree houses, so how could it not be awesome? Insane stuff. I mean, anything people want can happen. I saw a tree house being used as an office, and it had a lookout over the ocean and a hand-carved desk. And...and...oh, Pearce is designing a house now with a pulley system, so the owner can get her two-legged golden retriever up and down. Like, it's a fucking elevator for the dog! Nice lady but even nicer dog. He's almost fifteen, and he lost his legs when some asshole ran over him. Sad.

"Anyhow, yeah, I really like this job. You gotta see the ocean here. I know you're on the coast right now, too, but the West Coast isn't like the Maine waters. Just a different feeling and flavor. Pearce's property is huge, and it feels like I'm in the middle of nowhere because there are trees all around. His house is buried far back from where I am. We're not that far north of downtown San Diego, really, and I don't mind the drive."

"That's great, Sabe. So, if you're going out with friends and being all Sabin*ish*, why aren't you meeting girls? You were stuck in boring Bar Harbor with us for so long. I thought you'd get to the big city and go wild."

He laughs a little. "Yeah, I dunno. I'm out of practice."

"Aw, you need a little lovin', huh?"

"Maybe. We'll see."

I roll onto my side and stare at the empty fireplace. There's a stack of wood next to it that we never use. "Sabin?"

"Yeah?"

"How come you kept bringing in new firewood when you were here?"

Sabin routinely chopped logs and replaced those stacked by the fireplace with new ones. We never burned them because I still can't tolerate the sight of flames.

"Did it bother you?"

"No. I liked it for some reason. But why did you do it?"

I can tell he's a bit uncomfortable with my questions.

"Oh, I'm not sure. It's nice to be prepared. Maybe, one day, you'll be ready. You go through the motions, keep stacking the firewood, and maybe things get easier."

"I miss having you do that." I didn't realize it until now, but I do. The same firewood has been here since he left.

There's another long silence.

"I'm sure Chris will do it for you."

"I want *you* to do it." Suddenly, while I'm staring at the empty fireplace that might never light, my heart absolutely aches for Sabin to be next to me. "I wish you were here. Tomorrow won't be the same without you."

"You don't need me crashing your party."

"You can crash my party anytime, dummy."

"Hey, that's Luke Bryan's line."

I hear his guitar through the phone, and he sings a few lines of "Crash My Party," which cracks me up.

"You have a song for everything," I point out.

"I'm playing at a few open mic nights, did I tell you? And a few paying gigs."

"What? No. Why...Sabe, why don't I know this shit?" I'm so frustrated now. "This long distance–friendship thing sucks."

Music keeps coming through my earpiece because neither of us knows what to say. So, I just listen while he sings to me. When he's done, we stay on the line without talking. I don't know why this isn't uncomfortable, but it's not.

Finally, he says, "Kiddo, I gotta go. You're right that I need to bring some fucking side dish tomorrow, so I have to hit the store. I'm thinking something involving green beans and marshmallow goop or sweet potatoes and a can of onion rings."

"Ew, no! First of all, you've mixed up two dishes, but neither is good anyway. Make something nice, like scalloped potatoes with heavy cream and lots of cheese. Crusty top and whatnot."

"Oh. That actually sounds good. How do I do that?"

"I'll text you a link to the recipe. We're having that tomorrow, too. Do you have a mandoline?"

"Hello? I have a guitar."

I laugh. "The other kind of mandoline, the one that slices."

"The one that gourmet cooks use and the one that, more often than not, removes fingers? No, I do not have a fucking mandoline."

"Okay, just use a knife and thinly slice the potatoes."

"I'll give it a go."

"And if it doesn't turn out right, then we can make it together when you're here for Christmas and perfect your cooking."

"So, listen...I don't know how to tell you this—"

I sit up sharply. There's already an apologetic tone from him that I strongly dislike. "No, don't you say what I think you're going to say."

"I just can't take a month off from work. Or even more than a few days. Chris has a slow season, and you both can telecommute. By the way, is that not the most obnoxious word ever? *Telecommute*. Ugh. Makes me sick to say it. So pretentious and smug. Let's just say *work from home*. How's the magazine writing going anyway?"

"What? Fine. Who cares? What are you saying? That you're not coming home for Christmas? We have all these plans. I wanted to do a huge tree in the living room, and I ordered new stockings for everyone. And...snowball fights and big dinners and horrible carols."

"I just...can't. I'm really sorry. I feel awful about this. There's no way that I can take off enough time for such a long trip. I'd fly in and have to leave practically the next day."

"Okay." I'm trying with all I have to conceal my absolute misery over this.

I get it though. Sabin has a new job that he's committed to, and I have to be supportive. On a practical level, I understand all the reasons he won't be with us for the holidays, but that doesn't change the fact that my heart feels as though it's been sliced out of my chest.

It didn't occur to me that this move to California might permanently separate us, that we might never live ten feet from each other again. Of course that sounds idiotic, but I don't care. Sabin has every right to go off and have a life of his own. I just didn't realize how much I felt that part of his life belonged with me. I'm embarrassed at the wave of devastation running through me.

I can't do this now. The only right thing to do is rally and let him know that I support him. It's just that finding the right words seems impossible.

"Sabe, I love you, and I want you to do whatever it is that you need to do. I'll send you a crazy huge care package."

His voice has more rasp than usual. "Will there be a forty-pound fruit cake in it?"

"Yes. Also, fruit cake angels and fruit cake reindeer." I listen to him breathe for a few moments. "It's okay. They're just stupid holidays."

"They're not stupid holidays. You love them," he says.

"I love you more."

"More than snowmen?"

"They are cold and have stick limbs. Also, notoriously shitty attitudes about US foreign policy. Yes, I love you more than snowmen."

His gravelly laugh echoes into my ear. "But you'll build one for me anyway?" he asks.

"With three noses. And I'll put that disgusting parka that you shipped here on it."

"What kind of fucking creepy snowman are you making? And that parka is super gangsta, I'll have you know."

"Just for that, I'm adding on a hat with a veil."

Sabe laughs. "God, I miss you. You always make me feel better. It doesn't make any sense because…" He trails off.

"Because why? We're best friends. We *should* make each other feel better."

"Yeah. It's just…it seems like that should be true for…I mean…" He pauses. "It's just, usually guys have a guy best friend, and girls have a girl best friend."

I think for a minute. "And we have us. We don't follow rules."

"No, I guess not." He strums his guitar, and then I hear him slap his hand over the strings to stop the music. "I gotta run to the market. You talked me into making this potato nonsense. Send me the recipe as soon as you hang up, okay?"

"Okay. Happy Thanksgiving. I'll call you tomorrow."

"I'll try to pick up. Busy day with the potato eaters here."

"I imagine so."

"Have fun with Chris," he says. "But don't go traying."

"Not without you."

I hang up and stare into the unlit fireplace. *Fuck. Fuck!*

I sit numbly for twenty minutes and only shake off my daze when Sabin texts me and points out that, while we are very emotionally connected, he is not actually telepathic and cannot envision the recipe without text message dialogue. I text back the link and try to talk myself out of sulking.

I've been gone so long that Chris eventually sticks his head into the living room. "Hey, did you abandon me?"

"No, no. Of course not," I say rather flatly. "It's just…" I aimlessly wave a hand around.

Chris throws a dish towel over his shoulder and comes to sit next to me on the couch. "What's wrong? Is Sabin all right? Did he fall out of a tree house? Big blow to the head?"

I try to smile, but it's not working.

"Blythe, you're starting to freak me out. What's going on?"

"Sorry, everything is fine. Really." I lean against him. "Sabin isn't coming here for the holidays. He says he has to work."

Christopher runs a hand through my hair and wraps a long curl over his finger. "I was worried about that," he says, "which is why—"

"I mean, what the hell?" I yell out. "We're all supposed to be together! This isn't right. Everyone was broken and fucked up and all that, and then we sort of pieced ourselves back together, and…and…and we have to be together. All of us. I know he has a new job and real life, but…it's starting, isn't it? Eventually, everyone will start making their own plans. Holidays, summers…everything is going to change. We're fragmenting."

Chris puts a hand under my chin and makes me look at him. "Stop spazzing," he says with amusement, "and let me finish what I started to tell you."

I nod.

"We are not fragmenting," he states assuredly. "I was worried Sabin wouldn't be able to take off any time, which is why we're going to San Diego for three weeks."

I sit up straight. "What?"

"All of us—Estelle, Eric, James, you, and me. Then, Zach is going to come in right after Christmas." He kisses my cheek. "We're not fragmenting."

I throw my arms around his neck. "God, you're fucking amazing."

"Wait until you see the house I rented. *That's* fucking amazing. I was waiting to tell you and everyone else until the house was confirmed. Just got an email five minutes ago."

"Christopher…" I hardly know what to say, but then I remember one thing. "What about—"

"Jonah? Kevin from work is going to take him, if that's okay with you. He has a puppy, and I think he's hoping Jonah will tire him out."

"You think of everything, don't you? Now, I have even more to be grateful for this Thanksgiving." I lift my body and straddle him on the couch.

"And I," he starts, "also have so, so much to be grateful for." He looks at me with mischief and flirtation as he runs the back of his hand over the front of my shirt.

"Do you now?" I ask. "Whatever could you be talking about?"

"I'd be happy to give you a walk-through," he offers. His mouth is hot when he kisses my neck so softly and so teasingly that I already want to scream. "I'm grateful for you and for the way you inhale sharply when my tongue hits your skin."

"I do that?"

"You do." His mouth begins to trail over to my shoulders, and his hands go under the front of my shirt. "And how you still shiver when I first touch your breasts, as though you're still not used to me, even after all this time." His touch goes over my bra.

He's right. I do shiver.

"I'm grateful for this gorgeous body," he continues, "for the way you taste and move and sound when we fuck."

I lift my shirt over my head and toss it to the floor. "What else?"

"I'm grateful that there are so many ways to make you come and that you always seem to want me as much as I want you. I don't know how I got so damn fortunate." Chris smiles at me. "Most importantly, I'm grateful for the way you let me love you and the way you love me. I'm grateful that I'll never get enough of you."

I smile back at him. "We have similar lists."

"Yeah?"

"We do."

When I kiss him, I think of what I thought the first time we kissed. *He tastes like eternity and healing and completion.*

Because of this, I cannot imagine ever kissing anyone else.

6
THE IMPACT ON LANDING

YOU COULD NEVER TAKE MY HAND 'CAUSE YOU'D NEVER UNDERSTAND WHY WE RIDE.

IT'S BEEN A LONG TIME SINCE I'VE BEEN ON AN AIRPLANE OR IN A big city with crowds and noise and traffic.

I am more than slightly uncomfortable when Chris and I land at the San Diego Airport. It's taken us hours and hours to get here from Maine, and we're both exhausted. Unfortunately, I don't seem to be so exhausted that I'm free from feeling overwhelmed. Bangor International Airport wasn't a big deal, and then we had to run to catch our flight to Chicago, so I didn't have time to freak, but now that we're here, I'm getting wobbly.

"You okay?" Chris asks while we wait at baggage claim.

"Yeah. Just tired." I try to look relaxed and not focused on the hundreds of people gathered around the baggage carousel.

He takes my hand. "We're out in the real world, I know."

Chris gets it. I nod and step in closer to him.

Months in the safety of our Maine house have left me embarrassingly out of practice for life outside the cocoon. It's ridiculous. Apparently, I've developed some kind of agoraphobia, but there was a reason that we retreated to coastal Maine. We like the serenity.

I tell Chris that I have to use the restroom and dart off before he can worry about me too much. The ladies' room is inconveniently located by the massive security line, and I feel sick by the time I hide out in a stall. Of course, the restroom stinks like chemical cleaners, and there are lines and women crowded around mirrors and babies pooping and...

I lean against the stall door and try not to touch anything with my hands. Jesus, I'm sweating, and the phone shakes when I make a call.

"Is this the sexy escort I ordered?" Sabin asks immediately. "I don't want to hear any bitching about the tree-house situation, okay? It's very trendy right now. And you'd better be bringing the mermaid outfit I requested, or this whole thing is off. Also, I'll be paying you from my jar of pennies."

Sabin's voice cuts through my panic, and I let out a laugh of relief. "A mermaid outfit? Really?"

"Oh. Blythe," he says with mock disappointment. "Thought you were someone else. And don't question the mermaid outfit. I would look fucking amazing in it. Er, I mean, *she* would. Right. It's not for me. That would be weird." He pauses. "Or would it?"

"Sabin?"

"Yes, Blythe?"

"We're in San Diego."

"And you sound so...overjoyed about it. What's going on?"

"It's stupid. It's just that...there are a lot of people and noises and shit, and I'm sort of not doing well."

"It's December nineteenth. Of course it's a fucking mob scene everywhere. It's going to get better when you get away from the airport and downtown traffic."

The red light above the toilet is irritating me. It's as though it's waiting for me to sit on that germy seat, and that's not going to happen. I frown at the toilet, and then I lift my foot and push the flush button. It just turns red again.

"Oh my God, are you taking a piss while you're talking to me?" Sabin yells.

"No, I'm just hiding out for a minute."

"I wasn't mad. I was just concerned that I was missing out because I was going to go pee, too. I thought maybe that was a thing we were doing—peeing while we talk."

"That's not a thing we do." I nervously tap my feet.

"And what's *that* noise?" he asks.

"I'm tapping my feet."

"Stop that immediately. The lady in the stall next to you might think you're signaling her for sex, like you're a closeted senator or whatnot lookin' for action. I mean, unless that's what you're after, have at it, Senator."

"Sabin! I am doing no such thing! Besides, I think that signal is only for men's rooms." But I still stop tapping.

"B?"

"Yeah?"

"Get the fuck out of the restroom, get your bags, and go find some sunshine. It's gorgeous out. Better than your Maine winter."

"Okay," I say without conviction.

"Sweetness," Sabin says, "get the fucking fuck out of the restroom, and come get some Sabin love!"

I yank the phone away from my ear and giggle. "Okay, okay!"

"I'll meet you at the house in a bit, silly girl."

I hang up and knock my head on the door while I try to collect myself. This is humiliating, and I don't want Chris to see me like this, not that he'd care. He's seen me in much worse states. But he went to so much trouble to arrange this incredible trip and to get us out here, and here I am, being all bananas.

My phone sounds with a text.

> *Sabin: Get the fuck out of the restroom. I love you—you and mermaids.*

By the time I get to baggage claim, I'm half human.

When we're at long last in the huge rental SUV, heading away from the airport, I actually feel elated. It's impossible to ignore the spectacular bay scene. It's only mid afternoon here, and even though we've been up since three in the morning, East Coast time, I am suddenly energized. We really have left behind the bitter New England temperatures, and as I roll down the window, I do not for one second miss the wind chill that comes off the Atlantic all winter.

"It must be almost seventy degrees here!" I say with delight as the wind blows my hair across my face.

Chris points to the dashboard. "Seventy-one. Not bad, huh? That's warm for this time of year here, and we've got a great forecast ahead."

I put on my sunglasses and take in the view—sun smattering across the water, cruise ships loaded with passengers, smaller boats zipping by. I get that summer feeling back. Sunshine, I realize, will do me some good.

"It's going to be strange, not having snow for Christmas. I've never been anywhere warm over the holidays," I say.

"No? I guess it will be a little weird, but you'll love it. Not a traditional New England holiday, but we'll make it fun."

"Of course we will." I put my arm over his shoulder, and my fingers tickle the back of his neck.

Last year was our first Christmas in Maine, but before we were together, Chris always took his family off on some expensive exotic trip during college winter breaks.

"You're used to Hawaii and Tahiti and whatever, huh? Will you survive boring San Diego?"

He laughs. "I'm excited to be here. This is a great city."

"Thank you for doing this, Chris."

"We stay together," he says firmly. "If this is where Sabin is for the holidays, this is where we are. No question. It's important to me, but I know it's also important to you. You guys are very close, and you've missed him a lot."

"I feel like he's been so busy that we haven't talked as much recently," I say.

When Sabin first moved out here, we logged hours and hours video-chatting and talking on the phone, but as the weeks and months have gone on, it's been harder to find time, I guess. While we're out here, I plan on getting in lots of quality Sabin love, and of course, with everyone else, too. Estelle, Eric, and James get in the day after tomorrow and will drive up in another car.

"Sabin's been working hard. Have you gone on the company's website?" Chris asks. "They've got tons of pictures with really incredible structures, and I'm assuming that he's been learning a lot. This is good for him, really good for him."

I'm not sure if Chris is trying to convince me or himself.

We make the drive north to La Jolla, making a quick stop at a supermarket to start stocking up the house. In typical Christopher Shepherd fashion, he won't let me pay, and I promise myself that I'm going to sneak out of the house for the next grocery run and return with pricey steaks as payback.

It is only when we pull up to the house that I realize any grocery shopping I attempt will not come close to payback. "Jesus Christ, what did you do?"

"What?" he asks, feigning innocence. "It's La Jolla. What do you want?"

"Christopher Shepherd!" I shout, flabbergasted.

The house is more mansion than house, and it's smack on the water. I can't even form words right now. Just looking at the outside of this modern...compound...tells me that it is incomprehensibly luxurious inside.

"Christopher Shepherd!" I say again.

He laughs. "We need a house big enough to hold all of us. And who knows where James and Estelle will be sleeping? I didn't know if they needed one room or two—"

"This...this!" I stammer. "This must have cost a not-at-all-small fortune. It's way too much money to spend."

He shrugs and turns more serious. "I don't know if you really understand how much money we have."

I look at him. "I'm starting to."

"It's just money. And I have very mixed feelings about it." Although the car is parked, he grips the wheel and stares through the windshield.

"Part of me just wants to blow it all, so there's nothing left of my father. And part of me wants to use it for good, whether that's making sure everyone has the best education they can or taking crazy vacations. That money represents a shitty past, but maybe it also represents...you know, that we're all still here. I want to enjoy that. And I want the people I love, my family, to enjoy that. It's just a little spoiling on occasion. Besides," he says, turning to me now, "you know I'm happy anywhere. We all are. Look at Sabin. He won't take any money, and he's living in a tree house. We don't *require* luxury. It's just fun."

Chris has a point. While the Shepherds do tend to vacation in high-end spots, they're not a snobby bunch. Hell, they all waded through knee-deep muddy low tides, searching for clams, more times than I could count, and everyone worked like dogs on the house. This is not a family afraid of dirt and toil.

I open the car door. "So, let's go run around the house and play before everyone gets here."

The massive white boxy mansion sprawls over the property, and even Chris fumbles with the keys while letting us in.

He stands frozen when the door swings open, revealing a monstrous first floor with floor-to-ceiling windows that give us clear views of the Pacific Ocean. "Fine, I might have gone a little overboard."

We spend twenty minutes investigating. We drop our luggage when we find a bedroom with an ocean view and a skylight, and then we unload the groceries into the kitchen. While the kitchen we have in Maine is oversized, this one has such high-end appliances that I'm almost afraid to touch anything in here.

Chris rummages for glasses. "Drink?"

I nod. "Dirty martini. A hundred olives."

"Ah, a *drink* drink." He tosses a bag of chips at me. "Then, we have to eat, or we'll be on the floor."

The avocados we bought are perfectly ripe and creamy and a shade of green that is far more enticing than the dull hue I can get at home. I mix up the most delicious guacamole I've ever had. We stretch out on lounge chairs on the deck and eat mouthfuls of chips and dip as we stare, transfixed, at the ocean view.

"This is already the best Christmas ever," I say.

"I'm glad you're happy."

I call Sabin, but it goes to voice mail, so I text him and tell him to get over here.

"He's probably already on his way," Chris says. "Let's hope that fifty-year-old car he bought makes it."

My stomach is all fluttery, and my body is full of anticipation while I wait for Sabin to get here. The martini does little to settle me down, and I nervously eat half of the bag of tortilla chips while I keep checking the clock.

Chris falls asleep in his chair, and I spend the next two hours getting increasingly annoyed with Sabin. I call him three more times and text him a picture of me frowning.

Nothing.

I change my clothes and leave Chris to sleep while I walk down to the water. I wade and dig my feet into the sand. We must have a private beach here because it's beautifully quiet and soothing. There's no way that Sabin won't show up soon.

I call James and tell him how amazing the house is, and then I text Estelle and Eric pictures from my vantage point on the beach. This beach is totally different from the rocky shores of Maine, and it's easy for me to get dreamy and euphoric as I lie in the sand, not caring that I'm getting wet. The water is not warm by any means, but I have my bathing suit on under my sundress, so I rip off the dress and dunk myself in. The shock of the cold kills any jet lag I was feeling, and I let out a jubilant yell when I break through the surface.

"You kook!" I hear from the deck above.

I whip my head around, expecting to see Sabin, but it's Chris leaning over the railing.

"There's a swimming pool here, you know!" he calls down.

"It's not the same. I wanted real California ocean!" But I am shivering, so I run through the small waves and grab my dress from the sand. I check my phone.

Nothing.

I shield my eyes and look up at Chris. "Do you have a message from Sabin?"

He shakes his head. "No. It's pretty weird."

I take the wide steps back up to the house and wrap up in a towel. "Have you called him?"

"Doing it right now," he says. "Want another drink?"

I nod and wipe away salt water from dripping into my eyes. I brighten when I hear Chris talking in the kitchen. He must have finally reached his brother, so my heart lifts. Then, I realize the tone of the conversation is more serious than jovial.

I knot the towel over my bathing suit and poke my head inside. Chris has his back to me and is shaking a silver drink mixer with more force than necessary, slamming ice cubes and causing an echo through the cavernous first floor.

"Are you fucking kidding me? She's done nothing but talk about seeing you since you left Maine, and you can't get your ass up here? I don't care if you're busy. You knew we were getting in today, and you swore up and down that you had days off. It's *Blythe*, for fuck's sake. Why are you acting like she's an imposition?" He cracks the shaker against the counter. "No, I'm not telling her shit. You talk to her and tell her yourself."

"Chris," I say calmly. Despite my now dashed hopes of seeing Sabin today, I don't like to hear Chris spat with his brother.

63

He pivots and leans against the counter, throwing me an apologetic look.

"It's okay." I reach for his phone. "Sabe, you're not coming over?"

"Listen, I've just got so much to do. Really crazy right now."

Chris is staring at me, waiting to see how I'm going to react.

"If you can't, you can't," I say. "It's just that I talked to you earlier, and you didn't say anything about not seeing us today. I've been calling you all day."

"Yeah, I'm sorry. Sort of last minute, love. I had to run out and pick up some lumber for one of our projects. Now, I've got to help Pearce chop down a tree and haul it into their house. You must be jet-lagged anyway, right?" he asks.

"Right. Totally. So, tomorrow for sure?"

"Of course. Talk to you la—"

"Wait, Sabin!" I practically roll my eyes. "What time? Do you want to meet here?"

"Oh, right. What do you want?"

I take the martini Chris hands me and eat two olives before answering, "Maybe we can come see your tree house? Ten o'clock?"

"Perfect! Bring me sixty-eight blueberry bagels and a non-fat, no-whip decaf vegan mocha cappuccino with a foot-shaped cinnamon imprint."

I laugh, and Chris looks relieved.

"Ask, and ye shall receive."

"Welcome to California! The land of complicated and trendy ordering. See you tomorrow."

"See you tomorrow."

Chris takes his phone back and shakes another martini for himself. "I'm sorry. Sabin is being a prick for some reason," he says above the rattling.

I don't know what to say. I'm a bit embarrassed that I seem more eager to see Sabin than he does me, but he did say that he was busy.

It's very possible that it's true.

It's also possible that it's not.

There's a chenille blanket draped over one of the white leather couches, and it looks perfect for snuggling, so I grab it, and Chris follows me back to the deck.

"Let's just sit here and watch the sun set as we drink." I need a minute to regroup because this day has been more than and also less than I expected.

Chris sits, and I take my usual spot, lounging between his legs with my head leaning back against him. His body is rigid, and I know the exchange he had with his brother is bothering him, but we don't talk. We breathe, and we concentrate on the orange and pink colors that start to flood the sky.

When the water takes on the colors of the sunset, I feel more at ease—well, and more martini'd up. "We should get a tree tomorrow. A ginormous one. And we'll put a crazy red bow on top. And I'll hang up everyone's stockings. Oh, we have to get wrapping paper. Do we have more shopping to do? I can't remember."

"A few things," he says. "We'll bring Sabe back with us tomorrow and get the house ready."

"You can be my elves!" I suggest happily.

"Oh God, what are we in for?" But he hugs me in close. "How about we go out for sushi? It's a good West Coast thing to do, don't you think?"

"Can we get rolls with too many ingredients?"

"Yes."

"And can I drink too much sake and let you take advantage of me before jet lag kicks my ass, and I pass out on that beautiful king bed upstairs?"

"Yes."

"Then, sushi it is."

"And Sabin it is tomorrow," Chris says. Then, he's quiet for a moment. "You know what? Drive down by yourself, and I'll stay here. Take the whole day with him."

"Without you? I don't know."

He puts his mouth by my ear. *"Take the whole day with him."*

The sun drops halfway into the water.

"Okay."

7
COWBOY

AND WE LET IT FALL,
AND WE LET IT FALL,
AND WE LET IT BURN.

THE THIRTY-MINUTE DRIVE NORTH TO OLIVENHAIN IS RATHER nerve-wracking, but I grip the wheel and manage not to get killed on the freeway. So, that's a good start to the day.

I feel a little bad for stranding Chris at the house with no car, but he's not exactly locked in a hobbit-sized hovel, and he seemed fairly happy to sit by the pool and read. Besides, I have to be able to drive a car by myself. Obviously, I drive at home all the time, but it's on quiet roads for the most part. From what I can tell, it's impossible to go anywhere in California without having to hop on a convoluted freeway system with lanes designated for certain passes or carpools or exits. It's confusing. The nav system is the only reason I know what I'm doing at all.

But I don't die, and that seems to be my marker for success.

The name *Olivenhain* sounds quaint and cute to me, but as I cross the city line, it becomes clear that this is not a simple town. There is money here. It's more rural than I realized, but there is mountainous red-clay terrain that gives more of a desert feel. Properties are sprawling, many with wood fences marking the lines.

It's when I begin the drive up the winding dirt road to reach Sabin that I realize I'm on a farm of sorts. *Or a ranch maybe?* My experience with whatever kind of land I'm on is limited to what I've seen in movies or read in books, so I'm not sure what this is, but I know I like it.

Everything about California is giving me a bit of a culture shock, and I haven't been here for even twenty-four hours. The architecture, the weather, the way stores are all set up in strip malls—everything is new to me. And, my God, the palm trees! They really are everywhere, and I've already fallen in love with them. And while it might take some acclimating to handle the more urban aspects of this area, there's a beauty here in this place that Sabin now calls home, out of the congestion of the traffic, and I can see why he likes it.

He told me to take the dirt road past the main house on the left, and I admire the single-level tan stucco house. I continue past what I think might be fruit trees of some kind, and then I pass four horses roaming in a large pen.

Horses?

Sabin never mentioned horses, but I find this all rather exciting.

I'm almost tearing up now that I'm a few minutes from seeing him, and I park the car next to a wooden shed, as he told me to do. I take the tray of to-go coffee cups and the paper bag from the floor by the passenger seat and make my way ahead. A path starts with an arched bridge that runs over a man-made pond filled with ducks, and I'm utterly charmed that Sabin has such a magical entrance to where he lives.

The path continues between leafy plants that remind me of something more prehistoric than of this age, and I emerge in a field spotted with much larger trees. I look up and smile. There is Sabin's tree house, seemingly impossibly suspended so high up with supports running from under the house to the wraparound deck before lodging against the solid trunk. The wood is beautiful, with lots of texture and color patterns, and I am enchanted to see shutters and shingles.

It's a real house! Just…not on the ground.

Because I've never been a guest at a tree house, this feels totally bizarre, and I'm suddenly unsure how one enters a tree house. *Do I climb the winding stairs and just knock on the door?* I don't know. It's not a traditional house, so perhaps one does not make a traditional approach. I don't know if I expect to be airlifted by some kind of rope-and-platform system or what, so I decide that I'll just cup my hands to my mouth and scream out his name. I figure it's kind of a jungle call, which seems appropriate.

I'm about to yell up when I notice movement ahead. Then, I freeze. Someone is coming down the steps, but it's not Sabin.

It's a girl—and a skanky one at that, if I'm going to go with my gut and be judgmental—with rich brown hair tousled around her face, a skintight pink dress, and sunglasses so big that they're almost comical.

Except that I don't find anything the least bit funny about this.

Nausea tears through me, and I hear Christopher's words in my head.

"It's Blythe, for fuck's sake. Why are you acting like she's an imposition?"

The answer seems to be because I *am* an imposition. Getting laid last night took precedence over seeing Chris and me. While I understand the lure of good sex, I have a feeling the girl in the pink dress is not exactly the great love of Sabin's life, and I wonder whether his hooker joke yesterday was really a joke.

The other thing that I cannot deny is a distinct and painful feeling of jealousy. Not that I want to be stumbling out of a tree house, looking like a cheap whore, but I am jealous.

She walks past me and gives a little wave, as though there is nothing fucking creepy about this at all.

I stand, unmoving, for ten minutes while I get my emotions under control. There's something humiliating about being ditched for a cheap lay. When my heart stops pounding, I try to grow the hell up and push aside the fact that this reunion so far has not gone as I envisioned.

Despite my now shitty mood, I'm struck by how unique it is to take stairs surrounded by leafy limbs. Because my hands are full, I have to kick the door to knock, and then I kick again after he doesn't answer.

"Sabin!" I yell as I keep kicking.

The door whips open, and I find myself facing a shirtless Sabin.

"Jesus Christ, what?" His black hair is in messy waves that practically hit his shoulders, and he's got at least three days' worth of facial hair darkening his face.

"Really?" I shove the bag into his hands. "Here are your fucking blueberry bagels. Good thing I only got you a fraction of what you asked for because, based on the size of your belly, you don't need more carbs."

His face registers shock. "Oh God, Blythe. Shit, what time is it? I forgot you were…I mean…*fuck!*" The bag crinkles in his hand, and he looks at me with a mix of embarrassment and apology. "I'm so sorry."

I put the coffee tray on the floor of the deck and turn to go back down the stairs. "You suck, Sabin."

He grabs me by the arm and pulls me against him, forcing me into a hug. I try to shove him away, but he won't let me.

"Fuck! I'm so sorry. I'm an asswipe! A total jerk! Tie me up, and eat all the bagels in front of me in a form of weird but possibly titillating torture." He lifts me off my feet and squeezes harder. "Please forgive me!"

"I…can't…breathe…" I eke out the words.

He sets me down and steps back. "Now, let me get a look at you." He squints and peers intently at me. "Not bad for a bagel delivery girl."

"I brought stupid coffees, too," I snarl.

"Oh, hell. Someone is very, very mad at Sabin," he says.

"Someone did not realize she had been penciled in for a visit between prostitutes," I spit out with a bit more venom than I intended.

Sabin blanches. "Well, shit. I didn't realize you'd crossed paths with, um…um…"

"Oh my God, Sabin! You don't even know her name?"

"I do. Just give me a minute."

"I don't care what her name is."

"Evidently, neither did I." His smile pisses me off. "But she wasn't a hooker."

"I'm so glad that I flew thousands of miles for this welcome. Thanks, Sabin."

I've run halfway down the stairs when he says in the most pathetic voice, "I fucked up, okay?"

I stop and wait.

"I'm really, really sorry," he says. "Blythe, don't go. You can't. I'm going to make this all up to you. Look, I fucked up real bad, but you have to forgive me. Please?"

I stomp back up the stairs and push my way into his tree house. "The croissant and the black coffee are mine."

"Now, we're talking!" he whoops.

Despite my severe irritation, the sight of the interior forces me to smile genuinely. It's absolutely adorable, a studio apartment like no other, with stunning wood walls and floors. It's a small space, but one that appears to have everything he needs. I walk into an area with a love seat, armchair, and coffee table. Then, I go through the eat-in kitchen, passing a small dining table, and I enter another sitting area—this one, a perfect circle—that's next to a window overlooking a small pond with a view of the mountains.

A full-sized futon is propped up for lounging, and Sabin's guitar rests on the cushion. I trace the shape of it with one finger. This guitar is so familiar to me that I know every shade of color streaking the front, the few scratches and dings from years of being hauled from place to place, and a couple of marks from old drunken sloppiness.

Sabin keeps quiet as I explore. I'm trying to take in everything so that I can connect with this new life he's built, but right now, I just feel overwhelmed with how much I don't know. The guitar is about the only thing of his that I recognize.

I stand by the window and watch the ducks flapping in the water. Sabin comes to stand next to me, and without looking at him, I take the coffee he hands me.

"Where do you sleep?" I ask.

"Look up."

So, I do, and that's when I see the raised ceiling that rises into a tower of sorts with a loft area off to one side.

Sabin reaches above his head and pulls down a ladder. "After you."

The steps are wide, and it's less of a rickety climb than I thought, which is good because I'm not parting with my coffee. I emerge to a platform king-sized bed under a sloped ceiling. There are built-in shelves where he's put folded clothes, and I set my cup on the top shelf.

Because there's not really anywhere else to go, I crawl onto the bed. I look up through the skylight and watch as branches blow in the light breeze.

Sabin lies down next to me. "Hi."

"Hi."

"Are you going to look at me?"

"It smells like dirty prostitute up here," I say.

He laughs. "I told you, she's not a prostitute. She's a paralegal."

I practically snort. "Yeah, right."

"Maybe it wasn't paralegal. But it was para-something. Paraglider? Paragraph? Parallelogram?"

"Parasite?" I offer.

Sabin rolls onto his side and props himself up on an elbow. "Would you please look at me?"

Reluctantly, I turn my head.

The hint of a smile hits the outer edges of his eyes. "I missed you."

I'm having trouble believing him, so I don't say anything.

"I deeply apologize for being such a dick," he says. "I'm really glad you're here."

"Okay." I don't ask him why he blew us off yesterday or how in the hell he could apparently forget about this morning. "I'm not an imposition?"

He looks as though I'd smacked him across the face. "How could you even ask that? Because of what Chris said? Don't listen to him. You could never be an imposition."

"Okay."

"Where is Chris? I thought he was coming with you?"

I shrug. "He thought you and I might want to spend the day together." Shadows dance through the skylight. "If you're not too busy."

Sabin stretches out an arm and returns with a cowboy hat that he sets on his head. Leaning over me, he brushes hair from my face and tucks it behind my ear. "I would love nothing more than to spend the day with you. I want to take you to see the horses here. Did I tell you that I ride a little now? Pearce—you know, the guy who owns this joint and the tree-house company—has been teaching me about horses and stuff." He grins. "Blythe McGuire," he says loudly and gleefully, "I'm a real fuckin' cowboy now!"

I can't help but laugh. "You are, for sure."

"Now, stop with the pouting, and let's have fun!" He sneaks his hands to the sides of my rib cage and starts tickling me until I'm giggling and shrieking for him to stop. "There's my happy girl!" He goes back on his side and smiles down at me.

When I can catch my breath, I tell him a truth that I have to get out, "Sabe...I've missed you so much that it hurts. I feel so disconnected from you."

His face softens. "Then, let's reconnect. First, I'll show you the horses here, and then we'll get real tacos with the most awesome corn tortillas you've ever had. Not that shit you get in the supermarkets back East. The real stuff. You'll love it. And we'll eat too much and fart. Then, we'll...what else do you want to do? Go downtown?"

"Just talk. Listen to you play guitar. Eat more. Fart more. Take you to the house in La Jolla. Go buy a Christmas tree, decorate, cook for the kids."

He laughs. "The kids? I love that you say that."

"Why?"

"Because you nurture us all. You're kind of motherly."

I frown. "I am not motherly! I hate children. They're loud and annoying."

"You are motherly. You watch over all of us, and we're all loud and annoying. And you're working hard to make the holidays good when they're something we all used to hate."

"A lot of suicides happen around the holidays," I say.

"Oh, gee, that's cheerful. Were any of us planning on offing ourselves this year?"

I smack his arm. "No, I just mean that we're all probably prone to getting sad this time of year, and I don't want that for any of us. Everything changed when my mom and dad died." I pause. "And I imagine that you guys did not have anything resembling a happy holiday season when you were growing up."

"Not so much," he says softly.

"So, I just want to undo whatever I can. But this is not the easiest time of year. I miss my parents."

"I know you do. They were great people, weren't they? I have no doubt that they would have been extraordinarily proud of you with the way you got through everything, the way you took care of James. All of it."

I think for a minute while I look at him, take in how he's changed, how he's stayed the same. "Sabin?"

"Yeah, love?"

"Chris says that he's glad your father is dead. Are you?"

"Yep. Every fucking second." He sits up and reaches for our coffees, so I sit up, too. "But I don't want to talk about him."

I take a sip from the cup and peer at him over the edge as I do. "Sabin?" I say again.

He smiles. "Yes, love?"

"You're half-naked and stink like a paralegal parasite who's just been parasailing with a parallelogram."

"Very funny. I'll shower and get dressed."

"Will some of that belly wash down the drain?"

"Oh, low blow, B! Yeah, yeah, I haven't exactly been dieting here, but you'll understand after I stuff your face with authentic tacos. I can eat ten at one time!"

I nod at his gut. "Not exactly something to brag about."

"Just because you run ninety-seven miles a day and have a bangin' body doesn't mean you get to taunt us flabbies."

I raise one eyebrow and crack a smile. "I have a bangin' body, you say? Really? Tell me more."

Sabin actually blushes a little, which cracks me up. "You know what I mean, but that's my cue." He slides himself to the ladder. "I'm taking my morbidly obese self to the shower to clean up. And to cry. Please ignore any wailing noises that waft your way."

I scooch to the edge of the loft and hang my head down. "Sabin?"

He looks up at me from the bottom of the ladder and beams. "Yeah, love?"

"I like your tree house."

"I'm glad. Don't eat my bagels while I'm gone."

"Don't worry. Nobody in their right mind would eat a blueberry bagel. Barf."

I hear the shower run, and then Sabin's beautiful raspy voice reaches me as he sings a song I've heard many times. He knows it's one of my favorites. It's upbeat, and it makes him reach deep into his chest to belt out some of the lines. Listening to him takes away the last edge of my worry that there is some kind of rift between us.

RESTLESS
WATERS

OH, LAST NIGHT, I TRIED NOT TO DRINK,
BUT I WAS SCARED I MIGHT NOT GET MY SLEEP.
MID AFTERNOON, STUCK IN A BAR SEAT,
AND SHE SAID, "BABY, WHAT CAN I GET FOR YOU
TODAY?"

OH, BUT SHE GOT
MORE HONEY,
MORE HONEY,
MORE HONEY THAN I CARE FOR.
OH, AND SHE GOT
MORE HONEY,
MORE HONEY,
MORE HONEY THAN I NEED.

OH, SHE BLEW MY HAIR BACK.
MY MIND SAID LOOK AWAY.
I DON'T WANT NOTHING TO DO WITH THIS PLACE.
IT AIN'T MY SOUND,
AIN'T MY SCENE,
AIN'T MY TASTE.
BUT, OH, IF SHE HAD HER WAY.

AND SHE DON'T KNOW ME.
SHE DON'T KNOW ME AT ALL.

I sit back on the bed and look around while his song continues.

Maybe Sabin was nervous about seeing me and everyone else again, and he panicked a bit or something. Whatever it was, I feel better now that we've gotten past it. And I feel even better when I see that he has a picture of the two of us on one of the shelves here.

Last summer, Sabin persuaded a local fisherman to take us out on his boat, so we could avoid the more touristy charters, and we spent the day fishing until we both caught a surprisingly good number of bluefish, cod, and striped bass. We had so much success that we ended up freezing plenty.

The picture shows us both sunburned, our hair windblown and wild, but we're smiling and very happy. He's got an arm over my shoulder, and mine are wrapped around his waist, holding him closely. We're looking at each other with so much contentment, and we're so obviously physically comfortable with each other that anyone else looking at this picture might think we're a couple.

I've seen this picture a thousand times, but still, I'm compelled to pick it up and study it, study *us*. My finger traces our outline while I think. The photograph, the dynamic between us, looks different to me than it has before. I can't get a handle on why that is...or even *how* that is.

8
HIDDEN RIPTIDES

I KNOW THAT YOU KNOW BECAUSE YOU'VE SEEN MY SOUL. I WAS A LONELY ONE, IN THE SHADOWS.

"LADY DUCHESS MADEMOISELLE SEÑORITA BLYTHE?" SABIN YELLS from downstairs. "Are you ready to discover your inner cowgirl?"

I set down the picture, inexplicably rattled.

"B? Did you ditch me?"

"No, I'm here. Coming down."

We walk the path back to the car, and Sabin points out all the different trees. Avocado and orange trees are starting to blossom, and I love the idea that he'll be able to simply go outside and have fresh produce. People who live out here probably take things like this for granted, but I find the whole idea delightful. It turns out that the trees I thought belonged in dinosaur times are actually banana trees.

"I'd have hundreds of these planted at my house if I lived here," I tell him. "What else do I need to know about California?"

The weight of Sabin's arm over my shoulder feels good, as does the kiss he lands on the top of my head.

"I don't know that I'm an expert yet, but...you might see a lot of lizards—cute ones, not disgusting huge ones. You might—and don't freak when I say this—see a rattlesnake. The weather is pretty amazing, as you can tell. I hear this is warm for this time of year, so yay for climate change. But, man, the fall here? October was really beautiful. What else? Um...I originally thought I'd want to live downtown, but then this job came up, so I'm little more north than I planned. But it's only half an hour or so to get in to downtown, so that's cool. The restaurants are amazing—or so I hear. I'm mostly a taco-truck dude." He claps his free hand over my mouth before I say anything. "Yes, yes. I know I'm fat."

I lick his palm, and he yanks it away.

"You're not fat."

"A little bit."

"You're…cushiony."

He gasps. "Cushiony! I rather like that!"

"Sabin, I was being mean before. I don't care how much you weigh. You should know that. I just want you to be happy."

"Fat and happy?"

"Whatever you like, my friend. Or you could come running with me," I suggest. "You used to work out with Chris. So, you slacked off without him. It's not a big deal."

"Trying to compete with Chris didn't work out so well." Sabin kicks a rock off the path and guides us to the left toward the stables. "He's always been stronger. He's got more drive and willpower than a human should. I'd rather be cushiony. I can't win against that shit."

"It wasn't a competition. There was no prize, goofball. He had so much fun with you."

"He just liked that I'd sit on his feet when he did sit-ups. Look ahead in the paddock!" Sabin points. "There's my girl, Mia. Isn't she a beauty?"

I know next to nothing about horses, but the horse coming toward us is indeed beautiful. I laugh when she makes a noise as we get closer.

"She likes you, huh?"

"Ah, we are good friends, this girl and me."

We get to the fence, and I hang back while Sabin rubs his hand over her nose. He turns back and sees that I'm a bit daunted, so he pulls me forward.

"Don't you worry, B. She's a gentle girl. Relax. Horses are very sensitive and intelligent, and they'll pick up on your feelings. Think of her like a big dog. Dogs know when you're nervous, sad, all that. Let her know you're okay." He faces the calm horse. "Mia, this is Blythe. Blythe, say hello to Mia. Go on, B. Give 'er a little pat, right here on her side. She likes that."

Tentatively at first, I pat Mia's shiny coat. She doesn't rear up or otherwise freak me out, so I get more comfortable and even inch my pat up her neck.

"You are a very sweet girl, aren't you?" I keep talking, partially to convince myself not to be frightened but partially because it really is a thrill. "I bet Sabin gives you extra treats and spoils you rotten, huh?"

"I certainly do. Isn't her color awesome? She's an American Quarter Horse, which is sort of the Labrador of horses. Super friendly breed, really nice temperament. Smart and just all-around good horses."

"Her color is lovely."

Mia has a light-tan coat that darkens to black on her legs, as though she were wearing boots. Her black mane and tail blow in the breeze sweeping through.

"And she's so shiny."

"Good diet. Pearce makes sure all his horses are fed high-quality products and good supplements. Plus, I groom her all the time, and that doesn't hurt."

Three other horses are in the hundred-foot-long area where Mia is, but Sabin only has eyes for her. It's rather sweet.

"So, this is called a paddock?" I ask.

"Yep. They hang out here and graze on the grass and stuff. Hey, wanna feed her a carrot?"

"I don't know. Do I?"

He laughs. "You do. Here."

I take a carrot from the bag he's brought over, and I take a big breath, hoping Mia won't swallow my arm. Sabe puts his hand over mine while we feed her. I have never been this close to a horse before, and it's exhilarating. Mia flutters her lips as she makes what I can only compare to a giant purr, and I laugh with delight.

"She's so funny!"

"This one's a character, for sure."

"Do you ride her?"

"Oh, sure, all the time."

"Get on now! Let me see you!"

"Yeah? Well, if you want. Let me grab a halter. I'll walk her around the ring here for you."

Sabin runs to the barn and returns with a halter. He hops into the paddock, slips the halter over Mia's head, and then leads her out.

I stay outside the fence, but I follow him to an area by the barn. "Now, what are you doing?"

"These are the cross ties. I just temporarily tie her up here while I brush her to get any dirt off. I love this girl, but she's a messy one, and I got on these fancy duds to impress you."

"Jeans and a T-shirt?"

"Whatever. I'm a sexy beast, and I don't need Mia ruining my look. So, now, I'm gonna tack her up." He looks at my confused face and laughs sheepishly. "Sorry, that means I'll put on her saddle pad and saddle and then cinch her up. Tighten her saddle with the cinch," he explains. "Then, on goes the bridle, which is the piece that goes over her ears and forehead and has the metal bit for her mouth. The reins are part of that, too."

I have my phone out, and I'm taking tons of pictures and video while Sabin seamlessly readies Mia. I'm so impressed with what he knows how to do and how at ease he is.

"Now, off to the arena. That's the large circular area right there." He points next to us.

I go around the outside of the area and lean on the rails to watch him.

He leads Mia into the area and brings her closer to me. "So, you always do everything on the left. I stand on her left, mount from the left, all that."

In one smooth move, Sabin steps a foot into the left side stirrup, grabs Mia's mane, and pushes up, swinging his right leg over her. I see how perfectly suited he is for this. He takes her on a slow walk around the edge of the circular pen, all the while talking to her and stroking her mane. Not that I have any expertise, but Mia seems very responsive to Sabin, very tuned in to him.

He loosely holds her reins and makes a clicking sound, and she picks up her pace a bit so that they are trotting rhythmically. When he slows her down and looks as though he might stop, I call out for him to keep going. I drop my arms on the railing and rest my chin down.

I could watch him forever. This is Sabin at peace.

It seems he's been wearing that cowboy hat all these years for a reason.

I hear footsteps scraping across the gravelly road behind me, and I tense. If that parallelogram parasite has come back for more, I'm going to beat her to a pulp. Ready to do battle, I turn.

Mercifully, it's not her. It's a man with brown hair and gray streaks, a thin but solid build, fitted Wranglers that hug him well, and intoxicating pale blue eyes. He's a little Paul Newman*ish*, and I try not to giggle and blush when he introduces himself.

"Hi, there. I'm Pearce." He actually tips his hat to me.

I somehow refrain from curtsying in response when I shake his hand.

"I'm Blythe. It's very nice to meet you. You're Sabin's boss, right? And this is your property? It's just beautiful here."

"Well, thank you. And that's right. You're Blythe from Maine? Sabin's talked a lot about you. Happy to have you here. You and the family are all around for a few weeks, I believe."

"Yes, we're renting a place in La Jolla."

He whistles and gives me a smile. "Not too shabby. Glad it's slow right now with work. He'll have plenty of time to spend with you all. First time in California?"

"First time in California and first time this close to a horse," I say.

"Well then, let's do this right." He waves Sabin over, and when he gets within earshot, Pearce says, "Why don't you get your girl Blythe up on Mia?"

"Yeah? I didn't know if that'd be all right with you."

"Of course it's all right with me. You know what you're doing. You know how to be safe. And I don't think you'd let anything happen to this young lady, would you?"

"No, sir," Sabin says.

"Good. Get her a helmet though. Protect that pretty head."

"Wait, what?" I know my eyes are as wide as they can get. "You want me to ride? I don't know how to do that! I can't...I can't...um..."

"Sure you can," Sabin says.

"Sabin will take you nice and slow, right?"

Sabin nods. "I'll hold the reins and walk her around. You just sit there and enjoy." He looks to Pearce.

Pearce nods at him. "You're in good hands," he says as he backs up and waves. "Shepherd here has a way with all the animals, especially Mia. A natural rider, that boy is. Have fun, kids."

My knees might not be actually shaking, but I am a little nervous when Sabin buckles my helmet for me.

"You're gonna love this, B." He moves a small step stool next to Mia's left side and helps me get my foot into the stirrup. "Now, just grab on to her mane and then push up and throw your right leg over."

"I have to grab her mane? Doesn't that hurt her?"

"No, not at all. You can grab the horn if you want instead."

"There's a horn? Like a car?"

Sabin laughs loudly, and I glare at him until he stops.

"Okay, okay. Sorry. Not that kind of horn. This. The sort of knobby thing on the saddle."

"Oh. Okay. If you laugh at me again, I'm not getting on."

"I promise I won't."

Miraculously, I get up on the first try. Sabin does have to put his hands under my ass to push me all the way on, but I still count it as a success.

I sit up and exhale.

"Perhaps not the most graceful mount I've ever seen, but you did it!" Sabin says happily.

"And you got to touch my ass!"

"I did! Win-win!"

Sabin holds Mia's reins as he slowly walks us around the ring, and I love every second of it. Mia is incredibly gentle and calm, and soon enough, I relax into the ride. We go around the arena three times.

"Do you want to hold the reins and ride by yourself?" he asks. I must look hesitant because he adds, "I'll walk right next to you."

I agree, and he hands me the reins.

"How do I tell her where to go?"

"If you want her to head right, just open up your right arm a bit—don't pull on her mouth or anything—and take your right calf and put a little pressure on Mia's right flank. She'll understand what to do. Give it a try."

So, I do, and I'm surprised when just the pressure of my leg on her side gets her to turn. "She did it!"

Sabin smiles. "She did. What's interesting is, when horses are in the wild, the alpha mare always nips at the flank or shoulder of the other horses to direct them where to go. A lot like a dog herding sheep. So, we just copy that. In a sense, we become the alpha. They understand pecking order. Pearce says horses are like toddlers. They like structure and boundaries, and they love being praised."

I make Sabin take my picture, but right after, I wave him back to my side. I ride like this—technically on my own but with Sabin only a few feet away—for twenty minutes. We don't talk. We just walk and ride, and it's utterly perfect. I see why he loves this so much. It's almost meditative.

"You look very handsome, Sabe."

He does. The cowboy hat, the sun hitting his cheeks, the stunning backdrop of this priceless property—it all enhances how good he looks. I have tremendously missed him.

Sabin rolls his eyes. "Shut up."

"I'm serious."

"Okay, whatever. Hey, you getting hungry?"

"Totally. You'll help me down?"

"Of course. So, you'll want to shift your weight into the left stirrup, and then as you kind of half-lie across the seat of the saddle, you'll kick out that left foot and basically hop down by pushing with your hands and chest. Kick your left leg from the stirrup, and swing your right leg back over and off."

I do what he says, and again, my dismount is as ungainly as I predicted. I pretty much slide off the horse and then stumble back.

"Easy there." Sabin catches me with two hands and rights me before I totally wipe out.

I take his hands and pull them around my waist as I lean back into him. "Thank you."

"It's not a big deal. Just didn't want you to crash on your landing."

"Not for that. For today, for this. For being you. For being my best friend."

Sabin tightly hugs me, and in this moment, everything is right.

We spend the rest of the day eating tacos, driving by the coast, and stopping at a few produce stands. Then, we go back to the tree house and pack up a few things for Sabin to bring up to the La Jolla house. I assume that Sabin will ride up with me, and I am beyond appalled when he informs me that he'll be taking his motorcycle.

"Motorcycle?" I nearly scream. "Since when do you ride a motorcycle? They're dangerous. Oh God, Sabin."

For a minute, I try to believe that he's joking, but he walks to a lush area near the base of the tree house and shows me his bike. I feel ill. I don't like the idea of Sabin zipping around on this thing.

"Don't you worry for one second. I got me very good noggin protection." He grins and sets a helmet on his head. "And it's got a lucky horse painted on it. See?" He taps the shiny helmet and drops the visor down. "Let's roll, baby!"

I white-knuckle the steering wheel on the drive back to the house as I try to pay attention to the road in front of me and not the fact that Sabin is riding too fast and constantly changing lanes. He's probably intentionally riding like an asshole, and I'm nothing but relieved when we both pull up to the house.

Chris comes out to greet us just as I'm about to clobber Sabin.

"Are you trying to kill yourself?" I scream while Sabin looks annoyingly bemused. "What the hell?"

"Ah, saved by the brother." Sabin turns to Chris. "Again."

Chris tackles him in a hug. "Nice bike, man."

"See? Chris gets me." Sabin hugs him back, but I could swear that I see restraint there.

I only notice it because I know Sabin so well—or at least, I think I do. Maybe I'm wrong because Chris just seems thrilled to see his brother, and he's not reacting as though Sabin is not himself.

I grab some of the stuff from the car while Chris examines Sabin's death mobile and asks lots of questions.

"We have to get a tree!" I call back to them as I head inside.

"We will!" they answer.

"Christmas is coming!"

"We know!"

"Everyone will be here soon, and we have shit to do!"

"We get it!"

"So, come on!"

Now that Sabin is at the house with us, I'm really geared up for the rest of the group to arrive, and I call a meeting of sorts on the deck, so we can make a list of everything to do.

Sabin flops into a chair and faces the water.

I rest my head in Chris's lap while I type on my phone. "Okay, so we obviously need a tree and ornaments. Wrapping paper, name tags for presents. And food. What are our Christmas Eve and Christmas Day menus?"

Chris and I bounce around ideas, but Sabin mostly stays out of the conversation, either scrolling through his phone or staring at the water view.

Chris gets up to assess where to set up a tree in the living room. Before he goes inside, he kisses me on the mouth. "Glad you got to ride a horse. The pictures you sent were awesome."

"And did you see the videos of Sabin riding? He's amazing."

"I did. Very, very cool. I'm happy that you two had such a good day. He's a good brother and a good friend." Chris kisses me again and pats Sabin's arm before he leaves the deck.

Sabin still hasn't moved, so I stick out a leg and lightly kick him.

"What's up there? You've been very quiet."

"Just looking for dolphins."

He seems tense now, edgy even, and I don't know why.

"Such a big fucking ocean, huh? It just goes on forever. All that water, full of currents and riptides, with hidden dangers everywhere. But it looks so damn pretty, doesn't it? You'd never know." He shifts in his chair. "Look, it's kind of silly for me to stay here. I've got a place. I think I should just sleep at home."

I sharply sit up. "What are you talking about? Why would you do that?"

"I have work to do, horses to feed and stuff."

"You don't have work now. Pearce told me you're free, and I'm sure he'll feed the horses. Sabe, you have to stay here. We're *all* staying here. That was the plan. I don't...Sabin..."

"Okay, okay. Easy there..."

"Besides, I put three rubber duckies in your bathtub for you. You can't leave now."

He cracks a smile but keeps his eyes on the water. "Well, in that case, I guess I do have to stay."

I feel an underlying anxiety creeping through my system. I felt it yesterday and this morning and again now as I watch Sabin while he watches the ocean.

9
MARTYR

YOUR LOVER IS A SONG MAN, OH, HE IS A STRONG MAN, REACHING OUT FOR YOUR HAND. CAN'T YOU SEE?

ESTELLE IS WEARING THE MOST INAPPROPRIATE AND TIGHTEST RED spaghetti-strap nightgown, and she's sitting on my brother's lap with her arms around his neck. If I weren't so damn happy to see her and if it weren't Christmas morning—or closer to Christmas afternoon, given how late the college kids slept—I might casually throw a poncho over her. As it is, I've decided to embrace all that is Estelle. That also meant that I had to turn up the ceiling fan in our room last night to muffle the noise coming from the bedroom she was sharing with James. Both of them look so unbelievably gooey in love that I can't be mad.

And at least she threw on a bra under her nightgown, so Christmas miracles do exist.

In lieu of his usual cowboy hat, Sabin has on a Santa hat and is handing out presents. "As we have about reached the end of the whole point of Christmas—the whopping gifts—Estelle, my favorite sister, this is for you. I expect that the high-quality nature of this gift will excuse me from any other gift-buying over the years to come." He lugs a large rectangular item from behind the tree.

"Oh, no." Eric covers his face with his hands. "I can't look. I just can't."

"What?" Sitting next to him, I lean in. "What is it?"

"I'm pretty sure I have an idea, and just be happy that you don't room with her anymore." But he's smiling.

Estelle leaps from James and claps her hands together. "Gimme, gimme, gimme! Gimme the goods, baby!"

Chris is smirking in the corner, so I imagine that Sabin filled him in. "Estelle, get ready to have your socks knocked off."

She tears open the paper and absolutely squeals with pure delight. "Oh my fucking God, Sabin Shepherd! How in the hell are you so goddamn fucking brilliantly perfect?"

She's bouncing around and totally blocking my view until she turns the gift toward the room and holds it above her head.

"Holy...shit," I mutter.

"It's a goddamn Rhinestone Jesus!" she shrieks.

It is, in all its freakish glory. I can hardly believe it. How Sabin managed to find a framed Jesus image done entirely in rhinestones is beyond me.

"I fucking love it!" Estelle is beside herself. "RJ's in the house, baby!"

She sets it down, and James catches it just as Estelle jumps into Sabin's arms and wraps her legs around his waist. It's a good thing her nightgown has such a high slit on the side.

"And I fucking love you!" Repeatedly, she noisily kisses him on the cheek until Sabin is rolling his eyes and trying to detach her from his body.

"If I'd known you'd freak out like this, I would have left it at the flea market." But he's still grinning.

The scene before me is what I was hoping for—well, maybe not the Rhinestone Jesus part—and I scan the room to take it all in.

Chris and Sabin found the most massive tree, which I'm still surprised fits in the room, and we decorated it very simply with white lights, red bows, and a few handmade ornaments that we bought at a local shop. Not that a tree is the most important thing about this holiday, but it's a nice backdrop for being with the people I love most in the world. I feel settled and complete when we're all together.

Eric retreats from Estelle's continued whooping and comes with me to the kitchen to help cook. I've mapped out a rather elaborate meal. I might have gone overboard with how much food we'll have, but the college students have been eating dorm food for months, and

Sabin's clearly been gorging on fast food. Granted, the tacos we had the other day were delicious, but I'm afraid he hasn't eaten anything healthy in months.

Opening the oven, I check on the standing rib roast that I started a while ago, and then I start peeling and thinly slicing potatoes for the gratin. Eric fills me in on his classes while he simultaneously starts a chocolate mousse and assembles a giant salad. If I find a green pepper in my dessert, I'm going to be annoyed, but he seems to have a handle on things.

"So, one more semester, and you're done. You ready for it to be over?" I ask.

"For sure. I'm really glad I took this extra year, but I'm pretty over studying all the time." Eric does look tired, but he is also as bubbly as always about his academics. "I've been doing an independent study. Did I tell you that? My professor is so great. She lets me pick out all my own reading materials, and I can write about whatever I want. My room has been filled with thick books on ancient Greece. It's so fun. The Internet only gets me so far, and you know that I kinda dig the library."

"What are you going to do after graduation?"

"Well," he says, "I actually wanted to talk to you about that."

For a second, I have some silly fantasy that he wants to move to Maine, but that can't possibly be on his agenda. Then, I know. "Oh! You and Zach?"

He smiles but keeps his head down as he adds freshly washed arugula to the salad. "Yeah. I'm thinking about asking him to live together."

"Okay, I love that you're all Martha Stewart while focusing on your salad when there's a more pressing issue, but stop salading, and give me details! Where do you want to live? What's he doing next year? Tell me!"

Eric sets his hands on the counter and looks at me. "I had a feeling you'd like this idea. Zach is looking at a few job possibilities in Chicago, and we could be happy there. We haven't talked about plans too much, and I think he's being cautious, not wanting to push me or anything. But here's the thing…" He lowers his voice a bit. "I don't know if I can leave Estelle. I don't know what she's doing next year, and…Blythe, you know, she switched majors before me. Do you really think she had a burning need to study sociology, and that was worth an extra year of college? What's she going to do? Become a sociologist?"

"I don't understand."

"She didn't want to leave Matthews. I think she feels safe there."

"Oh, Eric. Did you switch your major to stay with her?"

He starts chopping a cucumber. "Yeah. Kind of."

"Why?"

He shrugs. "She got kind of messed up for a while. You know that. I didn't want to leave her. But now, I'm going to have to—unless she wants to come to Chicago or wherever I end up. But there's James now, and...I'm just not sure what to do."

"Eric, listen to me. Estelle is a tough chick. Don't forget that. Let her work out her stuff, but you have to talk to her about this."

"You know Estelle. She doesn't make that easy. Our bond is a little more unspoken," he says, laughing lightly.

"I know. But if you push her a little, she'll open up. Okay?"

He nods. "Okay. Thanks, Blythe."

We spend another hour cooking and listening to the raucous noise from the other room. Every single sound is exhilarating to me. We eventually lure in everyone's help with the promise of an outstanding dinner. Chris turns on loud music and stands next to me, occasionally leaning in for a kiss, while we cook. The bustle of activity now reminds me so much of the bliss we all had last summer, and I am extremely grateful that we're able to recapture that.

Dinner goes off smoothly, and it turns out that I did not radically over shop. I forgot how much James could put away. When we've polished off a shocking amount of food, Sabin, Chris, Eric, and Estelle move to the living room while I sit with James and pick from the salad bowl.

"This is the best part of dinner." I stab at a now wilted piece of arugula. "You know, when the salad has been sitting and marinating for a few hours, and it's all soggy."

"You're weird." But he peers into the salad bowl and grabs a fork.

"I missed you, little brother."

"And I missed your cooking," he teases. "Fine, fine. I missed you, too. Thanks for the gift, Blythe," he says quietly. "It was very cool of you."

I gave him an airline ticket to use, so he can go visit Estelle for spring break. When he opened the envelope, both of them lit up—and then made out for a little too long.

"Happy to do it. It's good to see you two back together. Just keep it down at night."

He blushes. "Oh God. Sorry, sorry. Although, I have suffered plenty over the years because of you and Chris."

"Fine. Let's call it even."

We clink forks.

"Blythe! Get in here!" Sabin's voice booms. "You didn't open your present!"

I wipe my hands. "Dear God, I can only imagine what it might be."

"Good luck," James says. "Be strong."

I laugh and go to meet my fate.

"Did you think I forgot about you?" Sabin makes an exaggerated frown. "Sit down, and receive the blessings of the day."

I cautiously kneel on the floor next to him.

He pushes a rather large present my way. "You can never say that I don't pay attention to everything you say."

I take off the paper and lift the top off the box. Then, I smile and bust out laughing. "Estelle is right. You really are goddamn fucking brilliantly perfect."

In the box are thousands of green mini swords.

Because they are the best and make everything taste better.

I kiss Sabin on the cheek. "These are the most awesome green mini swords a girl could ever ask for. And you're the best Sabin a girl could ask for." I scoop my hand through the cocktail swords. "I cannot believe you remembered this."

"A raging drunk Blythe is hard to forget."

"I think we all remember that day," Chris says.

"Yep," Sabin says a little too loudly. "Christopher's non-wedding wedding day. *That* was interesting."

"Gee, thanks for bringing that up." Chris shoots him an irritated glare.

"What? It's true. Don't kill the messenger. What was her name? Oh, yeah. Jennifer. Wonder whatever happened to her."

Chris has a look of disbelief coupled with growing anger. "Nobody cares what happened to her."

Sabin stands up. "Who's up for a Christmas Day sunset swim?"

"Dude, I'm totally in!" Estelle says with more cheer than the moment warrants. James makes a face, but she widens her eyes and grabs his hand. "We'll all run into the water, wearing our clothes!"

I cannot imagine that she has any real urge to dunk into the freezing water, but the room has grown tense enough that she's probably as eager as the rest of us to defuse this conversation.

"Yeah, that'll be fun," Eric says halfheartedly.

Sabin is out the door before anyone can ask what in the hell that little outburst was about.

When we're alone, Chris takes my hand. "Don't let him bother you."

"I'm trying not to. Just…he seems pretty moody. Up and down, you know?"

"Yeah, I'm starting to get that. Let's give him a few days. See what happens."

"Okay." I feel unsettled, but I have an idea that might wash away some of the unpleasantness. "Come with me." I take Chris by the hand and laugh at the curious expression he makes when I lead him to the tree. "We're going to lie down under the tree and look up through the branches."

"Please tell me you're kidding."

"No. It's romantic," I insist. "I read about it in a book. I want to try it."

"Whatever you want. It's your day."

Chris follows my lead, and we lie on the floor and push back until we are under the branches and bows and lights.

"Now what?" he asks.

"It's up to us. Maybe we think about the future. Or the past or the present. The New Year coming up. I don't know." I think for a minute. It turns out that this wasn't a bad idea. I gaze up into the lights, take in the detail of the many pine needles, and inhale the smell. "Maybe we just lie here and breathe."

So, that's what we do. Chris takes my hand, and we breathe.

As the minutes tick by, the room darkens as the sun fades, and the lights on the tree get brighter and sharper. In the distance, there is shrieking and laughter coming from the shore, but we block that out. Right now, it's just us.

I shut my eyes and focus on my hand entwined with Chris's, feeling the familiarity and comfort of him but also the energy and momentum he gives me. Our connection remains as exciting as it always has been. There is just the addition of security and stability.

"I have something for you," he says. "Don't get mad."

I turn my head, and I'm about to snap at him because we agreed that we weren't exchanging presents, but he looks too thoughtful and in love for me to be annoyed.

"Christopher..."

He slips out from the tree, and I giggle when he grabs my legs and yanks so that I glide across the floor a good five feet.

In a flash, he's on his side next to me, setting a small box on my chest. "Open."

"I wish you'd told me that you—"

"Shh." He holds a finger to my lips and smiles at me. "Open."

Inside the box is a silver sea urchin with a pale blue stone pendant that hangs from a thin chain. His gift leaves me emotional and moved. Chris is not one for fate or destiny or anything that he can't explain with fact and logic, but he has latched on to how undeniably tied we are to each other, and this necklace is a symbol of that. He's made an exception when it comes to us.

"Put it on for me." I can hardly talk, so I just watch him while he delicately undoes the clasp and then gently brushes my hair aside before he hooks it around my neck.

Now, I have on the necklace that belonged to Chris's mother and also this one. It's a damn good set.

"You're beautiful," he says.

"The *necklace* is beauti—"

He stops me with a kiss—a long one.

Sometimes, our kissing is brief, a quick show of affection in passing. Sometimes, our kisses are heated, urgent, loaded with sexual need. Then, there are kisses like this one—tender, unhurried, and patient—that are not about anything but love. This kiss is romance at its best.

"Good fucking God, get a fucking room!" Sabin hollers as he crashes loudly through the doorway. "Oh, wait. You have one," he says gratingly. "It's just upstairs. Feel free to use it. I don't think we all need to see you two going at it on the floor, do we?"

Chris lifts his mouth from mine. He remains remarkably calm, considering how obnoxious Sabin is being. Chris whispers under his breath so that only I can hear, "Don't say anything." He pulls back, takes my hand, and helps me to stand. "I'm going to make coffee. There's a nice French press here. Anyone want some?"

Sabin is dripping water all over the floor and toweling off while looking snarly, and Estelle and Eric excuse themselves to go get changed.

I meet my brother's eyes and silently beg him for help. Sabin has always responded well to him.

James nods and approaches Sabin. "Dude, let's tank up on caffeine and warm up. That water was fierce, huh? I'm glad we went in though. That was a great idea. Refreshing." He claps a hand on Sabin's shoulder, I think, in an effort to ground him or get him to ease up.

"Yeah," Sabin says reluctantly. "Yeah, sure."

Sabin starts to step past me with an uncharacteristic coldness in his eyes, but then he stops in front of me. He reaches out to touch my necklace, and then he lets out a callous laugh. "Oh God, really? You two still harping on that?" He drops the sea urchin back against my chest and walks toward the kitchen area, waving his hands in the air. "Ain't nothin' going to top that shit, huh?" His tone is filled with a nasty ridicule that I've not heard from him in years, and he saunters to the kitchen island with a level of casualness that infuriates me. "The great love affair to beat all others. You guys are just that *fucking* epic, aren't you?"

Chris lifts the teakettle and slams it hard onto the burner. "That's about enough." Now, he's angry. Now, he's working to control himself. "I don't know what the fuck is wrong with you all of a sudden, but get it together."

Sabin opens a container of mixed nuts and pours some into his hand before he starts tossing them up in the air and catching them in his mouth. "I'm just saying, these displays are all a bit much. Not to mention, you get off on throwing your money around." He frenetically gestures around. "This house? Not exactly necessary. And God knows what you paid for the jewelry."

James grabs his arm and tries to pull him away, but Sabin shakes him off hard, harder than Chris would like. He strides forward while I beckon James to come near me. There are certain family dynamics that I know to stay out of. I'm not sure what is happening here, but I keep my mouth shut, and I want James to do the same.

"You and your fucking money, Chris," Sabin continues. "And always the martyr, never spending shit on yourself. Making the big sacrifices, so you can look like some fucking hero who swooped in and spoiled us all. Like we're supposed to be grateful that you know how to use a credit card."

There is a fury emanating from Chris that I've never seen, and I'm terrified he's going to blow.

But he doesn't. Instead, he speaks with a measured voice that scares me more than if he'd simply lashed out and punched Sabin across the face, "I think you should go. Now."

"Fine by me." Sabin tosses another nut, and it bounces off his mouth when he tries to catch it.

Chris grabs the container and hurls it across the room. "Now."

"Whatever you want, Christopher. I didn't ask to stay here, and I certainly didn't ask for everyone to come and invade my life here. A little fucking space isn't a bad thing. Jesus. What? You guys can't function unless we're all glued together at the hip?" He grabs his wallet from the counter and walks out the door.

Chris puts a hand on the counter and looks down. James touches my back and guides me to the table so that I can sit. I'm not sure I would have been able to walk there on my own.

The three of us listen to the roar of Sabin's motorcycle as he takes off.

"What...what just happened?" The break in my voice tells me that I'm on the verge of crying, but I can hardly allow myself to feel anything through the shock. "I don't even know who that was."

Finally, Chris looks at me. "Welcome to the Shepherd Family Christmas."

10
BINGO AND KISSES

OH, SHE BLEW MY HAIR BACK.
MY MIND SAID LOOK AWAY.
I DON'T WANT NOTHING TO DO WITH THIS PLACE.

IT'S AFTER ELEVEN ON CHRISTMAS NIGHT, AND I'M CURLED UP ON the couch, staring at the tree, with my phone in my hand. I've been calling and texting Sabin for hours with no response. Since drawing out this day held less than no appeal, everyone but Chris and I went to bed a while ago.

Chris comes from behind the kitchen counter with a drink in his hand. Scotch, I'm guessing.

"You sure you don't want one?" He drops onto the cushion next to me.

"No, thanks." Maybe getting loaded would help me drown out Sabin's behavior, but I want to stay clearheaded in case I can make sense of it. Plus, I'm already depressed, and I know from experience that drinking does nothing to lift my mood.

"Blythe, I'm so sorry about today."

"It's not your fault." I haven't mentioned the details of the morning I first saw Sabin. I'd rather not worry Chris more than necessary.

"I feel like somehow it is. I don't know exactly what triggered him, but I can say for certain that holidays for us have never been great. You know, the pressure to have perfection when we never had that growing up. I think this whole season is pretty hard on him—less so for Estelle and Eric but still."

"And you?"

"You make it a lot easier." He pauses. "More than that. I love seeing you happy. When you get caught up in what to put in the stockings or what would make the perfect breakfast for Christmas morning, I like it. You spread this happy energy around, and it's infectious—for me, at least. But we are not a family with a good history, Blythe, and you can't change that."

"I'm so stupid," I say. "I actually thought I could cut through that a little. I wanted to—not because we're supposed to like holidays, but because…I wanted everyone to feel safe and loved. I didn't do that—at least, not for Sabin." I pause. "And he's the one who needs it the most, isn't he?"

"Yes, he's the one who needs it the most," Chris confirms.

This breaks my heart to hear, and I should have understood it sooner.

"But you did a wonderful job. If we can push aside Sabin's shitstorm, the truth is, you gave everyone else the best day imaginable. We're pretty used to imperfection."

I see perfection in things that are likely considered imperfections by others. My own thought from years ago rings loudly in my head.

"I think he's lonely." The lights on the tree grow blurry the longer I focus on them, so I wipe my eyes and shoot for clarity. "Estelle and James, Eric and Zach…"

"And then, there's us. Clearly a sore spot for him."

"Why is that? Why all of a sudden?"

Chris takes a deep breath and slowly blows it out. "I'm not sure. He's not drinking, so that's not it. You guys have a very close friendship, and maybe he thinks I'm in the way of that or that I resent it. I don't want to hinder your relationship. I never have. I'm glad you have each other. You're the closest friend he has, and I know that he's very good to you—well, usually. You know that he has his moments when he erupts. He picked a hell of a night to do it." Chris takes a long drink. "I can tell how much he hurt you tonight, and I wish that hadn't happened. If it's any consolation, he's going to feel terrible about it when he calms down. He adores you, sometimes maybe a little too much."

I don't know what to say to this because perhaps I adore Sabin a little too much, too. While Sabin's rant today did hurt, I'm more focused on it being an indication that he's in pain of some sort, and that is intolerable to me. I can't stand to know he's hurting so much.

"Today started out so nicely," I say dejectedly.

"It did."

"And I didn't overcook the rib roast or screw up the hollandaise sauce for the asparagus. Those were indicators that the day should have been a success."

"Blythe, you gave us the best holiday anyone could. We're not easy to take. I should have expected something like this, and I probably should have warned you. Listen, remember the year that I took them to Hawaii when we were still in college?"

"Of course. Sabin sent me thousands of pictures of him in terrible shirts and a few of you in swim trunks. You were all glistening in the ocean, and that made me drooly and crap."

Chris laughs. "Well, what he didn't send you were pictures from Christmas Eve when Eric flipped out about the food being terrible before overturning his plate and leaving the table. Or when Sabin interrupted a private luau and started a fight with some flame-thrower guy. Oh, and then he took a swing at me when I pulled him away before he could really get into a fight. If I remember correctly, he called me a 'psychotic, narcissist punk' and 'the lamest superhero there ever was.' I believe he said something about my not deserving a cape and certainly not a place with the Justice League. We all have our moments."

"Great. So, explosions are considered a holiday tradition? That sort of sucks."

"We might consider putting that tradition to rest, huh?" Chris tousles my hair and kisses my head. "It's not all jumping off docks and fishing and lobsters with us. You took on a lot."

"It's worth it. You know that."

He kisses me again. "I'm going to head to bed. There's something on the dining room table for you from Annie. I thought you might want to be alone when you opened it."

"Okay." I try to smile, but I feel shitty, as though I'd failed everyone today by not preventing what happened. If I had paid better attention or done a better job or kept us busier…I don't know. That's stupid thinking, and I shouldn't blame myself. "I love you, Christopher."

"I love you, Blythe." He slams back the rest of his drink and sends me a soft smile. "Merry Christmas. Go enjoy Annie's present."

I take a few minutes before I go to the table and find an envelope with my name on it. I slip out the card. The front shows a vintage-style Santa Claus in lovely soft colors, and inside, she's handwritten a note.

> *Blythe,*
>
> *Merry Christmas, my dear! I hope you are having a spectacular time in California, and I'm sure that the gang is keeping you on your toes.*
>
> *I made you something this year. Don't worry. It's not a horrid crocheted tissue-box cover or anything. I'm hoping that you'll like it and that it'll bring you some...well, comfort and joy. Forgive the seasonal phrasing, but I do want those for you. And I know that your parents would, too.*
>
> *Shall we plan for a spring visit? I miss my room at the Maine house, but I miss you even more.*
>
> *All my love,*
>
> *Annie*

She's slipped in a small piece of paper with a web address, which I find very curious, so I retrieve my laptop from the end table and type it in.

She's put together a video compilation.

Oh God.

Music plays while images of me and James and my parents move before my eyes. I immediately burst into tears at seeing the videos and photographs. There are formal posed stills from my parents' wedding, pictures of my mother pregnant with me, video of her talking to the camera and rubbing her stomach, followed by hospital pictures of a newborn me in a bassinet. Later, my mother is shown pregnant with James, and I see a video of me holding him for the first time.

There are a bunch of pictures of me in daycare. I don't know if the staff there took them and gave them to my parents or if Mom and Dad came in. I barely remember this place. I just have some hazy memories. I do know that I liked it there, that I was happy. There are a few pictures of me with two little boys. In one, I am standing between them, holding hands, and in another, we are all lying on the floor with our chins in our hands, listening to the teacher read a story. I smile at these because this was a time in which everything was easy, blissful.

I had no idea a fire would take half my family and leave James and me destroyed.

I also had no idea that I would survive that tragedy, that I would rebuild.

There's video of my family, presumably taken by my father. My mother is holding a young James on her lap, and I'm having some kind of toddler tantrum.

"Where Bingo?"

"I don't know," my mother says. "Look on the toy shelf, Blythe."

"Here it is. There," my father says from behind the camera. He stretches an arm and retrieves a game from under the coffee table. "Here's Bingo! She likes the farm animals on the tokens," he tells my mother.

But I bat away the game. "No! Where Bingo? Where Bingo?"

"Not this one? Don't cry, honey. Do we have another?" my mother asks as she touches a hand to my face and wipes away my tears. "I don't know why she's so obsessed with Bingo these days. We'll have to find another version that she likes better."

My toddler face crumples, and the adult me almost has to laugh at the pathetically sad face I'm making.

"My kiss?"

My mom leans over and smooches my cheek, but I push her away while wrinkling my face and rubbing my eyes.

"My kiss, my kiss," I whimper.

My dad kisses me now, too, but I'm clearly not satisfied.

Mom sighs. "I think someone needs a nap."

"I totally do. It's exhausting being a parent," my father jokes.

I clap my hand over my mouth and nearly crack under the emotion when I hear my mother laughing at him. The sound of their voices…is too much and not nearly enough.

I watch my mother put down James, and he toddles for a moment and then sits on the floor to play with blocks. Mom picks me up and holds me against her, stroking my hair.

"My kiss, Mama? My kiss."

She rocks me and pats my back, kissing my head and trying to soothe me.

"Where Bingo?" My tired voice gets softer as I talk myself to sleep in her arms. "Kiss, my kiss…"

"Kisses and Bingo," my mother whispers. She looks at the camera and smiles. "Is she out yet?"

"Yeah. Sleepy girl today," my father says softly.

I didn't know we had any of these early videos. Annie must have found them on my parents' computer or in some of the boxes she helped clear out from the house. My entire life seems to pan before me. The movie Annie's made shows me in grade school, middle school, and high school. There are no graduation photos though because that was after the fire. By then, I'd pushed Annie out of my life, and Aunt Lisa was too selfish and thoughtless to think to capture the moment. Of course, I was a walking zombie during that time, so I'm not sure I'd want to see myself as I was back then anyway.

I pause the video when a family photo of the four of us flashes. This was taken just days before the fire. My father put the camera on a self-timer and then ran to stand with us. He had to try this almost a dozen times before he made it back in time to the top of the huge boulder we were sitting on, so by the time he got the picture, we were all laughing. This is the best picture I've ever seen.

I watch the movie two more times. When I am done, I am left with an ache that I cannot resolve. Annie would never intentionally upset me, and I'm sure she thought enough time had passed that seeing these images wouldn't hurt me so much. In some ways, they don't.

Right now, I feel everything—joy, pain, loss, elation, love, anger…

My phone rings, and I look down. It's Sabin. I let it ring a few times while I sniff and clear my throat.

"Hi," I say.

"Did I tell you that Mia is a rescue horse?" he says.

"No, you didn't."

"Well, she is. Pearce went to a horse auction, looking for a younger horse, but he found Mia. She's twelve, and no one was going to take her, not because of her age though. Twelve isn't old for a horse. She's phobic about water. Won't go near it apparently. You pretty much get one chance to teach a horse that water isn't a danger. They don't understand that they won't fall through a puddle. Don't like when they can't see the bottom of things, where they go. They have to learn. Mia obviously had some kind of traumatic experience with water that we'll never know about, so she wasn't an appealing horse at the auction. There are people who go to those auctions just to buy up horses for meat for France and Japan. Killers, they're called. Pearce ended up bidding against some of those guys. He overpaid and saved her. She wasn't what he was looking for. She's not perfect, but he loves her."

The sound of his guitar trickles through the phone, and I listen silently for a while.

Sabin waits me out.

I shut my laptop and close my eyes. "She doesn't have to be perfect. That's okay. She's perfect for you."

"She is."

"I'm glad he saved her."

"Me, too." Sabin plucks out a few notes. "Blythe?"

"Yeah?"

"I'm really sorry."

I start crying.

"Ah, shit, B. Please don't cry. I'm not worth it. I'm just a complete tool."

"It's not you," I get out. "Well, not just you. Annie sent me this movie thing she made…with all these pictures. Seeing my parents again…before this, I haven't really looked at many pictures at all. There's video and everything." I wipe my eyes with the back of my hand. "It was the best and the worst."

He lets me cry for a few minutes. "So, you know the swords that I gave you?"

"I love them."

"I have another present for you. Your real one. Want to come over and get it?"

"Okay. Sabin? You're not a tool," I say. "Just prone to being snotty and mean."

"I know."

"I'll see you soon."

I tiptoe upstairs to my bedroom and gently shake Chris. "I have to go see Sabin."

He rolls over and yawns. "Now?"

"Yeah."

Chris opens his eyes and takes my hand. "Okay. I can't drive you. I had three scotches, and they were all very big."

I smile. "I know. I can drive. It's okay."

"Text me when you get there. And tell him I love him even though he's a fucking moron."

"Okay. Go back to sleep, love."

Chris rolls over and starts snoring immediately. I tussle my fingers through his hair and watch him for a few minutes. Then, I kiss his cheek and head out.

11
UNICORNS AND RAINBOWS

YOU COULD HOLD ME TIGHT, BUT I STILL DON'T FEEL I FIT INSIDE THIS LIFE.

THE DRIVE THIS TIME IS EASIER BECAUSE THERE'S LITTLE TRAFFIC on Christmas night. My headlights flash over Sabin, who is waiting for me in the parking area before the bridge. I get out and run into his arms, and he buries his face in my neck.

Apologies don't have to be spoken now. It's easy for me to forgive Sabin.

We stand in each other's hold for what feels like an eternity, and I don't want it to end because we are both safe and calm like this. There is no room for dead parents or hurling of insults or holiday-induced rage. There is just us.

"You're shivering," he says.

So, I tuck my arms up between us, and soon, his heat warms me.

"Let's go inside, love." Sabin rubs my back and then takes my hand in his.

We walk to the tree house, and inside, he grabs a blanket and sits me on the futon. He sits in the chair across from me, and we look at each other for a while.

This is decidedly very awkward *and* very comfortable.

"Do you want to tell me about the video stuff Annie sent?" he asks gently.

I shake my head. "Not really. Do you want to tell me why you freaked the fuck out today?"

He shakes his head. "Not really."

"Should we not have come to San Diego? Was this a bad idea?"

It takes him a moment to respond. "It wasn't a bad idea at all. I'm sorry I said what I said. I'm...I'm in a really weird place right now. I don't know what's going on with me, but it's not your fault. I love you guys. And it was really cool of everyone to come here just for me."

His words are not enough to ease the worry, but I don't push.

"Do you want to give me my present?" I give him a small smile to let him know that we're going to be all right.

He smiles back. "Okay."

Sabin takes his guitar and sits back. "So, I, uh...I wrote you a song. For Christmas. It doesn't have elves or reindeer in it, but it's still for Christmas. It's nothing much. I hope you don't hate it. Just a little song, you know." He clears his throat.

"Sabin Shepherd, are you actually nervous?"

"What? No!" Sabin rolls his eyes.

"You are! After all the times you've sung to me, you're nervous. I think it's cute."

"Oh, shut up."

"You shut up and start singing."

"Fine, fine." He sets the guitar on his leg and looks down.

From the moment he starts, I have this strong reaction to his voice, more than I usually do. He has a way of reaching into my gut and tearing at my emotions. Even when the lyrics aren't overtly emotional, his delivery, his intensity...I am invariably pulled closer to him, and our connection is strengthened, just as it is now. The song is classically Sabin in that it's slow and gutsy, but in its simplicity, it's also one of the sweetest, most joyous songs he's written.

THESE CITY LIGHTS
SHINE SO BRIGHT.
BUT ONCE A YEAR,
WE PUT 'EM IN OUR MIRROR.

DIRT ROAD ON TIRES,
FIREWOOD ON FIRE,
SNOW-COVERED HILLS,
OUR COUNTRYSIDE HILLS.

No, I won't catch a wink,
Not on this Christmas Eve,
'Cause my love shines so bright
In this countryside,
Brighter than your city lights.

These country nights
Feel so right,
But all the year,
We put 'em in our mirror.

Dirt road on tires,
Firewood on fire,
Snow-covered hills,
Our countryside hills.

No, I won't catch a wink,
Not on this Christmas Eve,
'Cause my love shines so bright
In this countryside,
Brighter than your city lights.

He finishes and keeps his head down.

I hardly know what to say. No one has ever written a song just for me. "Sabin, it's so beautiful, so peaceful."

"That's why it's for you."

"Sabe…" I move from my spot and go to kneel in front of him. "You couldn't have given me a better gift. I love it. I *love* it."

Finally, he looks at me. "Yeah?"

"Yeah."

"It's no expensive necklace."

"Why would you even say that?" I shake my head. "What is this shit about?"

He shrugs. "I don't know. I'm sorry. Again. It's just…I don't have that kind of connection."

I shake my head. "What do you mean? With me? With another woman?"

"I don't know. Forget it. I don't want to do this." He puts down his guitar. "Are we okay, you and me?"

"Yes, we're okay."

But here's what I recognize to be undeniably true: While he and I are okay, *he* is not. Sabin is in pain. Of that, I am sure. I cannot tolerate seeing anyone I love hurting, and while Christopher's trauma and the aftereffects have given me my own kind of sympathetic pain, I believe that he has a resilience that Sabin might not. And that resilience, I think, Sabin might resent.

I see vulnerability and fragility in front of me, and I would do anything to repair what is broken. I just have no idea how, and he doesn't want to talk. There's a push-and-pull from him that, if I'm honest with myself, started last summer. He's either all in or shoving me and everyone else away. And I am left with no clear way to manage this.

"Let's do something," he says.

"What?"

"Wanna count stars?" His big smile is back.

"It's cold out now, silly boy."

He stands up and pulls down the ladder to the loft. "Through the skylight! How magical to be in a tree house on Christmas, right?"

"Technically, it's the day after Christmas now."

"Then, how magical to be in a tree house the day *after* Christmas, right?"

"Right. Let's count stars."

"After you, Lady Blythe."

I scramble up the ladder and dive onto the futon. "I see one!" I say with a giggle.

Sabin rolls next to me and points. "And I see another." He claps a hand over my face so that I can't see, and he says excitedly, "And, Blythe, there's another one! And another one! Oh, look. Another three. So, that's six for me and just one for you. You're not having much luck with this."

"Sabin!" I yell. "You're cheating! And I didn't say this was a contest."

He pulls away his hand. "Oh. So, we can add our stars together?"

"Yes. This is a team effort."

We spend the next ten minutes counting real stars and making up ones that are not there until we reach an even one hundred, which we decide is a success.

I move to lie on my side and notice something new on one of his shelves. "Hey, what's that?" I scoot over, take a snow globe from its spot, and return to lying down. "It's so pretty."

"Oh, yeah." Sabin waves a hand. "That's from Mollie, Pearce's daughter."

I feel around it in the relative dark up here and locate a knob that I turn. The globe lights up and plays a twinkly tune. "There's a horse inside. It looks like Mia, huh?"

He rolls to face me, and I set the globe between us.

"I guess it does."

"That was very nice of her." I raise one eyebrow. "How old is this Mollie?"

He shrugs. "Our age, I guess."

"Any chance she has a little crush going on?"

"Ha! I don't think so. And she's real quiet and sort of plain. Nice girl and all, but she's not exactly my type."

"Why? Because she's not a parasitic paralegal paragra—"

"Oh my God!" He laughs. "No. She's a sweet gal, but that's it. Not exactly the love of my life."

"You have one, you know. Somewhere out there."

He pauses and smiles softly. "I know." He seems embarrassed all of a sudden, and he looks down at the globe again and picks it up. The lights change from white to red to green to blue. He winds it up again and hums along to the tune. "I guess it is kind of cool, huh? Pearce gave me a pair of cowboy boots. Did I tell you that? Real ones, too. Not junky shit."

"That was thoughtful of him. I think you've made a very nice home for yourself here."

Sabin looks at me for a long time. So, I look back at him.

"What is it?" I ask.

"Okay, so I wasn't going to give you this, but…" He digs into the front pocket of his jeans and pulls out a small fabric bag. "It's stupid, but…well, here."

I undo the thin drawstring and empty the bag into my hand. I have to hold it to the light coming from the snow globe, and then I smile when I see it—a unicorn charm.

"Do you know why?" he asks tentatively.

"I do." Then, I smile, even while my eyes grow wet. "Because," I say, "unicorns shit rainbows. And because this is about when you made me part of your family. When I was lost and scared, you helped pull me from the wreckage."

He nods. "Yeah…and then you pulled all of us from ours."

It's hard to see, but I think his eyes are also brimming with tears.

He's wrong though. I didn't save them, not all of them.

"It's not as nice as what Chris gave you. I know that—"

"Stop," I say forcefully. "You stop that." I hold my hand with the necklace against my chest. "Sabin…" I struggle for words. I don't know how to tell him how much he means to me, how integral he is to my happiness, to my entire world. There is no way to verbalize how Sabin is as much a part of me as Chris is. So, I say the only thing that I can, "I love you."

He puts his hand over mine, both resting over my heart. "I love you, too, Blythe."

We've said *I love you* a thousand times. We say it without thinking and without parameters. We say it because it's true.

This time though feels different. I can't define how. I just know that we are more tied to each other than ever.

I move the snow globe from between us and inch closer. My fingers find the clasp on my necklace, and I undo it before slipping on the unicorn next to the sea urchin. Sabin intently watches me, and when I'm done, I wrap my arm around him and tightly hug him. Sabe rolls onto his back, settling me into the crook of his arm.

He pushes my hair back over my shoulder. "It's late, huh?"

"Yeah. I should go." I am exhausted, but I don't want to break this moment, this tie I have with him.

"Just stay here. I'll sleep on the futon."

"No," I whisper. "Don't leave." I'm afraid that he'll leave my hold, and I'll never get him back.

He waits a long time before replying, "Okay." He rubs my back. "We'll have a sleepover?"

"Yes."

"Will there be sexy pillow fights and hair-braiding and gossiping about the hottest boy?"

"Yes."

"Discussions about celebrity crushes?"

I yawn. "Okay." I reach into my pocket and pull out my phone.

"Texting Chris?"

"Yeah. Don't want him to worry when he wakes up, and I'm not there."

"Is he upset that you came here?"

"Not at all. He asked me to tell you that he loves you. Also, you're a moron, but he does love you."

"Chris is way too forgiving." Sabin blows out a long breath. "So are you. I'm sorry that I destroyed Christmas for everyone."

I send my text and then set my phone next to the bed. "You didn't destroy anything. We're all still here. We're all in one piece."

He sets a hand on his forehead. "Sometimes, I feel like...fuck, I don't know."

But I do know. I have been there.

"Like you were left drowning."

"Yes."

"And you're struggling to breathe."

"Yes."

"So, do it. Breathe. Just breathe."

"There's no air, Blythe."

"Reach for me. I won't let you drown. I'm right here."

He rubs my back some more and then laughs lightly. "You're already taken."

"I have two hands, Sabin. Grab one."

He thinks for a while, and I feel him take hold of his own hands to fully encircle me in his embrace. "I'm trying, love. I'm trying."

12
THE SWEAT OF YOUR SKIN

I FEEL THE SWEAT OF YOUR SKIN, THE TANGLE WITHIN. YOUR ACTIONS ARE MY DREAMS.

IT'S EARLY WHEN MY EYES OPEN, AND I'M STILL NESTLED AGAINST Sabin.

I leave before he wakes.

I need to run. I need to burn off...something. Anxiety maybe. I'm nervous for some reason.

Everyone is still asleep at the house when I get there, and I slip in, change into my running gear, and hit the pavement for five miles. I don't think during this run. I just focus on the strength in my legs, the rhythm I keep, the in and out of my breaths.

The shower I take when I get back does nothing to quell my edginess. Or maybe it's an energy. I'm having trouble pinpointing where I am, but the run didn't calm me.

It's when I'm toweling off that I know what I want.

The noise from the shower in the master bath didn't wake Chris, so I do. I'm still a little damp as I slide the sheet down and crawl between his legs. My boyfriend likes to sleep naked, for which I'm very grateful for right now because I don't have the patience to ease boxers off a sleeping guy. My sexual appetite has soared, and I cannot get his cock in my mouth fast enough. Within seconds, he's hard and starting to move his hips with the pace I've set.

"Blythe," he murmurs.

My hand slides under his ass, and I dig in, pushing him deeper into my mouth, making him groan and put both hands in my hair. Because my mouth is moving fast and my tongue is pressing so firmly against him, I get him panting in no time.

Before he gets too close, I lift up and lay my body over his, rubbing my clit against his wet cock. "I need you, Chris. Now."

It just takes a small movement for me to position him, and I rock back to sink his cock inside me.

He lets out a hard moan, and I immediately lift up and drop back down.

And then, again.

I'm starting to feel better.

I brace my hands on either side of his head and grind against him. "Tell me how good my pussy feels."

"Your pussy is so fucking perfect," he growls, clamping his hands on my ass.

"Tell me how hard I get you."

"You get me hard as steel."

"Tell me how I make you come."

"You make me fucking detonate." Chris is having trouble talking, but I don't stop.

"Baby, tell me how much you love hearing me come." I'm rubbing my clit against his body, bringing myself closer and closer.

"You coming is the hottest sound on earth."

"So, make me come," I pant. "Get me there."

He lifts me up and down, working his cock back and forth inside me. His movements are making me more demanding, more desperate.

"Get rough," I beg. "Show me how much you want it. Make me feel it."

He moves one hand to knot in my hair, pulling firmly, and he smacks the other hand against my ass once and then again.

"You need me to prove how much I want you, huh?" In one slick move, he flips me onto my back and pins my hands above my head.

Chris pushes his cock so far up inside me that I can hardly breathe. He stays closely pressed against me while he curls his waist back and forth in just the slightest movement. "You feel that?"

I look at him and smile. "No."

He pulls out almost fully and slams back into me so that I cry out. "Better?"

"Getting there."

So, he spreads my legs open wider with his, and he starts to fuck me hard, long strokes with no pause in between. His weight keeps me locked against the bed, and my hands are immobilized under his. All I can do now is feel how my orgasm is building, how he's going to get me there.

"Look at me, Blythe. You see now how much I want you?" He keeps driving himself inside me. "You feel that?"

"Yes." I nod almost imperceptibly. "Don't stop, Chris. Don't stop..." I'm in such a haze now, and it's heaven.

"Now, Blythe. Come for me." His breathing has escalated, his groaning deep and ragged. "Give me that sound. Let me feel that pussy."

Balancing on the edge of coming, I am raw and in my own world with him. "Tell me...we're unbreakable. Tell me, we're forever." I'm gasping for air. "Tell me, tell me..."

He releases my hands and cups my head, and then he lowers his mouth to my ear. "We *are* unbreakable. We *are* forever." He moans against me. "Don't you ever forget that. So, come for me. Come *with* me."

My orgasm pounds through, causing Chris to release his own. With his lips grazing over my neck now, I can hear every nuance in the sound of his pleasure.

He stays inside me until our breathing evens out, until we can see straight. "Good morning, beautiful. I don't know what brought that on, but holy shit." He kisses my shoulder, and his smile rubs against my skin.

"Good morning to you."

"I think you fucked away the hangover I would have had."

I laugh. "A surprising added bonus, huh?"

"Indeed." Chris lifts up. "Hi."

"Hi, baby."

"Things all right with you and Sabin?" he asks. "You stayed there? Up late talking?"

I nod. "Yeah. We're good. He still feels totally crummy about everything though."

Chris touches the unicorn charm on my necklace. "This from him?"

It takes me a second to reply, "Yes."

"I like it." But there's a hint of melancholy when he smiles. "Shitting rainbows, huh?"

"Is it okay that I put it on your chain?"

He almost seems confused that I asked this. "Of course, Blythe."

He traces his fingers over my eyebrows, my cheekbones, down to my jaw. I know how he looks when he's thinking hard, so I wait until he figures out what he wants to say.

"You get to have both of us, you know. You do."

"Chris, it's not like that—"

He stops me. "It is a little bit. It's not what we have, but it's something strong. And you get to have us both."

I start to protest, but he stops me.

"And another thing? I smell like scotch sweat, and I'm starving. How about I shower and then take you out to lunch?"

"How about I shower with you and then you take me out to lunch?"

"Almost the best offer I've had today." He winks and stands next to the bed. Then, he grabs my hand and pulls me to follow him to the shower.

13

YOU'RE HURT

AND WE RIDE
IN THE CORNER OF MY ENTIRE LIFE,
ON DOWN SOUTH NOW
WITH DRAGONS AND MOONSHINE.

As MUCH AS I COULD HAPPILY SPEND EVERY MOMENT OF THIS vacation sitting on the deck and staring out at the California seashore, I take Zach's arrival as impetus to get us all into downtown San Diego to explore. One night, we explore the Gaslamp Quarter and grab dinner at Searsucker, and on another night, we feast in Little Italy.

Yesterday, I insisted that we all go on a whale watch. Yes, we have similar tours that leave from Bar Harbor.

"But these are California whales!" I said enthusiastically.

The eye-rolling and grumbling about "stupid tourist activities" quickly quieted down though when we were treated to a dramatic display of breaching by gray whales migrating to Mexico. Not to mention, we saw plenty of dolphins and sea lions.

This morning, there's a winter festival downtown, so the seven of us have been strolling through parades, eating at food carts, and stopping at tables displaying local businesses with plenty of handmade crafts.

"Arts and craps," Sabin keeps muttering under his breath.

The air is a bit chilly, but the sky is a stunning bright blue. I zip up my jacket and stand near Zach while he gets a giant pretzel from a vendor.

"I think this is five meals in one," he says happily as he slathers it in mustard.

Steam rises off the hot pretzel, and the salty smell makes me salivate.

I've already eaten plenty, but I go ahead and get one, too. "Oh my God, this is amazing," I manage to say through mouthfuls.

"Right?"

We walk together and stop when Estelle and James pull our group over to watch a street performer hurling bowling pins up in the air while somehow juggling and riding a unicycle at the same time.

"I'm glad you could come out here for a bit," I say.

He nods. "So am I."

"Eric seems to be doing really well, huh?"

"He is," Zach agrees. "Estelle and James are totally back together, too, I see. They have a nice feel this time around—more settled, less extreme."

"I agree."

"And you and Chris—you guys are in good shape, too. I like being around you both."

There's a roar of applause that we use as a good excuse not to say anything for a minute. There is one person he has not mentioned.

So, I do. "How do you think Sabin is doing?"

Zach takes another bite and delays answering. "Well," he says, "something seems to be going on."

Sometimes, Zach is the only person I can talk to about certain things. He has a similar perspective, and we are bonded because we each love a Shepherd boy, and therefore, we love a boy with damage. As much as we are enmeshed in this family, we are also outsiders, observers of what they cannot always see. There is a code of silence that Zach and I have learned to follow, and only when we talk alone are we able to break that.

"What do you see?" I ask him.

He shrugs. "He's a little distant. A little angry. Snarky one minute, charming the next."

"He's not predictable right now."

"He's not. Sabin watches you a lot, you know," Zach says. "And you and Chris."

"Yet," I say as we start to walk to watch a drummer pounding out a rhythm on steel drums, "he won't look at me today, not directly. I don't know if he's pissed at me."

"Blythe, I think it's quite the opposite."

Before I can ask what he's talking about, Estelle appears and excitedly waves a flyer in front of my face. "Come on, we have to head up a few blocks. We have to see this break-dancing harpist magician!"

I don't have any idea what this means, and it sounds idiotic, but she looks enthralled with the idea, so we scurry to keep up with her. Zach drifts back to hold hands with Eric, and I'm pleased to see how comfortable Eric has gotten with being affectionate in public. He's always been okay with touching Zach in front of his family and me and James, but this is one of the first times I've seen him like this out in the big, scary world.

Sabin has been a little quiet today, so I seek him out to walk next to him. Because he's always loud and bubbly, his demeanor is noticeable and concerning.

"Hi." I put a hand on his lower back, and I'm surprised that he doesn't move his arm over my shoulder. It's what he normally does. So, today, I realize it's decidedly not normal. "You having fun?"

"Of course, love. Fried dough?" He offers me the paper-wrapped dough.

I hold up my pretzel. "Already stuffing my face."

He taps his food against mine. "Then, cheers to us both."

He smiles, but that doesn't make me feel much better. Sabin is, after all, an actor at heart.

"You okay today? You don't seem quite like yourself."

"Just kind of mellow. That's all."

We stop by Estelle's coveted street performer, and I squint in disbelief while a man indeed makes a few dance moves that are followed by strumming a harp and pulling two baby bunnies from the strings. Estelle's shrieks of delight carry over the crowd, and I laugh.

I look around for Chris and finally locate him. He's on the other side of the closed-off street, standing by an open tent that houses an art gallery's display. I weave my way through the dense crowd. Before I am even within talking distance, I feel the tension radiating from him. His body language is as familiar to me as my own, and something in his stance sets off alarm bells.

Chris stands, unmoving, midway down the long aisle with some framed paintings and photographs on easels and others secured to temporary walls.

"Chris." I keep my voice quiet as I slowly approach him.

His eyes are riveted on the painting in front of him, and I turn to look at the large canvas. I might not be an art expert, but it's a stunning piece. Vivid colors streak and swirl in front of me, creating an abstract work filled with electric reds and oranges and greens. Swipes of textured black and gray give the painting a three-dimensional edge. It should be beautiful, I can see that, but I find it markedly unsettling.

I glance at Christopher, who remains transfixed.

"Chris?" I say again.

He steps forward and touches the painting, his fingers tracing over the nubby black marks.

From behind me, I hear Sabin say, "Jesus fucking Christ."

Sabin steps to my left and goes to the painting next to the one that has Christopher's attention. Then, he moves to another one. Finally, he stops next to Chris. "He just won't go away, will he? He just won't *fucking go away.*"

"He's dead," Chris says flatly.

"But he's still goddamn here, isn't he?" Sabin sounds shaky, anxious, desperate. "There's no outrunning him, is there? There's just no fucking outrunning him."

My stomach drops when I scan the painting again and then the ones nearby. Sabin's disbelief and fear become my own.

Their father painted these.

Chris has his hand on the painting still when a woman approaches us.

"Excuse me, but you can't touch the artwork," she says tersely.

We all ignore her, and I move closer to the boys. "Your father's?"

Chris drops his hand and numbly backs up. "Yes," he confirms.

Sabin is ashen, stepping in closer to the painting with the black smudges. He studies it, his expression one of curiosity that turns darker the longer he looks. That turns fearful.

"This is your father's work?" the woman asks. "I'm the gallery owner, and we're tremendous fans of his. What a thrill to meet you." She extends a hand that no one accepts, yet she continues to gush, "He donated a significant number of pieces to us, and we have a showing dedicated to his work coming up. I had no idea he had children, or we would have invited you to attend. Do you live in the area? It's this coming Saturday, and you must be there. What an incredibly talented artist he was, and I was terribly sorry to hear of his passing."

Christopher and Sabin both look as afraid as I've ever seen them, both unmoving and in shock.

"Each painting alone is worth a substantial amount, and the number of pieces that he arranged to leave to us was so generous." She steps in closer to them, but both are frozen. "Do you know how many he left to be sold for charities as well? Such a humanitarian, your father—"

Quickly, I insert myself between her and the boys. "Back up," I direct her.

She leans to the side, insistent that she be heard. "What? I'm just explaining how much they're worth—"

"They're not worth a goddamn thing!" I am nearly spitting out my words. "Destroy them. Destroy every single one."

The gallery owner's shocked expression means nothing to me. I turn and put my hands on Sabin and Chris, pushing them away, trying to lead them from this cruel reminder of their past. Both stumble back, both lost in whatever memories these paintings have triggered.

The woman's hand lands on my shoulder. "I don't understand. If you'll give me your numbers, we'd love to have—"

I whip around, shoving her hand away, and step in so that my face is just inches from her. I speak slowly and clearly because I will only say this once, "Shut the fuck up. Do you hear me?" There is so much venom and threat in my voice that she finally clamps her mouth. "You have no idea what you're doing, so just shut the fuck up. We are leaving. Do not talk to them. Do not ever contact them. They are no longer that man's sons. They do not exist to you. Clear?"

She nods.

Chris and Sabin are in the same spot where I left them, and I ignore the few onlookers who witnessed the scene.

"Come on. It's okay. Come on." It takes more force than I expected to get them to budge from their spots, but finally, I wordlessly move them away from the tent and get them down to the next cross street.

"Where are Estelle and Eric?" Chris asks, suddenly panicked.

"They're still back up where we left them."

"I don't want them to see. They can't see."

"Okay. I'll make sure Zach gets them past that gallery without stopping." I send a short text to Zach, explaining what's going on.

"Thank you." Christopher's usual steadiness has been shaken hard, but he's starting to come back to solid ground. He turns to his brother. "Sabin? It's okay now."

Sabin's eyes are unfocused. "Chris?"

"It's okay, Sabin," he repeats. "You're all right."

"But...you're hurt?"

Chris sounds more confident now. "No, I'm not. Look at me. Sabin, you have to look at me."

Slowly, Sabin turns his head to Chris. "You're hurt."

"I'm not. See?" Chris holds out his arms, and he turns around once, letting Sabin scan his body. "Do you see? I'm not hurt, and more importantly, you are not hurt. You're in one piece. I'm in one piece."

Sabin's eyes fall back to Christopher's upper arm area, to a place where I know there is damage from a burn. "You are hurt. I remember that."

"That's over." Chris takes a stride forward and puts both hands on Sabin's shoulders, forcing them to lock eyes. "Listen to me. We're safe, and we're free. Look around. Do you see where we are? We're not back there." He takes Sabin's hand and presses it under his arm. "See? It doesn't hurt anymore."

"I want to go home," Sabin says.

"Okay." Chris is so gentle with him, so caring. But it's as though he were speaking to a child.

And, I realize with pain, that is what he's doing. He's speaking to Sabin as he must have done years earlier.

"I need to go take care of Mia. She needs the exercise."

"If that's what you want to do, that's what we'll do."

A glimmer of brightness peeks through. "You haven't been to the ranch yet, Chrissy. You can see the tree house and Mia."

"I think that's a great plan," Chris says.

I've never heard Sabin call him Chrissy. I bet he used to though. It's something a little kid would say.

We usher Sabin back to the car, and I hurriedly text Zach again. I don't need to tell him more than that we had to get Sabin out of here. He'll understand.

Getting back to the ranch seems to restore a bit of whatever happened to Sabin downtown. It's the first time he's wanted to show Chris where he's made his home, and I stay in the background while he gives Chris the tour. The truth is that I'm too unnerved, too frightened, to do much else. Chris is very good with Sabin, whereas I'm afraid that, if I open my mouth, I'll fall apart. Chris is admiring the exquisite paneling of the tree-house walls and commenting on the view when I excuse myself to go visit Mia.

I walk the path back to the paddock and try to clear my head. Mia is by herself today, and she clops toward me.

"Hi, pretty," I say.

I'm not scared to reach my hand to her now, and she waves her tail and makes a few nickering sounds while she lets me pet her.

There is too much swirling through my mind, and I am overwhelmed by Sabin's evident pain. I don't think it was until today that I understood how he was still haunted. It sounds stupid to me now, but I thought he'd worked through so much. But maybe it's too much to escape—or too much to escape alone.

Estelle, Eric, and Chris all have a significant relationship. While we cannot undo childhood trauma, James, Zach, and I do provide the person we love with some level of help and comfort. Love doesn't fix everything, but it helps.

Sabin is alone. I'm not there enough. I'm not truly his—or his alone.

Alone. It's a word that fits here because I suddenly see how alone Sabin must feel.

The understanding surges through my system and crushes me. He has an added layer of pain that his brothers and sister don't have. In fact, I suspect he might have other layers that I don't see yet.

Each sibling had their own experience growing up in that sickening household.

I'm not sure I know what Sabin's was.

I'm not sure I can stomach knowing.

Sabin brings Chris out and introduces him to Mia. I stroll to the edge of the arena with Chris while Sabin gives the same riding demonstration he gave me. This time, however, we are all subdued.

Chris has managed to bring some peace and calm back, but something significant happened today that none of us can shake entirely.

We lean against the rails and watch.

"You're very quiet, Blythe," Chris finally says.

I nod.

"It must have been scary to see Sabin like that."

I nod again.

He blows out a long breath. "The painting..." he starts. "I didn't...I didn't know Sabin remembered that day. I tried to protect him from that, but I guess I didn't do a very good job because he remembers something."

I watch Sabin. I just watch him ride and watch him be free for a few moments.

"The painting..." Chris continues. "The black on it? It's from coal. Burned into the canvas. Then, caked on. I could see some ash in there, too."

It's as though these stories are endless. When I think that maybe I know them all, there are more.

"Sabin was there?" I ask.

Chris shakes his head. "No, actually. I made sure. He was outside. I thought...I don't know how he knows. My intention was for him to be shut off from it all."

"But he had a very strong reaction today."

"Yeah. I was..." He inhales and exhales so sharply that I feel his pain. "He must have heard or seen more than I knew. So, today hit him hard. Gave him...some kind of flashback." Chris pauses. "We get those sometimes. We always will probably. It's part of the post-traumatic stress. He and I have it worse than the twins. I get mine at night, mostly when I sleep. You deal with that all the time, I know. I got it a bit today, but Sabin and I handle things differently...or we process things differently when they happen."

Chris, I'm aware, was unusually logical and present, even while growing up in his father's house. He stayed focused on the idea that there was a finite end to what they were suffering, that they would all get out of their father's control, and that there would be life after. What kept him sane was, ironically, putting himself in his father's path so that the other children would be safe. He routinely had Sabin take charge of Estelle and Eric to shield them from whatever abuse

124

their father was unleashing. But that wasn't always possible, and I see how Chris is faulting himself for that right now, as he has done many times before.

"I didn't do enough," Chris says.

"You did everything that you possibly could. You have got to forgive yourself for this crazy idea you have that you had to be some kind of superhero. No one could have done what you did for Sabin, for everyone."

"I thought he was doing well. Maybe he was. Maybe today was just a bad day."

"Maybe it was."

"But it was scary for you. I know that. It's hard to be present for someone else's pain."

"Sometimes, I feel helpless."

"There are many layers of hell, Blythe, and you've watched us go through a lot of them. It can't be easy for you. On days like this, I think you should run."

"That's not going to happen."

He turns to me and smiles softly. "I know. It took me a while to accept that because I could not understand how you would choose to be in this with us, but I know you won't leave. And you do more for me and for Sabin than we could ever explain. Some of what you do is so intangible that we can't break it down to thank you, but we are grateful for every moment that you stay."

"And I'm grateful for every moment that you let me."

Chris and Sabin have been and might always be enveloped in some degree of darkness. But I will always love them both.

"Sabin's pain feels worse than my own," he says.

"I know it does." I understand this because it's what happens when you love someone more than yourself. You would take on their suffering. You would do anything to bring them relief. "But...but look at him with Mia. For right now, just for right now, in this moment, he's happy."

Chris takes my hand. "That's something."

"That's an important something. So, let's take it."

Sabin has picked up his riding pace with Mia, and it's a beautiful thing to watch. The two of them move as though they've been together for years, and Sabin has some punch back in his voice when he nears us. "Chris, you want to ride?"

"You bet I do, cowboy!"

"Bet you don't do as well as Blythe did her first time."

"We'll see about that." Chris hops the wood fence and winks at me. "Although, I think Blythe was outstanding her first time."

Sabin's laugh is a welcome sound. "Yee-haw to that then!"

"Oh my God, Chris! Really? Sabe, make sure he falls off."

Sabin strides toward me and takes my hand as he eloquently removes his hat and gets down on one knee. "Whatever my darlin' cowgirl wants." He kisses my hand and then looks up as though he's going to say something, but then he stops himself. He holds my hand in his while he struggles for words.

I shake my head a touch. "I hear you. You don't have to say anything at all. I hear you."

He kisses my hand again. "Your boyfriend is about to fall off a horse. Get ready!"

Sabin, of course, does not let Chris fall, and for the next thirty minutes, I escape the troubled afternoon and just watch. The strength of the bond between these brothers is strong, but that strength is grounded in turmoil, and that worries me. There is endless love, but an additional piece is beginning to show, and I cannot identify it. It's a dynamic that hasn't yet fully played out.

"We have to stop meeting like this."

I turn and blush a bit when I see Pearce. "Hello, again."

Sabin waves enthusiastically. "Pearce! This is my big brother, Chris! Look how well he's doing."

Pearce waves and gives a thumbs-up. "Lookin' good there! You're a solid teacher, Sabin. Nice job." He leans against the railing with me and squints before he taps down his cowboy hat. "You enjoying your trip?" he asks.

"I am. Been exploring the city a bit, being a little touristy on occasion, but I think that's allowed. It's nice to see where Sabin lives. I especially like being here, watching him with Mia. It's a peaceful place to be."

"We could all use a little peace now and then, huh?"

I sigh. "You're not kidding."

He follows Sabin with his eyes for a minute. "Sabin doing all right?"

I look at Pearce. "Yeah. Why do you ask?"

He tips his head to the side a bit. "He's been working when he doesn't have to. Trying to keep busy. Probably avoiding a few things. Sabin's a drinker, right?"

"How did you know?" I can't hide my surprise.

He shrugs. "I might know a thing or a hundred about that." Pearce smiles a bit. "It's easy for me to see it. That's all."

"You used to drink?" I ask hesitantly. I don't know the rules about talking about this stuff, but he brought it up.

"Yes, ma'am. That's why I'm not married anymore. Been sober for twenty years now. Drinking away your problems only makes new ones, I learned. So, I quit. Carrying around a lot though, that boy. I'm guessing booze was the least of it."

"You know Sabin pretty well."

"Not details, but I don't need details to know Sabin has a story. And it's a whopper."

"Yeah," I agree. "It's a whopper." There's no disguising the sadness in my voice.

"He's a good kid. Really good kid. Tough as nails. Just a little unsteady right now. Sabin's got some shit to work through, and this is as good a place as any to do it."

"You watch over him, don't you?"

"As long as he lives here, you bet I do." Pearce stands up and gestures to Sabin. "Watch the reins, Sabin. Getting too loose there."

Sabin nods and tightens the reins in Chris's hands while he continues to walk next to his brother and Mia.

"There you go. See how that's better?" Pearce rubs his palm over the stubble on his cheek. "I'll be here if he needs anything, Blythe, okay? He's good people. He's got a home here, no matter what."

14
ROADIE

**AND TONIGHT, TONIGHT, WE DRIVE
THROUGH THEM HILLS,
BLACK AS ALL NIGHT.**

SABIN IS SINGING AT A CLUB THIS EVENING. HE'S ALWAYS LOVED
the spotlight, and I'm excited to see him on stage. *Stage* might be a
grander term than necessary, given that we're going to a
restaurant/bar that probably doesn't offer up a massive performance
area, but that's fine. It's the night before New Year's Eve, so I don't
know what kind of crowd will be out tonight, but the six of us will be
there to cheer him on.

I'm picking up Sabin so that he can get there early, and the others
will meet us. I'm a little stressed because I'm running late. It took me
forever to get ready tonight, which is unusual for me because—much
to Estelle's dislike—I'm not much for fashion. Yet I couldn't figure
out what to wear or how to do my hair or makeup, so I eventually
caved and called on Estelle for help. It's not as though we're going to
a formal gala, but I wanted to look nice. It's a night on the town. It's
for Sabin.

I'm parked under a tree outside the path to Sabin's place, but I sit
in the car for a few minutes and fuss with my lip gloss and then curl
my hair around my fingers, trying to feel comfortable. Estelle fluffed
out my hair into a wild mane of curls and assigned me fitted boot-cut
jeans paired with heels and a shirt that shows more cleavage than I
usually do. I pull on the back of the shirt to raise the fabric in the

front, and then I pull down the front. It's just going to slip back that way anyhow. Might as well go with it.

It's dark out now, but solar lights have come on to shine the way over the bridge. I'm pleased that I'm managing the heels better than expected although I do take the walk slowly. I hear voices when I reach his door. It's open, and I'm about to step in when I see that he's not alone.

A young woman, near our age, is sitting on the floor in front of him while he leans back on the sofa. His pant leg is rolled up, and she's holding a hand to his calf.

"Well, ow! Shit! That hurts!" He throws his hands into his hair.

"I'm sorry. I'm sorry." She keeps her hand pressed to him but apologetically looks up. "We just need to make sure it's clean. I'm really sorry." Her voice is soft and even, a bit motherly.

I don't know why I don't come out from the shadows I'm in, but I stand still.

"I'm sure it's fine," he says. "You don't have to do this."

"I'm glad that I saw you limping when you came back, or you might have just walked around with gravel and dirt in this. It's a pretty bad cut. That motorcycle is a bad idea. Are you sure you won't let me drive you to the hospital?"

"It's okay, darlin'. I'm fine." But he winces a bit.

"I'm just going to coat it in antibacterial ointment now and then bandage it up."

"Thanks, Mollie. You're real sweet."

She drops her head and focuses on his leg, but I can see her cheeks turning pink. Tenderly, she takes a handful of gauze from him, and I can see the significant scrape he's given himself.

I knock on the open door and step in. "Hey," I say tentatively. "You all right?"

"Blythe!" Sabin sits up. "Shit, is it that late already? Sorry. Minor bang up."

I take a seat next to him and peer down. "That's a rather bloody mess."

He's got a nasty deep scrape that runs most of the length of his calf.

"It's nothing. Blythe, this is Mollie, Pearce's daughter. Mollie, this is my friend Blythe."

I smile at her. "Hi. Thanks for patching him up."

130

Mollie smiles shyly at me. "Hi. No problem." Her light-brown bangs hang over her eyes.

She's pretty, I notice—petite, simple blunt haircut, no makeup, T-shirt, and cargo pants. Sabin was right when he mentioned she wasn't really his type, but I can't help noticing that she seems nervous and a bit flustered. Her hand shakes a bit when she tears open a few large bandages and applies the ointment to his leg, but she does a very good job of securing the gauze with white hospital tape.

"So, you wiped out on that stupid bike, huh?" I can't keep the scolding tone out of my voice.

He waves a hand. "Whatever."

Mollie packs away the supplies she brought into a tote bag. "I'm sure he was going too fast," she says quietly. "It's not safe."

"Where did this happen? On the highway?" I ask, alarmed.

Sabin shakes his head. "Just...you know, up the road. It's fine. I just took a turn too fast. Don't overreact."

"His arm is cut, too," Mollie adds. "Not as bad. But it's still cut."

I grab his arm and pull up the sleeve. Another large bandage is wrapped around his upper arm. "God, Sabin!"

"Relax! And we have to leave, B. I go on at eleven."

"Are you sure you still want to do this? You just had a motorcycle accident. And Mollie's right. You should probably go to the hospital."

"What? This is nothing, kid." He stands up and does some exaggerated knee bends. "See? Check me out! All in working order."

Mollie stands awkwardly and looks at her feet. "Okay. Well, good night," she says. "Please don't ride so fast. It's dangerous," she speaks so softly that I can hardly hear her, but her tone is kind and concerned. She starts for the door.

"Thanks again, Molls!" Sabin moves to the far side of the tree house to collect his guitar.

I stop Mollie at the door. "Thank you. Really."

She tucks her hair behind an ear and bites her lip. "Blythe? Um...he could have really hurt himself. Much worse."

She's worried. I can see that.

"I know. I'll talk to him." I smile and try to reassure her. "He'll be okay. He's tough."

She looks me in the eyes. "Everyone can break though. I don't want Sabin to break."

"I don't want him to break either."

I should ask her if she'd like to come out with us. I know that. It would be the polite thing to do.

Yet I don't. I'm not sure why, but I don't.

Mollie gives a little wave and rushes out.

Sabin doesn't seem to be walking funny or having any trouble carrying his stuff to the car, so I decide to forgo a lecture on motorcycle safety. The larger concern I have is that his behavior feels unsafe. He's risk-taking and chasing danger. I don't like it.

"Mollie seems nice," I say on the drive.

"Yeah, she's all right." Sabin has his window down and is letting the wind rush over his face while he closes his eyes.

"She seems to like you."

He turns and grins. "Why wouldn't she like me? The ladies love Sabin."

I laugh. "I'm serious."

"Yeah, well, don't get excited. That's not gonna happen. She looks about twelve."

"She does not. She's cute."

"Don't be ridiculous. But she had a bag full of every kind of bandage anyone could need. Jesus, I could have chopped off an arm, and she probably would've had something for that. Oh, I love this song!"

Sabin turns up the indie radio station we have on, which is fine with me because I need a minute. I'm taken aback at how undeniably and markedly relieved I am that he doesn't pounce on the idea of Mollie as anything more than the girl who bandaged him up. Sabin is my best friend, so I reason that it's normal to feel protective. Of course, the jealousy piece here is a little weird and creepy. It's not true jealousy though. It's just...

Okay, I'm a little possessive over Sabin. Fine. I can admit that.

Sabin turns down the radio. "By the way..."

"Yeah?"

"You look really good tonight, B. The..." He waves his hand around. "The hair and stuff. You look nice."

He turns the music back up, louder than before, so I don't have a chance to reply. But I do smile.

The traffic isn't awful, so we make good time.

We walk in to loud cheers of, "Sabin," from Chris, Eric, Estelle, James, and Zach, who have taken up a long table by the stage.

This place appears to have more of a bar scene than I thought, but Sabin doesn't seem to flinch. In fact, he looks elated and energized to be here. He high-fives James, and then the manager directs Sabin to a back room, so I go with him to see if he needs anything else.

"Sabin!" I pat his back as we set down his things. "I'm a roadie!"

He laughs. "You are the best roadie ever, B."

"Are you nervous?"

"I'm really not," he says. "Singing's kinda my thing. It'll be fun. You'll stay the whole time, right?"

"Are you crazy? Of course, you nut. You couldn't drag me away. Listen, Sabe…" I start. "Look, I didn't know this place had a bar scene at all. You okay with that?"

"It's not a problem, sweets. To be honest, I really don't miss the booze. But you go have a drink, and I'll drive us home, okay?"

"Maybe. I'm just here to see you." I give him a hug. It was going to be a short hug. That's what I intended, but instead, I'm finding myself holding on to him for longer. "You're going to be great."

Sabin's arms tightly embrace me, and we just stand there. He's supposed to be unpacking and warming up and doing whatever pre-gig thing he needs to do, but instead, we are clinging to each other.

"Okay," he finally whispers.

"Okay," I whisper back.

Slowly, he drops his arms and turns to open his guitar case without looking at me. "Love you, B."

"Love you, too, Sabe." I stop in the doorway. "We'll be the people screaming and clapping two feet from the stage. Try not to miss us."

Sabe laughs and turns my way now. "I'll won't."

15
JUST A SONG

**YOU WILL LOVE ME ALL,
OR YOU WON'T LOVE ME AT ALL.
I WILL NOT BE PIECES OF YOUR FAVORITE SONG.**

CHRIS IS DRINKING SELTZER WHEN I SIT DOWN NEXT TO HIM, BUT based on the clutter of glassware on the table, he's the only one.

"You look smokin' tonight," he says, draping an arm over my shoulder. "How's Sabin tonight? He doing okay?"

"I think so, yeah." I signal our waitress and order a grapefruit and vodka.

"Nervous for him?" he asks.

"Not really nervous. Just antsy. Did you get to talk to him more yesterday?"

Chris shakes his head. "No. It felt like he needed a little space to come down, you know? I'm glad he stayed at the house with us though."

Eric plops into the chair next to me. "Psst, Blythe! Blythe!"

His attempt at being hush-hush fails significantly, and I have a feeling that the beer in his hand might not be his first of the night.

"Hi, Eric." I smile warmly. I adore him, and I'm glad he's letting loose tonight because he's so often on the more controlled side.

"Psst!" he says again. "I just wanted to tell you that I'm gay. And I am in love with a boy."

Chris and I both burst out laughing.

I fake gasp. "You are not!"

He nods energetically. "I am!" Then, he inches in a little more. "Okay, seriously, I'm going to ask Zach to live together after graduation. Wherever he wants."

"I think that's wonderful," Chris says.

"So awesome," I agree.

"Okay, cool. Just needed your blessing to live in sin." He bounces away and sits comfortably on Zach's lap.

As if that didn't already make me happy, he then actually moves in and kisses Zach. And it's not a token short kiss. Eric *kisses* Zach. The entire table whoops, and we all raise our glasses. Eric doesn't even pull away. He just continues the kiss while lifting his own glass.

Estelle leans over the table. "Dudes, I need to talk to you about something." She's liquored up for sure, but she's better at holding her drink than her twin.

"Shoot," Chris says. "Seems to be a night of confessions already."

"I don't know what to do after graduation." She takes a swig of her beer. "Eric's gonna live with Zach, isn't he? Is that what he said?"

"Maybe," I say.

She doesn't often look worried, but she does now. "Chris? I don't know how…it's just…" she stammers. Estelle is not one to stammer.

Chris stops her. "Do you want to come stay with us in Maine for a while?"

She brightens and looks relieved. "Could I? With…James?" She looks at me.

"Estelle, of course," I say insistently. "You're welcome anytime at all. It's your home, too."

I realize that they've never had anywhere to go home to during summer and college breaks. It was always up to Chris to corral them somewhere, figure out a plan for each time away from school. Even after my own parents died, James and I had a home base with Aunt Lisa. Not that we liked her all that much, but we still flew back home to familiar territory and had some semblance of family. It's pretty normal for kids to stay with their families during their off times, to always have a backup place to stay.

The Shepherds have never had that, but they do now.

"James wants to talk to you about redoing the front porch, expanding it and adding in a larger patio area. Then…he's thinking about grad school or an architecture internship in Boston." She strums her nails on the table surface and looks around. "It's going to be fucked up, being apart from Eric, but it has to happen, I guess, so I'd feel better…being with you. We won't be in your hair, and you can just kick us out anytime you want."

"We would love to have you," Chris assures her. "You don't have to walk on eggshells."

"I'm not walking on fucking eggshells." Estelle sticks out her tongue. "Have we met? I don't do eggshells. I'm just telling you that we won't interfere with your exceedingly loud sex life this time around."

Chris covers his face with a hand. "Oh my God, did you have to throw that in?"

She polishes off her beer and clunks it loudly on the table. "I did. And that means you don't get to interfere in my exceedingly loud sex life either. This is going to be beautiful!" She grins and blows me a kiss, and then she makes a dramatic show of kissing my brother—with a lot of tongue.

When James can breathe, he looks bashfully at me. "Sorry, Blythe. Sorry…but since Estelle can't keep her voice down and I heard all of that, thank you. You guys are the best."

"And because you're so fabulous and all that," Estelle says, "maybe you won't mind that Zach invited Eric, James, and me to go skiing with him and his family in Jackson Hole. We'd leave in a few days, cutting this trip short." She squeezes her eyes shut and crosses her fingers after she drops this bomb.

"Oh." I'm hit with disappointment, but…well, they're college kids who want to go skiing.

James glares at her. "We totally don't have to. He just asked us tonight."

Rather quickly, Chris answers, "I think you should go. You'll have an awesome time, and it's been ages since you've been skiing."

I'm about to say something, but Chris rubs his fingers against my arm. He has a reason for thinking this is a good idea. I just don't know what it is.

"Really? You won't be mad?" Estelle claps her hands. "Fuckin' bitchin', James! We're going skiing! Sexy snow-bunny outfits for me. You slipping your cold hands under my—"

"Hey, hey!" Chris rolls his eyes. "Don't make me change my mind."

She makes an overly serious face. "Yes, brother dear. Understood." Then, she stands and yells toward the stage, "Sabin! Woohoo!"

I turn in time to catch him winking at his sister before he launches into a song. This might be a small bar, but they've got a stage light shining on him. This is his element, and I feel an onset of relief to see him as he is tonight. Despite a rough afternoon the other day, he is still the Sabin with all the strength and character I know he has. It's just good to be reminded of that.

He spends over an hour doing crowd-pleasing cover songs, including "Sister Christian." He dedicates it to Estelle and even lets her sing loudly and off-key into his mic. While it might be a drunken audience, they are wholly enthusiastic, and Sabin easily gets them all to sing along with him.

It's a happy group tonight, and I don't want this all to end, but at twelve thirty, Sabin announces that his set is over. I can barely hear what he's saying over the audience's applause and particularly over Eric's thumping on the table. We all join in though, and it creates one of the only embarrassed expressions I've ever seen from Sabin. He thanks the crowd and hops off the stage to grab a seat with us.

Chris jumps up and stands behind him, putting his hands on Sabin's shoulders and shaking him. "Who's my rock-star brother, huh? That's right! This boy! So proud of you, man."

Sabin pats Chris's hand. "Thanks."

"We're getting *marrieeeeeed!*" Eric hollers.

We all whip our heads to Eric and Zach.

"You're *what?*" Sabin asks.

Zach smacks his forehead. "We're not getting *married*. We're moving in together," he explains.

"Oh!" Eric claps the table. "That's right! We're moving in together!"

We cheer and congratulate them.

But Eric wrinkles his brow. "Wait a minute. If we got married, there'd be cake, and I could totally go for some cake right now."

"And maybe a gallon of water and a few aspirin," Chris mutters. "Actually, there is that late-night bakery we walked past on the way here. Just a few doors down."

"Let them eat cake!" Eric hollers.

"Chris, why don't you take the drunks out for cake, and I'll help Sabin pack up?" I suggest.

"Take your time. Eric has to sober up a little before I put him in the car. If he pukes everywhere, I'm gonna be pissed."

Chris manages to wrangle them all outside, leaving just Sabin and me.

"So?" He sits across from me now and fidgets with a napkin on the table.

I feign confusion. "So…what?"

"Blythe! Come on." The napkin is in shreds.

"You were amazing."

"Yeah?"

"Outstanding. Perfect. I've never seen you do better."

Suddenly, the manager rushes over with a panicked but hopeful look on his face. "Sabin? That was great, and obviously, the crowd loves you. Here's the thing. Another guy was supposed to close out the night, and he no-showed. I try to end the nights with something kind of mellow. It helps calm the place down and all that. Fewer bar fights. Any chance you want to do a few more songs? Just twenty minutes even? It'd really help me out."

"I don't know," Sabin says. "I mean, I guess."

"Sabe, you have to!" I insist. "You're the king of the slow song!"

He laughs lightly. "Okay. Sure."

Sabin gets back on stage, and the applause is immediate and loud. "All right, kiddos. We're going to bring it down a notch here, so sit back and listen to the mellow stylings of yours truly."

It's as though the entire room is under his command, and I'm not surprised when the room quiets down to listen to him. Sabin has a magnetism that reaches every person here, and I cannot take my eyes off of him. A few couples slow dance near the stage, and the atmosphere he creates with his music puts us all in a bubble where the outside world does not exist. We are all simply here with Sabin. He plays a few songs, and then he taps his guitar and thinks for a moment.

"So, uh…Blythe," he says, looking directly at me, "this one is for you."

I can't help but smile when he starts, "When You Say Nothing at All." It's an older song that I adore. A little sappy, a little syrupy, but it's one of the sweetest songs ever. I had no idea that he knew I loved this.

It's a song about communicating without words, about being there for each other always, about deep connectedness—the way we did the other day after the turmoil following the gallery showing.

It's a song about us. And it's beautiful. And I love every second of it.

The only problem is that I might love it too much because I realize that I am holding back tears and not doing a particularly good job of it. So, I just let my cheeks get wet because these are happy tears that come from how much I care for this person singing to me and how much I value every part of him.

The clapping throughout the bar is the only thing that snaps me from the moment. I realize that the song is over, and he's starting another one.

He looks away from me now. "This song is called 'Daisy.' I wrote it last summer, and it goes a little somethin' like this…"

SO LONG, MY LOVE.
YOU KNOW YOU WERE THE ONE.
YOU RIPPED MY HEART IN TWO,
BUT I'LL STILL SAVE HALF FOR YOU.

IF YOU WALKED INTO THIS ROOM RIGHT NOW,
I'D TELL YOU HOW I FEEL FOR YOU STILL.
YOU'RE THE ONE I LOVE,
BUT NOW I'M GOING AWAY.

If there weren't already tears in my eyes, there would be now. The other problem, I realize, is that not every bit of me feels purely happy. There is a nagging ache, a pull, on my heart that I cannot decipher because it's too strong and too confusing. And I don't want to deal with it. So, I brush it aside and just stay with Sabin and his song.

So, IF I AM LONELY,
I GUESS I'LL HAVE TO BE,
FOR A WHILE ANYWAY.
THE ONE I LOVE
ALWAYS ON MY MIND.
YOU'RE STILL WITH ME
ALL OF THE TIME.

So LONG, MY LOVE.
DAISY, YOU WERE MY ONE,
BUT YOU RIPPED MY HEART IN TWO,
AND NOW IT BLEEDS FOR YOU

TAKE CARE OF YOURSELF.
I'LL HOLD ON HOPE.
YOU KNOW IT'S ALWAYS
HERE TO CLAIM.

I can't even hear the rest of the song because my head is swimming, and I have some emotion that I cannot identify pounding through me. I have panic and anxiety and…and…and a longing of some sort that sends me spiraling.

More abruptly than he did before, he says good night and thanks the crowd before getting off the stage. He heads for the back room to get his things faster than I can stop him. So, I wait. I need a minute anyway. A minute to do what, I don't know. To think maybe, but I don't really want to.

I grab a fast shot at the bar. Not that a Mind Eraser is going to help me much, but I can still hope it'll erase what's eating at me.

He wrote that song last summer, I think over and over. *Then, he left— without warning, without a plan.*

He ran.

Did he run from me?

Oh God…

I see Sabin make his way across the room. He stops to talk to the manager for a moment, and then he hesitantly comes to stand next to me.

"You ready?" he asks.

"Sabe…" I start.

"Why do you look like that? It's just a song," he says, preempting whatever I might have come up with. He's smiling, but it feels forced.

Maybe I'm wrong. I hope I'm wrong.

"It's a powerful song," I tell him.

"That's how I do things. Come on. Let's go find everyone. Chris has probably had all he can take."

He rushes out the door, and I go after him, hoping to say…*what?*

I want it to be a few minutes ago when we were locked together in a song. This? This moment feels shattering, as though we might be on the brink of our friendship turning inside out.

Chris and the rest of our group are only a few feet from the entrance. He watches them stumble and then rolls his eyes at me. "Well, I fed them cake. Still drunk though."

Chris and I are parked in the same area, so we all walk together with us up front. Sabin has positioned himself behind the others, and I suppose that's for the best. I put my arm around Chris's waist and try to regain my sense of stability, to remind myself what the boundaries and dynamics are.

The sidewalks are filled with people leaving bars now, and traffic is tight. We maneuver around groups talking outside of clubs, and we're only a block away from our cars when we pass two guys leaning against a signpost.

"Fucking homos," one of them says loudly.

Chris slows to give them the benefit of his attention, but he keeps walking.

"Like this town doesn't have enough faggots already," the other says.

Chris comes to a halt and then moves in front of me as he faces the two. Eric and Zach don't appear to have heard what was said because they are still talking with James and Estelle, but Sabin clearly has because he lowers his guitar to the ground and steps forward.

"Sabin, don't," Chris says sharply. "Don't. Let it go."

He's not going to let it go though, which seems pretty obvious as he approaches the duo. "What the fuck did you say?"

"*Shit*," Chris mutters under his breath.

The others have just bypassed Chris when Sabin lunges forward and grabs the guy with a baseball hat by the collar. "Tell me what you fucking said," he demands through clenched teeth.

The guy smirks. "I said, 'Fucking homos.'"

"I'm gonna rip your fucking face off, you goddamn piece of shit!" Sabin's rage builds quickly, too quickly.

"So, you're one of them, too? Bet you're getting off from just touching me."

Chris moves toward them and tries to intervene.

After seeing this, the thug turns his head back toward Sabin. "What's the matter, little pussy? Can't fight your own battles? Need him to come save you?"

My chest tightens as those words leave his mouth. That was precisely the wrong thing to say.

Before Chris can reach them, Sabin explodes.

He sinks a brutal kick dead center in the guy's chest, forcing him to fly back. The victim knocks over several trash cans before he makes his landing, and I hear the hollow *thud* of his body as it slams mercilessly into the unforgiving concrete.

"Sabin!" I scream.

Blood pours from the victim's nose as Sabin stands over him. His eyes are wide with fury as he pulls his arm back, poised to continue his attack.

Chris tries to launch himself into the mix, but the second guy grabs him and swings a punch. Chris is too fast though, and he manages to duck while reaching for Sabin, who is now repeatedly pummeling a fist into his partner's face.

I wince when I see bare knuckles sinking into Sabin's cheekbone, and I scream his name again. James pushes past me and goes after Sabin, but I don't see what happens because Chris goes flying back against the wall. The *crack* from his head slamming against brick scares me to the core, and for a brief second on impact, we make eye contact.

I am too terrified to make a sound, but I get to him as he drops onto the sidewalk. "Oh God, Chris."

The hit he took is serious enough to jolt everyone apart, and the guy in the hat signals his friend to make fast tracks out of here. Sabin manages to take a parting shot at his victim, driving a fist into his stomach, before they run off.

"Christopher, look at me! Look at me!" I might be crying. I can't tell. I can't tell what's happening, where anyone else is.

The only thing I see is that Chris has lost consciousness, and Sabin is now kneeling beside us.

"Oh, Jesus Christ. Fuck!" he hollers. "He always gets the brunt of it. He always does. Fuck, make it stop. He always takes everything. Oh God, oh God..." Sabin is panting and nearly drowning on his words.

I have never heard this kind of mayhem and chaos from him, and it rips my heart in half.

"Chrissy, please wake up. Please wake up. I'm so sorry. I'm so sorry. Why can't you just let me take the hit for you? Please. Just once? Just once." He is pounding his fists on the pavement now, slamming his skin into concrete, as he begs for redemption that I cannot give him.

I roll back on my knees and look before me. Two people I love are before me, and both are in substantial agony.

I don't know who needs me more or who to help first.

16

THERE ARE DOLPHINS, AND THERE IS DEATH VALLEY

THE THINGS THAT YOU LOVE ARE THE THINGS THAT WILL MAKE YOU CRY. NEVER HAVE TO TELL ME TWICE.

THERE WERE SIRENS. POLICE CARS AND AN AMBULANCE. THERE WAS the emergency room and a very nice doctor. I don't remember all of it because I was in a panic for most of the time. In the end, the only thing that matters is that Christopher woke up when the EMTs arrived and that he was discharged from the hospital with a concussion.

That was five days ago. I haven't seen or spoken to Sabin since. He won't take my calls.

Chris drove down to the ranch the other day and tried to talk to him, but Sabin kicked him out.

The kids left with Zach for their ski trip, so Chris and I are alone in the house.

The kids. I have to laugh that I've started calling them this, as though Chris and I have somehow become parents to the brood. I suppose in some ways we have.

I'm trying to be respectful that Sabin wants space right now because I believe in privacy and one's need to be alone during certain times. It's not easy though. Among other things, his mood fluctuations are concerning, but I'm hoping that he's sorting some of this shit out. Maybe I need space from him, too. It hurts to acknowledge that, but he and I are in an upheaval that I don't know what to do with.

I'm trying to focus on Chris—on Chris and me—but I'm feeling guilty while doing so, like I'm somehow abandoning Sabin...or betraying him. It doesn't feel right to talk to Chris about this, whatever *this* even is, because...it's fucked up.

I can't stand this.

I've kept busy with writing. My boss is having me do a few pieces on San Diego, and it's been easy enough to pour myself into detailing the various places I've visited here.

So, I write. And I watch the ocean from the deck. And I try not to think.

I just wait. Because Sabin will call. I know he will.

And the image of Christopher's head slamming into brick and the sound and the expression of pain on his face will all fade.

It's cloudy this morning, but the gray sky makes for a dramatic visual over the ocean.

"You cold?" Chris comes outside with a blanket.

"A little." I sit forward and let him drape the blanket around me.

"You doing all right?" He looks worried.

"Yeah. Just feels weird that everyone is gone."

"And that Sabin is MIA?"

I nod. "It's why you encouraged the ski trip, isn't it? You wanted them to clear out."

"Yeah," he admits.

"Because Sabin is going to blow at some point, and you didn't want them around."

He looks into my eyes. "I think so. I think you can handle it, but I don't want Eric and Estelle around for it. He's..." Chris sits in the chair next to me and thinks for a minute. "He's very angry with me, I think."

"What? Why?"

"I'm not sure. He's trying to hide it, but...I feel a lot of anger from him. Or resentment." He sighs. "Something. It might be why he won't talk to me. I'm so much a part of the problem that I can't be part of the resolution. At least not yet. Blythe...you might be the only person who can reach him."

"How? I don't want to push him."

"Just be here for him. Everything will unfold when it needs to."

In the distance, dolphins bound through the dark waters.

"Okay. I can do that."

"So, listen, I just got an interesting call." Chris pauses. "But I want you to tell me if you're not okay with it."

"All right," I say with a bit of hesitation.

"It's nothing bad. Don't worry. Some guys from Death Valley National Park—I know, cheery name—want me to head out there for four or five days and consult on part of the software they use for the park. I guess they like what I came up with for Acadia, and it's sort of a big deal to be asked."

Chris is not one to brag, but if ever there were a time to do so, now would be it.

"Chris, that's amazing! You should be really proud of yourself."

"So, um…you don't mind if I go?"

"You *have* to go," I insist. "God, Chris, I'm really happy for you."

"Thanks. They want to fly me out today though. Is that all right? I hate the idea of leaving you alone here, but…" He lifts his shoulders. "I don't know. Maybe you can get Sabin to talk to you if I'm not here."

"I'll do what I can. Go pack. It's totally fine."

"All right. They'll send a car to take me to the airport, and then I've got a two-hour drive to reach them after I land. Should be quite the experience. Kind of going into the middle of nowhere, it feels like."

The idea of being in the middle of nowhere actually sounds good to me right now. It has to be better than this chaos with Sabin.

While Chris is packing, I scribble a note that just says, *I love you*, and I tuck it in his wallet. It seems old-fashioned, but it'll give him a little something to find. Texting is fine, but I like the idea of him coming across this unexpectedly. I tuck it between credit cards, and I'm about to shut his wallet when something catches my eye.

Snooping is wrong. It's an awful thing to do, but something about the textured paper compels me to tug on it. The ivory paper has been folded in half, and while it's a torn section from a larger piece, I don't need the full paper to know what this is. Because I see the names *Christopher* and *Jennifer* inked in elaborate cursive writing.

It's his wedding invitation.

I feel sick to my stomach. And angry and resentful and betrayed. *Why in the world did he save this, nonetheless carried it around?*

My hands shake as I replace it.

I busy myself with cleaning the kitchen so that I don't have to talk to Chris much before he leaves, and I time it so that my gloved hands are busy scrubbing a pot when his ride outside beeps the horn.

"It's just a few nights," he says as he comes up behind me and wraps his arms around my waist.

"No problem." I keep scrubbing.

"Blythe? You seem upset."

There has got to be a reason he kept the invitation, and I'm not going to overreact—or I shouldn't. So, I fight it.

I force a smile and tilt my head back to kiss him. "I'm not upset at all. Just preoccupied. I want you to have a good trip, and I'm not exactly trapped in a hovel here."

"Okay." He kisses me again, but I can tell he's not convinced. "I'll call you later. Love you."

"Love you, too."

I spend two hours needlessly scouring the kitchen and trying not to think. It does occur to me that I've spent a lot of time intentionally *not* thinking about things.

It's fruitless, I know, but I text Sabin again. Then, I leave him another voice message.

I go for a draining long run and try to excise the tension consuming me.

It's been a while since I've been alone for more than a few hours at a time, and making dinner just for myself sharply reminds me of the year after graduation when I was alone in my parents' house in Massachusetts. It was a year when I focused on rebuilding my world and being functional while learning to live again. It was not the happiest year of my life, but it certainly wasn't the worst. So, I should be able to tolerate being by myself tonight.

I call James to see how the ski trip is going, but I have to leave a voice message. Then, I watch a really terrible Lifetime movie while I eat chips and salsa in bed. Chris calls, but I ignore him. This is probably the first time I've refused his call, so he texts me and says he assumes I've gone to sleep, so he'll reach me tomorrow.

I fling the phone onto the floor. Maybe I'm being unreasonably angry, but I don't care right now. I turn off the light and pull the sheets over my head.

What if Chris is harboring some kind of regret over his wedding day, over Jennifer?

That's stupid. It was a long time ago. He loves me very much. He is devoted to me. He promised me that we were unbreakable.

Of course, I made him say that while I was fucking him.

He loves me. He loves me, I tell myself over and over.

I just feel like being angry right now, so I allow it.

I feel horrifically alone, and that reminds me of how alone Sabin is, how I cannot stand that for him. But I'm also reminded that I cannot deal with thinking about him too much right now.

He and I are in dangerous territory, that much is clear, and I am frightened to death that we will not emerge unharmed.

17
SHAKEN

**HOLDING ON TO SAD LOVE,
IN AND OUT OF MADNESS,
HOLDING ON TO SAVE IT.
YOU DON'T SEE I HAVEN'T KNOWN FAITH, FAITH.**

THE NEXT DAY FEELS ETERNAL. I CONTINUE TO AVOID CHRIS. I cannot call Sabin again. I cannot do anything.

I pace around the quiet house—again. I'm midway between the kitchen and living room on my umpteenth lap circling the huge room when I hear a loud plane. Or a train. Or...

What is that?

I stop walking and listen. Then, I look down at my feet because I think they're moving, but they don't appear to be. The noise gets louder, and suddenly, I hear dishes rattling. Quickly, I turn to the kitchen. Yes, the dishes are indeed clinking. The rumbling sound continues to roar through the house, and a growing panic grips me because I finally understand that this must be an earthquake.

I don't know if it's going to get worse, if the house is going to collapse or be swallowed up in some kind of fault line.

I don't know the first fucking thing about earthquakes.

My heart is pounding through my shirt as I stand, unmoving, in the middle of the room.

The middle of the room? Wait, that's not right. I'm not supposed to be here. I'm supposed to be in a doorway maybe.

I get my legs to work, and I move myself to stand with my back glued to the entrance of the mudroom.

Then, there is silence again, except for my breathing. I hear the sound of my panting.

My head is buzzing from the fear, and my arms are tingling. So, I just stay where I am because I'm not sure I still know how to walk, and I don't know if this earthquake is over or if there'll be another one.

I don't know the first fucking thing about earthquakes!

Well, except that one should not stand in stupid places like under chandeliers and such, so I press myself harder into the molding and pray this is a support beam.

My phone rings, and I pick it up without even looking at who is calling.

"Hello?" I can tell that my voice sounds weird.

"Are you all right?"

"Sabin?"

"Yeah. Are you guys all right?"

"It's just me," I say robotically. "Chris is out of town for a few days. My feet feel funny."

"Are you all right?" he asks more insistently.

"I did not like that. Is…is there going to be another one now? How does this work?"

"I'm ten minutes away. I'll be there soon."

He hangs up before I can say anything else. I'm not particularly interested in getting out from under the archway, so I stay where I am and suspiciously eye the room, waiting for something else to happen.

"California sucks!" I scream out. "You are supposed to be beautiful and perfect, and this vacation kind of fucking sucks!"

Not surprisingly, California does not reply to my complaint.

I'm still holding my position when the front door flies open, causing me to jump and let out a fearful cry.

"Sorry! God, I'm sorry!" Sabin holds up his hands and stays where he is. "It's just me. Apologizing again, it seems. Everything's okay."

I put my hand on my chest and try to get my breathing under control. "Everything is not fucking okay."

The sight of him jars me back into emotion, and I am hit with how difficult it is to see him—how I have been wanting nothing more and how much I've been dreading it.

"Everything is *not* fucking okay," I say again more forcefully.

"I know," he says. "I know it isn't."

"We need to talk, you and me."

Sabin looks at me for a long time. "I know that also." He steps toward me. He's still got a good bruise on his cheekbone from the fight the other night. "Are you going to come out of that doorway?"

"Is there going to be another earthquake?"

"Maybe. Maybe not. Hard to tell. The world isn't a stable place, is it?"

This is one of the only times I've seen him in a serious mood. No joking, no snappy quips, no deflecting.

Sabin takes off his leather jacket and sets it on the counter. Then, he walks calmly across the room and extends a hand. "The ground could give out beneath us at any time, but we can't stop that. So, come on."

I take his hand. It is the best feeling in the world to feel his familiar touch again, but I just look at my hand in his with sadness. "Everything feels broken," I say.

"It does feel broken."

I look him in the eyes now. He's as destroyed as I am. I can see that.

"I'm scared to talk to you. I'm scared of how you've been acting. I don't want to make things worse, but we have to have a conversation—about Chris because you've got some kind of huge issue there that I'm not getting. And…" I pause. "We need to talk about us, Sabin. And it has to be an honest talk because something is really fucked up."

The nervous energy I have belongs to him also. I can feel it radiating from his body, and it burns through me.

He says nothing for a bit.

"I wish we didn't have to do this," he says.

"I wish we didn't either."

"But I guess we don't have a choice anymore."

I order myself to breathe and to focus. The ache in my heart, in my entire being, hurts like all hell. "Sabin, what is happening with us?"

It takes a long time for him to answer. "I'm not sure. I know that I feel safer and happier and better in every possible way when I'm with you. And that worries me. A lot."

"Sabin—"

"So, I've tried the one-night stands, and they don't get me anywhere. They don't make me need you less. Because there's no feeling, no attachment with anyone else. And maybe I also chase after that because I can't have the alternative. Fuck, I don't think I've ever kissed a girl who I felt anything for. I have no idea what that's like. Maybe I never will."

"Of course you will."

"I don't know, Blythe." Then, he lets out a ragged breath to control his emotions. "Because the girl I trust most in this world is taken."

Now, my heart is pounding again. "I love you. You know that."

"I do. The problem is, I might be *in* love with you."

He's just said what I've been unable to face. "Is that why you left Maine and moved here?"

"Yes," he says directly. "I thought leaving would make it better, but it's the same now. And I left because I already feel goddamn guilty enough when it comes to Chris. I get so happy when I'm with you, and then I just crash hard because...I can't...I'm not allowed to feel anything for you.

"You draw me in, and we're completely in sync. I'm fucking complete. And that makes me miserable because it shouldn't be like that. You're not mine. I *don't* get to feel like that. There are times when I watch you with Chris, and I'm so...I'm so jealous," he confesses. "I don't want to have to say that to you, but you wanted honesty. I'm jealous. I'm an asshole for that. It's wrong. So, I run and try to get you to stay away, but that doesn't work either. And I know it's all on my end, and it's my fault."

I have to think long and hard before I say what I do. "I don't know that it's all on your end. I don't know what it is, but there is something happening between us that's different than it's been. I understand...the jealousy. I've felt it, too."

He shakes his head. "You can't. You're in love with Chris."

"Yes, I am." I search for how to understand and explain what I feel. "But...Sabin, I get overwhelmed by you sometimes, by how much I care for you, by the force between us. We call each other best friends, but that doesn't capture it, does it? We're not just best friends."

"No, maybe not. So, what are we?"

154

"I can't define it. I mean, right now? Right in this moment, I cannot for the life of me figure out how to explain what you mean to me, how to make you feel everything that I do. To...to convey that I would fall apart without you. That I adore you on so many levels. There are no words to capture that in a way that feels satisfying. When I hug you, when we're close, it doesn't seem like enough. It doesn't show you the importance of the way I love you. Normally, when you feel this powerfully for someone, you...you show them. Physically. You make love."

"And we can't do that," he says.

I don't like what I have to ask. "Is that what you want? How you think about me?"

The rumbling sound reappears, and the ground beneath me vibrates. "Sabin, it's another one?" My words catch in my throat.

With my hand still in his, he takes the few steps forward to be close to me. He puts his other hand on the doorjamb above my head. "Just hang on. It's okay."

He looks down at me, and I squeeze his hand.

I do love him, so much. I just don't know what to do with these feelings, how to categorize them. And I am at a loss for how to fix what has been building between us. What has been so perfect and easy for so long now feels terribly complicated.

The earth shakes for another few seconds and then stops as suddenly as it started with no warning on either end.

"It's like you're in my blood," he says softly. "I can't get you out."

I feel his body touching mine, and as I look up at him, he moves in a bit closer. There's a charge between us, one I can't deny but one I can't label either. I have the urge to envelop him in my love, to protect him, to convince him how he moves me.

Now, he puts his hand on the back of my neck. There is such tenderness and care in his eyes.

"Sabin..." I can't move. I don't want him to stop, but I also don't want him to move in closer.

He does though. Just a hint. Just enough so that I feel his breath on my lips.

We are both still, waiting for some kind of divine intervention to tell us what to do.

But there is none. There is just us.

Finally, Sabin chooses, and his mouth moves in a fraction more.

I still can't move. I still can't react. This feels perfectly right and so horribly wrong.

"Sabe," I whisper.

He pounds the doorframe above me and sharply pulls away. "No! No! Chris has done everything for me, and I don't deserve any of it, so I cannot be in love with you. I won't."

Sabin backs away from me, his face showing that he is as stunned and confused by what is transpiring as I am.

"Please don't go," I say. "Please. Let's just…let's just…"

"What?" he demands as he continues to walk away. "Figure this out? How? Oh God, this is fucked. This is fucked." He shakes his head and gives me the most heartbreaking look. "I can't do this. I have to leave. I'm so sorry. I have to leave."

The door slams behind him, and I clap a hand over my mouth to stifle the sobs. Finally, my knees give out, and I sink to the floor.

I'm going to lose him, I can tell, and I don't know how to stop that from happening because I am so mixed up. It's been a long time since my thoughts have been so convoluted, so impossible to get a handle on, and I don't want to be back in that place.

My world is coming undone.

Earthquakes are the least of my problems.

18
BURN, BABY, BURN

**I'D GIVE ALL OF ME
AND EVERYTHING I OWN,
IF YOU'D JUST FOLLOW ME BACK HOME.**

I BARELY GET OUT OF BED THE NEXT DAY. I'M A WALKING ZOMBIE, unfocused, teary, my mind ringing with torment. Disappearing into depression is easy for me. I know how to do this all too well. Sheltering myself under the covers, shutting out the world—I can do that really well. I'm a fucking expert.

So, I do.

I don't bother with trying to call Sabin because I know he won't answer. I'm sure he's spiraling the way I am.

Chris calls repeatedly, and I answer and immediately hang up on every call.

Finally, when the sky just begins to darken, I answer just to make him stop.

"What?" I'm almost too tired to even say that one word.

"Blythe," he says softly, "what is going on?"

I close my eyes. "You're the one carrying your wedding invitation around. You tell me."

"I was afraid of that. I found your note. You can't possibly think that anything is wrong with us?"

"I can think whatever I want. Leave me alone." I hang up and turn off the ringer.

The phone flashes to show that he's calling back, but I ignore it.

Then, he texts me.

Chris: Please don't be upset. There's no reason to be. I'll explain it to you, but we're not doing this over text. Either pick up the phone, or we can talk when I get back.

I don't have the energy to reply. My heart is too shattered—because of him, because of Sabin.

The ceiling fan takes me into a trance, and I stare at it minute after minute until the sky is black and until I hear music. I should find it odd that the ceiling fan is making music, but I just listen. It's beautiful, and it lulls me into some kind of resemblance of peace. I let myself drown and be engulfed in it. Minutes tick by, and I don't question how long I've been buried under the sheets.

Only then, Sabin's voice cuts through my delusion. It's *his* music, I realize, coming from outside. It's barely audible, but that voice is like no other. So, I lift myself from the bed and stand by the open window. There's just enough moonlight that I can make him out. I would know him from any distance—the shape of him, the way he moves, the character he exudes. His entire being is so distinctive to me that I could pick him out of a crowd of a million.

I laugh at myself. *I would know him from any distance.* I've thought that about only one other person, Christopher, and right now, my ties to both of them are fucked up.

The walk from the bedroom out to the deck feels endless, but I make it. I can't imagine what he's doing here when he abandoned our last scene so quickly. Based on the dying campfire he's sitting next to, apparently, he's been here for a while.

My heart can't take another talk right now, and I'm about to turn and leave when he begins to sing.

WHY DID YOU RUN?
YOU WERE SO COLORFUL. YOU WERE SO BEAUTIFUL.
IF YOU'RE BORN IN THE FIRE, YOU WILL BURN.
WE AIN'T BORN ANY WISER. YOU WILL LEARN.

IT'S GETTING COLD IN THE WATER, MY LOVE.
COLD IN THE WATER, COLD IN THE WATER.

RESTLESS
WATERS

I WAS BESIDE MYSELF WHEN YOUR SOUL
LEFT THE ROOM
'CAUSE YOU'D TALKED OF MISTAKES YOU MADE
AND HOW YOU DON'T WANT THE SAME FOR ME.
NO, HOLD ON, BE STRONG
'CAUSE THE TEARS WILL STILL FALL AT WILL.

Sabin's been drinking. I can hear it. There's just a slight edge to his voice, and the only good thing about it is that it jerks me into alertness and fight mode. I am not going to let him drown if I can help it.

With determination and as much of a level head as I can maintain, I make my way down the stairs from the deck and cross the sand to reach him. I stop a few yards away.

"I don't think you're supposed to build fires on the beach," I say.

"Well, I did a nice job, didn't I? Rocks around the edges, well contained."

I kneel down and try to assess how drunk he is. "You've been drinking."

"So what? Can you blame me? And don't get all fucking preachy on me. I cut myself off an hour ago. It's not working."

"You've been totally out of touch...after what happened." It's excruciatingly hard to say even this. "Why are you here?"

Sabin takes his time setting his guitar back in the case before he stands and begins walking back and forth. He's a mess. His sleeveless shirt is dirty, his face is unshaven, and his black hair is unruly. More than that, he's boozy and volatile. That's easy to see.

"Here's the thing, Blythe. I can't do this anymore. I won't."

"Do what?"

He waves a hand between us. "This. You and me. It's over. I don't want to see you anymore. Not after tonight."

It's as though he'd hit me across the face. I stand up. "Sabin, don't you dare—"

"No!" he says sharply. "We can't be friends. Or anything. I'm just here to tell you that. We are over. Everything about us is over."

"You don't get to just announce that like it's no big fucking deal." Now, I'm angry with him. "You stick it out with me, and that's that. Because we *will* figure this out. So, no. You are not ending this. I won't let you."

"Actually, Blythe, I *am* ending this. I can do whatever I want. When it comes down to it, we don't really have any ties to each other, do we? No. I stole your coffee. You fell in love with my brother. That's the end of our story. You and he get the enviable connection, the whole aligned-with-the-stars one. Not you and me.

"And I need to take myself out of this mess and away from you and Chris because the guilt..." His pacing speeds up, the distress in his face increases. "Jesus, the guilt is impossible. I can't sleep. I can't be awake. I can't find anyplace that isn't filled with guilt. It's already bad enough over Chris, but I cannot add in all this bullshit with you on top of that. Do you fucking get that?"

"On top of what? What do you feel so guilty over?" I run my hands through my hair in frustration. "You are the most genuine and loving person. So, no, I don't get it. Explain it to me. Chris worships you. You know that. He would do anything for you."

"And that is the goddamn problem. Don't you see? He did *everything!*" Sabin's agitation is growing. "Christopher Shepherd motherfucking protected all of us, and he left nothing for me to do! He took the brunt of what my father dished out, and Chris never let me give back to him."

He is screaming at me now. "He always stepped in when he could, Blythe. Chris is a fucking saint. He is. He threw himself in the path of brutal bullshit over and over. He set himself up for it."

Sabin starts to cry, and his emotions tumble out fast. "Always. And I should be grateful for that. I am grateful, but...but I also hate him for that. Now, I am left standing here, all alone, having done nothing to shield him. I did nothing. I did nothing."

Watching Sabin, of all people, fall to pieces rips apart my entire system. I don't know how to face him or what he's saying. To some degree, I've had to get used to it with Chris, but Sabin has always convinced me that he tackled and beat his demons, which was a fucking trick that I stupidly allowed myself to fall for.

He went to rehab and got all fixed up. No follow-up needed. Done.

It was easier to believe that he'd somehow magically healed after such a short time.

"Chris did everything, Chris is a fucking saint," Sabin tells me again. He can't stress this enough. That is clear.

"Always the martyr."

"Making the big sacrifices."

"Hero."

Sabin's words from Christmas Day rush through my head.

"Chris has all the glory. He gets to be the strongest, the bravest, the one who stood in the path of danger so that we wouldn't have to. So, he deserves to be applauded. Really, he does. But I fucking hate him for it, too. I hate how he blocked me from getting to stand up for myself, but more than that...I never got to fight for Chris. After all he did, I couldn't fucking fight for him? I hate him. I hate him. And I can't stand that I hate him. How fucked up does that make me, huh? He has scars to show what a prince he is, and I have nearly nothing next to that."

"Oh God, Sabin." I take a step forward.

Approaching his agony takes a lot of strength because it's never easy to walk into someone else's storm. But I can't, nor would I ever, abandon him, no matter how destructive it proves to be.

"You have scars, too. Honey, you have scars just like Chris."

Sabin's arm flies down, and he grabs the bottle of whiskey. He unscrews the cap, and he flings it away. He looks at me with anger and takes a long drink. "It's not the same. You know that, Blythe. He took more than his share. He took way more."

The burning embers near me are hard to block out, and they are wreaking havoc with my thinking.

Fire, burning, flames, smoke, James, glass, blood, death, my family...

I have to shake that off, so I turn my gaze to the dark waters, searching for what to say. I don't matter right now. Only Sabin does. I'm someone he trusts, so I have a chance to get him to let go of whatever it is that he's been holding in. I know that something inside him needs to be discharged into the world. The release of what he's been trying to suppress could save him, and I will not accept anything less than that. Saving Sabin is the only acceptable option. I'm not sure that I can do it, but I will try.

"The paintings we saw the other day," I prompt. "There was one in particular...the burn Chris got under his arm."

Sabin flinches, and I keep my eyes glued on him until I understand.

God, I hate having to say this. "That was meant for you, wasn't it?"

He takes another drink and wipes his mouth. "Yeah. I wanted it. I practically *asked* for it. To help...even things out, you know? So, I could be Chris's partner in all that shit and not someone he had to suffer for."

He's breathing hard, sweat forming on his hairline. "I started it, you know? Our father was in his studio, working on that huge painting, devoting and caring for that fucking canvas like he never did for us. He had…he had smears of color everywhere. Palettes and whatever. Brushes bleeding red. And there was this little kiln he kept running in the winter, partially to keep warm in that huge room but also for when he worked with metal. He liked metal a lot. Heat it up and bend it to do what you want. I didn't think about that risk."

He stops and faces me. "I didn't think about that. All I wanted was to badger him. That was all it would take. Say one wrong thing. So, I walked into his studio without permission and told him that his painting sucked. That it was stupid and ugly. I don't know what else I said. I was fast back then, but I didn't even try to run because I wanted to get what I'd come for—something that was just for me and not for Chris. But my father only got in one good hit before Chris heard me screaming. I got too scared, and I screamed, Blythe. If I'd just kept my mouth shut—fuck!"

His desperate face wrecks me. Chris has told me a number of hideous stories, but Sabin never has. I've never heard one detail from him, and now, I am again watching someone I love explore levels of anguish that I can only imagine.

"Chris got there, and…he was in his shorts, still wet from swimming, and he put himself between our father and me. I can't remember exactly…Chris started taunting him, saying he was a better target. He's the one our father really wanted. Then, somehow…" Sabin shakes his head, trying to recall the details.

"Oh. I know. I do know. Chris told me to get out, to run. He pushed me. He literally pushed me out the door and slammed the deadbolt shut. God, I can still hear that sound. I pounded on the door. Really hard until my hands hurt so much. I was screaming and crying because they wouldn't let me back in. I think I was ten, maybe? Eleven?

"Chris forgot there was a window though. He forgot that I could go to it and watch. So, I did. I watched what was supposed to be mine. He smacked Chris. He slammed Chris's head on the table. And more. Then, my father, without thinking twice, just took one of the tools he had by the kiln. I don't know what it was, something metal

162

though. And he stuck it in the kiln, and he made Chris wait. Then, he burned Chris. Right in front of me. After, he rubbed the tool onto the canvas, so it was part of the painting forever. I can...I can still hear Chris."

Sabin's deluge of tears and guilt is nearly intolerable to take. There is no possibility that the abuse stories they tell me will ever make me less sick to my stomach, less full of rage that I cannot ever fully release. It is my job, however, to be a source of stability and strength now. I've learned that. So, I have to at least try.

"None of this was your fault. Not any of it. Even that day. Your father was a monster, Sabin. What he did to all of you, who he was...it's unforgivable. But you are just as brave and strong as Chris. You got through it. God knows how, but you did, and you are here. And you are worth everything. Don't do this to yourself. You got through it. You got through it." I am pleading with him, but it feels tragically useless.

"You think I got through it? Are you fucking crazy? Look at me. Look at me! It's never over. It will never be over. You think you're all healed and shit? You can't be that stupid." Swiftly, he takes a piece of driftwood and lunges it into the coals in the firepit, making a flame jump out.

Involuntarily, my breathing catches, and I let out a sound. My heart races as a flash of panic sears through me.

"See?" His tone is nasty, cutting. "Trauma—the gift that keeps on giving. Do you actually believe that you can run through the pain? You can't. You can't outrun shit. Keep putting on your sneakers and pounding pavement, but you'll never beat down that bitch."

He jabs the stick into the fire, creating another burst of flame and hot sparks. It's a hateful thing to do to me, and this time, I cannot contain myself, so I give up on trying to hold in my tears.

"I love you, but that was goddamn mean, Sabin," I choke out. "Even now."

"Just proving my point, darlin'," he says bitterly. "That fire you think you're over? You're not. You'll never be. And us fucked up Shepherds? We'll always be tainted with pieces of hell."

"You are *not* tainted," I say as strongly as I can. "Please. That is not who you are."

He drops his arms to his sides. "Of course I am. Everything about me is tainted. I love you. I hate you. I love Chris. I hate Chris.

You're both my idols and also the people I can't get away from fast enough. With you two, there is nothing but pain and guilt everywhere I turn."

I step directly in front of him and take his face in my hands. Immediately, my palms are covered in his tears. "Listen to me, Sabin. I am not leaving you. I won't. I refuse to let you shut me out of your life. I refuse to let you destroy yourself. That is not going to happen."

He pushes me away. "Get the fuck out of here."

Now, I grab his shirt and bring us close. "I love you. Don't do this."

"You have to stay away from me. I'm trashing everything around me, so just get the fuck out of here! You can't fucking help me!"

"Stop it! Stop it!" I'm as frenzied in my emotions as he is, and it's without full awareness of what I'm doing that I lift up on my toes, press my mouth tightly against his, and kiss him hard.

To get him to stop talking.

To get him to shut the hell up with his story of torture.

To get him to love himself. To feel my love in whatever form it's meant to take.

To make this explosion end.

I cannot take any more. I cannot pick up any more wreckage.

My hands knot in his shirt as my lips move over his, my tongue sinking into his mouth. Sabin tastes like whiskey and misery. I feel his hands on the back of my head, his fingers pulling at my hair, as he kisses me roughly. Too roughly. This kiss is angry, and it's heated for all the wrong reasons. I know that.

I try to pull back, but his hands keep us together, so I keep kissing him, trying to drown out his pain. I dig my fingers into his shoulders, pulling at him, silently begging him to feel loved and whole and unbroken.

His touch moves brusquely over my back as he claws his hands down my shirt until he hits my lower back. Sharply, he yanks my waist against him and takes his mouth away.

"Happy? You think you can fuck the life back into me like you did with Chris? Well, you can't. Because there is no life to get back. I never had one in the first place. All I have is damage. That's my baseline. That's all I know. And that's where I'm staying. So, you go back home and crawl into Christopher's bed. That's where you belong. I am fucking done with you."

There is such disgust in his eyes, in the way he speaks to me, that I move back four or five steps. I know how to handle Chris when he's upset, even when he's swimming in a sea of severe pain, but I do not have the slightest idea of how to handle Sabin.

Or how to handle myself. I'm only making things worse for him.

I keep backing up, slowly distancing myself from him. Just as I turn, I catch movement in the corner of my eye.

It happens so fast. He moves so fast. There is no time for me to stop him, to come up with anything to prevent what he does.

So, when he takes the burning stick from the fire and holds it to the skin under his right arm, all I can do is scream. Over and over, I scream.

Sabin's impulsive and violent act frightens me so much that I don't go to him. My attempts to get through to him, to help him in some way, only escalated what had already been a heightened situation, and I'm terrified that I'll just make things worse if I go to him now. That he'll do something even more awful or dangerous.

So, I just scream and stumble across the beach to reach the stairs.

19
SAME SHIT, DIFFERENT DAY

IF SHE COULD PAY WITH BLOOD, SHE'D BLEED. AND SHE'S HOLDING ON AS HARD AS SHE CAN, HOLDING ON BY THE SKIN OF HER HANDS.

FROM MY CHAIR ON THE DECK, I KEEP AN EYE ON SABIN. HE DRINKS a little more, but he leaves the bottle more untouched than I would have predicted. A drink now and then, but he doesn't down the bottle. That's a very small silver lining in all of this.

What hits me harder is the realization that, for the second time in my life, I am watching a boy on a beach. A boy on a beach who is drowning on dry land. This time, I cannot give a part of myself to him because he won't accept it.

My fear and my heartbreak are so present that it's difficult for me to think rationally, but I know that I cannot look away from Sabin, not even for a moment.

For an hour, I sit, unmoving, my sight glued on my best friend. His back is to me while he sits on the beach and faces the water. Later, he curls up in the sand, finally asleep after this evening of agony.

But I'm still going to stay.

After too much time, I break from my own deluge of hurt. My friend's destruction so far outweighs mine, but it's still a force of will to shake myself to function, and it takes great effort for me to hit the right buttons on my phone.

He picks up as soon as the phone rings. "Blythe."

"Chris." It's difficult to speak. "Chris…"

"Tell me what's wrong." He knows immediately that there is trouble far greater than what I found in his wallet, and the urgency in his tone is unmistakable. "Is it you or Sabin?"

"Both," the tremble as I speak is out of my control. "I need you. *He* needs you."

"Are either of you hurt?"

I'm not sure how to answer this, so I just say, "I'm at the house. Sabin is on the beach."

"Are you both safe?" This is a question only asked when it's clear the situation is extremely serious. Chris quickly understands that we're in a crisis. He wants to know about potential danger.

"Yes, yes. He's asleep now. But we need you. We really need you. Sabin…" I start to cry so hard that it becomes difficult to breathe. "Oh God, he's spiraling. He thinks he didn't do enough when you were kids. That you didn't let him help you the way he could have. He's a wreck because you stopped him and didn't allow him…you didn't allow him to be an equal victim, an equal target. He is angry and feels guilty, and he's totally losing it. He burned himself. Chris, he *burned* himself to be like you." My breathing and crying are out of hand. I'm nearing a place that borders on out of control. "The painting. He told me about the painting. He saw more than you thought."

"Fuck. *Fuck!*" Chris slaps his hand against something, and his impact tears through me. The sound of his reaction is too familiar. His sense of responsibility for his family is profound, almost too much so. "I already got a car, and I'm an hour into driving home. You not taking my calls was enough to tell me things were bad. But it's a lot worse, isn't it? It'll take me another four hours or so, but I'll get to you as fast as I can."

"There's…more…I have more to tell you." I don't know how I'm talking because my head is spinning so out of control. "Sabin and I…we're all screwed up. I am so alone right now, and I don't want to be. I am going back to that dark place I fought to get out of. Don't let me go there. Please don't let me go there again."

Sabin's disintegration is becoming my own. I'm together enough to identify it but not together enough to stop it myself.

"You'll tell me everything when I'm there. Right now, you're going to breathe for me. Just breathe for me. Let me hear you."

He's right. I'm hyperventilating. Heightened states take over my body and my breathing. I feel as though history keeps repeating itself because Chris has had to convince me to breathe normally before. This thought makes my panic escalate.

Maybe Sabin is right, and we'll just keep cycling through pain forever. There is no escape.

I let out another sob.

"Blythe!" Chris is aggressive enough in his tone to make me listen. "Breathe in for four, exhale for eight. Do it now."

So, I inhale slowly and listen to him count to four. Then, he counts to eight as I exhale. We do this for the next few minutes until I've come back down.

"A little better?" he asks.

"Yes." My head and body are together enough for me to tell him, "I'm sorry I wouldn't talk to you before. I'm so sorry. It was stupid. Especially now."

"It doesn't matter. I love you, and I'm coming home."

"Okay. I love you. God, I love you so much." I'm crying harder. "Please come home. Please come home."

"Baby, I'll be there soon."

I hang up with the knowledge that help is headed toward us. Chris knows how to stay calm right now because he's been through much worse storms than this. Despite *and* because of everything he has survived, he has become someone with a shockingly strong foundation, and it's one that I'm depending on right now. It seems appalling that I should lean on him when this situation is so strongly tied to him, but the truth is that Chris has a skill set and fortitude that can withstand my breakdown. And Sabin's.

It's part of why I'm so in love with Chris. He is competent and capable in ways that are striking and beautiful. He has insight and compassion that, even with his measured control, shine through and heal.

Even in my chaos, I finally become aware of how dependent I am on him. Not in a crazy, pathological way, but I see how much he brings to what I don't have, and my reliance on him is sharply in my consciousness tonight.

It's why we work so damn well. Together, we create balance. I give what he needs. He gives what I need. After that, we have immeasurable chemistry, and that chemistry goes way beyond the sexual. There is a pull and bond between us that surpasses definition. And in that, I trust.

I have let him fall into me more times than I can count, and tonight, I need to fall into him.

Hour after hour, I alternate between lifting my eyes to Sabin on the beach and staring at my phone. The video that Annie sent me plays repeatedly, and it's beyond me to stop it. I want to live in the past with my family and in the life I had before I knew what it meant to have my world blow up.

Sabin is likely right. I will never get over my losses and the vivid images I have of the precise seconds when those losses slammed into me. As much as I've tried to move through the memories of that fucking fire, I cannot forget. I'll never forget.

I will very possibly drown in those flames.

If Chris does not get here soon and pull me from the fire again, I might just fucking drown in flames.

Worse, maybe, Sabin will drown in himself.

My entire body is full of anger and sadness, and I stand up and slam my hands onto the railing as I scream out at the water, "A little less fucking drowning and a little more land would be nice! Do you hear me? Do you fucking hear me? Less drowning, more land!" I stay frozen as I squint into the dark, waiting for some sort of response from the universe.

When a car door slams, I start to cry again. I'm sick of crying. I've done enough of it in my life, and I hate coming undone, but I can't control myself. In a blur, I'm in Christopher's arms, and he wordlessly holds me against his chest until I begin to find some level of calm.

"Sabin's still out, so he's okay for right now," Chris says gently. "Let's take this one piece at a time. We're all going to get through this."

He lowers me down to a chair and then sits himself across from me.

"Annie made that video for me," I share. "And all it does is break my heart. I couldn't get myself to show you before. Or anyone. It's supposed to make me happy, and instead, it shreds me. Sabin knows that none of us will recover. We won't, Chris. We won't. That means that James and Estelle and Eric...we can't get better, can we? The video just shows how true that is."

170

"Oh, Blythe. Do you want me to watch it?" he asks. "I don't have to, but would it help you?"

I nod, so he starts it from the beginning. I now know every sound of every second, and I watch him as my family and my past move before his eyes. At one point, he stops the video and rewinds a particular section a few times, listening to a young me with my parents. I hear my mother talking to me as she rocks me to sleep while I murmur what sounds like nonsense.

Chris smiles, finishes the video, and turns off the phone.

"What Annie put together for you? It's extraordinary. Tonight, you only see the loss, but it's so much more than that. You got to experience something beautiful. Please don't forget that. By default, we grab on to the loss, but you can choose not to. Look at these pictures for what they are. It's just love here. Over and over, it's love."

"I'm sorry. I didn't think about how this compares…about how you didn't have this. God, I'm sorry." I'm awash with the level of selfishness I've allowed myself.

"You get to feel this loss. You had something that was stolen from you for no good reason. You're allowed grief—when it happened, now, and in the future. You can feel this pain for the rest of your life, and that's okay. One day, it will become tolerable, but it's all right if it's not today. You plan for healing. You have to assume that you'll get there. That's the fight we are in. Each day, we are fighting to heal."

"I don't know if we can. We'll never forget."

Chris runs a hand through his hair. "Jesus, Sabin did a number on you, didn't he? Look, we don't have to forget. There is no forgetting. Healing doesn't mean that the past doesn't exist. It means that we allow it, that we accept it, and that we continue to move on."

I want to believe him, I do, but I have doubts tonight.

He takes my hands in his. "Let's take care of the first thing. Look at me, and listen very carefully. The wedding invitation. You don't understand why I still have that, do you?"

I shake my head.

"I keep that with me as a reminder to never do anything so fucking stupid in my life ever again. To never shut myself off from you or run from closeness and intimacy. I keep it to remind myself that I was the one who should have never let things go that far and that I am the one who should have stopped the wedding. I'm ashamed of everything related to Jennifer and the wedding. I very nearly lost you for good, and it's only because of your faith in us and your profound trust in me that I got fucking lucky enough to get you back. Then, we got to build this relationship that we have today. That's why I keep the invitation. Blythe, you are my world. You know that, right?"

His adoration is so genuine that I actually smile. "You are the great love of my life that I get to have."

Chris kneels in front of me and wipes my eyes. "Yes. You will always have me. We are unbreakable."

"We are unbreakable," I repeat.

"Yes. Now, you need to tell me about Sabin. And about you and Sabin because I think you guys are a little mixed up about where you stand with each other."

So, I tell him everything. It's difficult to share the details because I know it must hurt Chris to hear about Sabin's anger toward him, and Chris already feels as though he should have done the impossible when they were growing up. But he listens patiently as I pour out what I know.

To his credit, he doesn't flinch when I tell him that Sabin thinks he might be in love with me and how that is contributing to his self-destruction.

I don't want to say what I'm about to, but I must. "And tonight, on the beach, when he was falling apart...I kissed him."

Chris actually has to suppress a smile. He clears his throat. "And how did that go?"

"Not very well." Now, I'm kind of embarrassed by all of this.

"About as well as it did the first time when Sabin got drunk on Thanksgiving in college?"

"Pretty much."

He laughs.

"Aren't you mad?"

"No, I'm not mad. I'm surprised this didn't happen sooner. I figured you guys would test the waters at some point. Although, I assumed it would be in a less extreme context."

"You did?"

"Of course. With as close as you are, as physically comfortable as you are together..." He shrugs. "It's a question you two would need to clear up at some point."

"I'm sorry. It was a dumb and awful thing to do. Not to mention, it made everything worse."

"Are you worried that you're in love with him?" he asks gently.

"No. I mean, maybe..." *God, I hate this conversation and this night.* "I don't know what is happening."

"I think I do." Chris wipes my cheeks again. Despite the circumstances, he is so peaceful and steady. "So, when you're with Sabin, do you feel sexually attracted to him? Do you get all tingly and aroused? Do you want to rip his clothes off?"

"What? No! Ew!" I wrinkle my face. "God, Chris, seriously."

He smiles again. "*What*, *no*, and *ew* are not really the reactions of someone who is feeling passionate, romantic love."

"Well, no," I agree.

He's right. While I've felt drawn to Sabin, I've never been turned on by him. I've never fantasized about him or wondered what it'd be like to—just no. I can't get myself to go there.

"But you have strong feelings for him, right?"

I nod.

"And that's what's making you confused. You feel like you should only have intensity with me and no one else, that you're betraying me."

"Yes."

"You're not betraying me, not at all."

"I don't understand how you can say that."

His expression is so soft, so sweet. "It might be easier for me to understand your relationship because I'm watching from the outside. I get a clarity that maybe you guys don't. So, I need to talk to both of you about this, and maybe I can help. But, for right now, it's after four in the morning. You need to get some sleep, and I need to get Sabin into the house and see how bad his burn is." He pauses. "I don't want you to see that, and he probably doesn't either."

It's true that I am utterly exhausted in every sense, and I can't take much more right now. "Okay."

"After I take care of Sabin, I'll come to bed, and I will hold you all night long. I am so fucking sorry all of this happened. I didn't quite see that Sabin was in such bad shape. Or I didn't want to. I knew he would blow, but I never dreamed it would be this rough on him or on you."

"You and Sabin need to talk about the past, Chris. With each other. There's a wall up between all of you, as though you were each in your own bubble. But you and Sabe especially need that wall down. There can't be secrets. And I understand why you don't talk about your father with him. It's because his pain hurts more than your own, and delving into it kills you. I get that. It's how I feel about you. But it's the only way."

I move to the edge of my seat. My lips go to his, and I kiss him with gratitude and devotion and hope.

What surfaces, what I needed reminding of, is that he is what true love tastes like.

20
TO HAVE THEM BOTH

NEW FIRE, NEW HOPE, WAS AN OVERLOAD. HEAVY AIR THINNED, BUT IT'S STILL THE SAME

THE MORNING ONLY BRINGS ME MORE EMOTION. I AM EDGY AND bolted awake by the pressuring need to know that all of us are still intact. I'm alone in bed, but I do remember Chris staying with me all night. His familiar hold, his smell, his breath as I slept has given me enough comfort to face whatever is next.

I stumble to the bathroom and douse my face with cold water. I look like all hell. I slept for seven hours, but that did little to prevent my eyes from getting red and puffy. I throw on a tank top and loose pants, and then I head downstairs to the kitchen.

Chris and Sabin are talking in the living room, but I avoid looking their way, and I take my time with brewing an espresso and frothing milk. I stand by the sink and drink half of it before I'm able to walk across the room and sit in an armchair.

Chris doesn't appear to have gotten any sleep. His eyes are dark and heavy, yet he exudes the same steadiness he had last night. He's on the couch next to Sabin, who has his head in his hands, as he listens to his brother.

"Sabin, I didn't mean to do this to you. The only thing that I could control at all back then was what I did to keep you guys as safe as I could." Chris pauses. "As much as I fucking hate talking about this, I've had a lot of therapy. It's all rough, and every minute in the office hurts, but it helps. It really does. It's taught me to see my life and to find the words to talk about it."

It's evident how difficult this is for him, but Chris is able to shake himself into doing what he needs to.

"The truth is, I haven't wanted to focus on you. That's another level of my own pain that fucks me up worse to think about. But I get what you're going through. It makes sense." Chris tenses for a second but pulls himself back in. "Now, I understand how the way I stepped in might have backfired because you feel like you didn't get to do what I did."

"I wanted to save you like you saved me," Sabin says through tears.

"Well, fuck. I *didn't* save you. I couldn't stop everything that happened, so don't fool yourself into thinking I did. And what you need to know is that you did help me. Tremendously. You did something I never could have, which was getting Eric and Estelle away from whatever the fuck our father was doing to me. You *hid* them. Think about *all* those times you hid them. No one else could have distracted them the way you did. You sang to them, you told stories, you played games, and you got them to laugh. Do you have any idea how important that was?

"So, you don't have anything to feel guilty about. I don't want that for you. But I also get that you're angry with me because there were a lot of times that I didn't let you get in his path. I can't apologize for that because I'd do it again. I wouldn't go back and let you suffer in that way."

Chris puts a hand on Sabin's back and leans on his shoulder. "There was no right way for us to handle that shitstorm we grew up in. We were going to come out damaged in one way or another, no matter what, and we were all in an impossible situation. We were just kids. We did the best we could. But I will always feel like I didn't do enough, that I should have been braver. And I'm sure you'll feel the same way, too."

Sabin continues crying, and Chris sits silently with him and lets the tears flow. I've never seen Sabin cry this way or for this long, and it's extraordinarily painful. It's necessary though, and I hope letting go like this will help him.

Chris wraps his other arm around his brother and tightly hugs him. "You were wonderful, and you still are wonderful. And I'm sorry if I made everything more fucked up for you than it already was. I'm far from perfect, but I love you, and I don't want you bottling all this up and torturing yourself. We've had enough of that.

"Last night, Blythe said to me that we have to talk about these things. She's right. This is probably the first time you and I have really been open about all this shit—how awful our childhood was and what it's doing to us now. I know it's hard, and it all sucks, but it's the only way we're going to get better."

Speaking fears and shame will do miraculous things. I'm proof of that.

Sabin nods into his hands and finally looks to Chris. "I'm not angry with you. I'm really not. How could I be? It's just that I let everything get all twisted up and distorted. It's true, what you said. I wanted to do more. I feel like I should have. But that's not your fault, Chris. It's not. Please know that. He's not here anymore for me to be angry at, so…I've been throwing my rage at you. It was wrong.

"I just wanted to erase everything that had happened, so you wouldn't have to be so fucking heroic, so you wouldn't have had to do what you did for me and the twins. Because you *were* heroic. You were wonderful. Thank you. Thank you, Chris. I've never told you that. I am…" His voice breaks. "I am so grateful. And I love you."

Now, he looks at me, his eyes so full of sadness and fear. "Blythe."

"It's all okay," I say immediately. "We're going to be okay."

"Did you…" he starts.

"Yes," I say softly. "I told Chris everything. I had to."

"Oh God." He rubs his eyes and stands up. "I need coffee."

When he walks past me to the kitchen, I notice that he touches a hand to where he burned himself, and I questioningly look at Chris.

"It's not that bad," he says softly. "It'll heal."

Sabin returns and now sits on the far end of the couch, away from Chris. "I don't even know what to say. You've got to be pissed about Blythe. I don't know why this is fucking happening."

Chris smiles. "I'm not pissed. I talked to Blythe a little bit last night, and I told her that I think I understand this better than you guys do. Look, Sabin, I don't think you're in love with her. I really don't. I'll ask you the same thing I asked her. Are you attracted to her? Do you think about getting her in bed? Are you getting hard left and right when you're—"

"God, Chris! Shut up! No! That's creepy. She's Blythe! She's my friend—" Sabin catches himself. "Oh. Huh. Well, that's interesting."

Monumental relief takes over, and I laugh when Sabin finally looks my way.

"I'll refrain from being insulted," I say with a smile.

He looks sheepish, but he smiles, too.

"See?" Chris says. "That's one reason to think that you're not in love. At least, you're not romantically in love with each other. What I do think though is that you guys kind of are in love as friends. And that is a beautiful thing. The kind of love you two have for each other is very strong and very rare. But it's beautiful, right? It's only because your feelings are so strong that you think it must be more, that it must be turning into a romance.

"Sabin, you give Blythe so many things that she needs. I am not her entire life, nor should I be. She needs you. You're fun and free and wild in ways I will never be. It's not who I am. But I also should have let you know ages ago that you don't always have to be the upbeat, endlessly entertaining guy. You get to have bad days, to be unhappy, or to feel whatever you want to." Chris sighs. "I don't think I've ever let you feel that's allowed. I want so much for you to be happy that maybe I've been blinding myself to the fact that you're not sometimes. And that, sometimes, it's really bad."

He looks so forlorn and apologetic, but then he rubs his hands on his jeans and tries to brighten. "But back to the good news. You and Blythe? You give her an amazing relationship, and I want that for her. Do you hear me, Sabe? You get to love her. That doesn't upset me at all."

"Okay." He doesn't sound convinced.

Chris laughs. "Sabin, I'm serious." He waits until Sabin begrudgingly faces him. "I'll say it again. I am *not* upset. Do you see that? Do you believe me? I love the friendship you two have. It's tremendously unique and special. I'm not threatened by it. I'm not jealous. I don't see anything between you guys that scares me or makes me worry that I'm losing Blythe. I'm on board. Understand?"

He looks to me. "And, Blythe? Remember what I told you the other week? You get to have us both."

I release a deep breath. "I get to have you both," I repeat this sentence because it's the happiest thing I've been able to say in days.

This realization brings me such peace. Chris has broken this down in a way that gives me a distinct reprieve from my anxiety, and he's also made it okay for me feel the joy of what I have with Sabin. Chris is right. Sabin and I are in love. I can see that now. It's not in the way one usually thinks of being in love. And I'm also aware that there is a degree of understanding and generosity in Chris's ability to allow and even celebrate this. How his heart can be so open after what he has survived astounds me.

Chris winks at me. "So, go hug your other boyfriend."

Sabin reaches over and playfully shoves Chris, but his face shows the same lightness I'm sure mine does now. I get up and walk to Sabin, accepting the tears streaming down my face. I throw my arms around his neck and tightly hold him as my tension and worry continue to drain from me.

I get them both. I get them both.

Sabin's hug brings me such faith that we will all be stronger because of this trip. His touch feels right. His energy and love feel right. In this hug, I have pure and uncomplicated happiness. And that's what my friendship with him is. We got way off track for a while, but because of Chris, we are repaired, and we can embrace our closeness.

Sabin kisses the top of my head. "I feel like I keep saying this, but I'm sorry—for everything I put you through, for confusing you, and for dragging you down with me last night. I did some awful shit. I said some awful shit—"

"Stop, Sabin. Stop. I think we had to go through that. There was a reason."

"What I did with the fire...that was vicious. It's unforgivable."

"It is forgivable. And I forgive you. That's what friends do for each other. We make exceptions for crazy circumstances. It's very simple."

Sabin squeezes me, and I turn my head to catch Chris's eye. He is truly happy right now, and that means an infinite amount.

Slowly, I separate myself from Sabin. "Your arm?" I ask tentatively. "It's okay?"

"You shouldn't have had to see that. But I'm okay," he says confidently. "I'm okay. Before you bring it up, yes, I'll go see a shrink." He rolls his eyes. "God, it's so cliché."

"It's a cliché that's going to help. I will be here, and Chris will be here…for whatever you need."

"Okay, Lady Countess Royal Highness Blythe McGuire."

"Good." I tousle his hair.

We drop down to the couch, and I'm sitting between them.

"So," Chris starts, "there's one more thing. I wasn't sure if I should tell you two this, but…Sabin, you seem to get a little touchy about the fact that Blythe and I have a history—from before Matthews. The idea of a…destined tie between us or whatever." He looks embarrassed, voicing this out loud to his brother, which I do understand. "It's important to me that Blythe and I are together because we choose to be, not because we have to. We are about more than that history. We are about the present. But that day, when she was on the dock…" He begins to stumble a bit. "That day is a part of us. Do you think that you're not entitled to feel so strongly about her because you don't have that with her?"

Sabin looks uncomfortable. "You guys have an…an almost unexplainable connection. I know that. It's…fine. Really. It's your thing together. I shouldn't have said anything because I'm not a part of that. And I shouldn't be."

"The fact is though, you are a part of that." Chris takes my phone from the table. "You have that past with her, too. The three of us have that together."

He pulls up the video I played nonstop last night, and I am totally confused.

"Watch. Sabin, watch this closely." Chris puts my phone in Sabin's hand.

"Chris, what are you doing?" I don't want to relive this pain again. "Please don't."

"Just wait." He takes my hand. "Just wait."

So, I do. I wait while the same pictures and video and sound play out, but I shut my eyes because I refuse to look again.

Until Sabin has a reaction I cannot ignore.

"Oh my God," he says with a catch in his throat. "Oh my God, this can't be right. Chris?"

So, I look to my left to see what he's watching. He stops the video, rewinds, and hits the Play button again so that photos of me as a toddler at school flash by.

"Keep going," Chris says with encouragement.

We all watch my former life play out.

Then, Chris says, "Right here. Listen. Listen closely."

I've heard it so many times now, and I can't bear to listen to my parents comfort me while I go on about Bingo and kisses.

"Do you hear it?" Chris puts his other hand on top of mine. "Do you hear it?"

I shake my head and look at Sabin. His face is one of such disbelief and confusion that I have to turn back to Chris. But I can't speak now because something is gripping my heart. Something has started to creep in and take hold.

It's Sabin who speaks first. "There are pictures here. Of me and Chris. With you, B."

"Yes," Chris whispers. "At daycare. We all...we were at school together. And based on those pictures, we were all friends back then. They were important enough for your parents to save, Blythe. They meant something."

Sabin rewinds the video so that he and I can study the pictures. Now, I see it. Maybe, had I focused more on them, on their eyes, I would have seen it. But there are pictures of me between a very young Chris and Sabin. My hand goes over my mouth, and I gasp as I try to contain myself.

"Now, go to the video," Chris says. "Listen. Blythe..." He almost laughs with disbelief. "Blythe, you're not saying, 'Bingo.' And you're not saying, 'My kiss,' like your parents thought.

"We...because of how crazy our dad was, we moved around so much. We were in Massachusetts at some point. This made me remember that. I don't think it was for long, and we probably left right before this video was taken. So, listen to what you're saying. You're missing us."

He lets it sink in.

And when it hits, when the reality hits, I nearly break. But in the most beautiful way.

"I'm saying..." I struggle to get it out. "I'm saying, 'Where Sabin go?'"

"Yes," Chris says.

"And I'm saying, 'My Chris.'"

"Yes, you are."

Sabin's reaction is audible. His breath is sharp as he inhales understanding and memory. "You used to tuck me in. I remember

181

bits and pieces. You used to sit next to me by my nap mat and rub my back. Chris?" He is alert with shock. "Chris, do you remember that? She used to rub my back. To watch over me."

He rewinds the video, and I can see how his mind is racing to catch up with the memories.

"Blythe? Blythe? I remember you. I can feel you. How you…how you…you mothered me. You hovered and made sure I could fall asleep. I can't see your face—it's like I can only see you in a shadow—but I remember the feeling."

"We must have moved. Again. And this video is Blythe asking for us," Chris says quietly. "Do you see how much she loved you back then?"

Sabin and I are both too wrought up with feelings to talk much, but he nods emphatically.

"Blythe and me," he gets out. "We were best friends even back then, weren't we?"

"You were. Still, every day, you get to choose to have that friendship. You're not friends because of this, but it's good proof that you belong together. That we all belong together. Somehow, we circled back to each other."

"Where Sabin go?"

"My Chris."

My heart is overwhelmed.

I take Sabin's hand with my left and squeeze Chris's with my right. "Of course we circled back to each other. This is where we all belong."

21

JUST WATER

OH, AND THE WIND WATERED MY EYES.

TWO DAYS LATER, THE THREE OF US ARE ON A BEACH IN DEL MAR. Chris and I are watching Sabin on Mia. This is one of the few beaches in the San Diego area where riding horses is allowed. The call I made to Pearce went better than I could have hoped, and it was his idea to bring us all here.

Sabin is at the upper edge of the shore, right now as far from the water as he can be. He looks moderately anxious, but I can see him trying to ride with confidence.

Pearce is standing with Chris and me. He crosses his arms and watches, much more at ease than Chris and I are right now. I feel as though a million things hinge on this happening, and I wasn't convinced it was a smart idea when Pearce had suggested it. However, it seemed to be a risk worth taking.

"He's got one chance to get her into the water," he explains. "If he's not careful, if he pushes too much or too fast, he'll miss the window, and she might never get over her fear."

"Can he do it?" I ask.

"Sure." Pearce squints and studies Sabin for a minute. "If anyone can, it's him. And if it doesn't work out, that'll be all right, too."

Sabin and Mia walk slowly and get closer to us.

"Start inching her down. If she gets nervous, let her back off a little, but keep encouraging her. She's got fear, sure, but she's smart, and if she can figure out how to get out of this, she will. It's your job to be the kind but firm parent, Sabin. Let her see it will all be okay," Pearce instructs.

Sabin nods and then glances at Chris and me.

"You look great, Sabin," Chris says. "Right at home."

Mia turns a bit and moves a few feet closer to the water, and Sabin praises her and strokes her mane. "That's my good girl. Just water. It's nothing to be afraid of. And I'm right here. You're doing really good."

Pearce lifts up and down on his toes a few times. I think he's more anxious about Sabin finding this success than he's letting on.

He smiles though and then takes a seat in the sand. "Sit down. This might take a while."

Chris and I get comfortable, and I take in the view. The sight of Sabin working with Mia, encouraging her to overcome her fears, is beautiful. The uncharacteristic clouds above lend a dark filtered light, but that just allows Sabin to shine more.

Chris and I stay quiet while Pearce periodically calls out encouragement or instruction. Mia moves from side to side, crossing her legs over one another, as she tries to move back, almost dancing in place, but with every minute that passes, Sabin gets her a bit closer to the lapping shore.

When she stops walking for a second, Pearce puts a hand to his mouth. "Keep talking to her. Let her know you're relaxed. I can see you tensing up, so knock that off. You've got this, Sabin. You've got this. Show her how it's done."

From my spot on the beach, I can see Sabin take a big breath and regroup. Although I can't make out what he's saying now, his gravelly voice carries up to me, and his tone and pace are calm, soothing. Mia responds well, and I grab Chris's hand when she turns to face the water. Without being able to hear, I know what Sabin is saying. I just know it.

"Reach for me. I won't let you drown. I'm right here."

"Now's the time," Pearce says as he leans back on his arms. "Let her face her fear. Stay with her, and make her understand she's in good hands. Not too fast. Talk her through it. Dig deep, Sabin, and pass on that confident energy. Right from your core. Give that to her."

Sabin is honed in on Mia now, no longer turning back to check in with Pearce, and he leans over, talking right into her ear while stroking her coat. She takes a few steps, pauses for a moment, and then takes a few more.

"Just about there," Chris whispers.

I'm pretty sure that I stop breathing when Mia's front hooves are a foot from the water. She looks off to the side, and then she faces the ocean again. She steps forward and wets her feet.

"Hot damn!" Pearce says happily.

Sabin throws a fist in the air, but then he immediately brings it back down and regains his composure as he guides her to walk parallel to the shore until they're just casually strolling through a few inches of water.

This time, I am watching a boy on the beach save himself, and it's a glorious feeling.

"Look at him." Pearce is nodding with approval. "He's showing her it's just like any other walk now. Nothing to get worked up about." He smiles broadly. "Smart, smart boy."

For the next fifteen minutes, Sabin and Mia walk back and forth along the shore. Their motion is fluid, and the aura they both give off is one of pure connection and joy. Sabin's determination and skill today assure me that he is ready to work on himself, that he has the capability to power through the dark and find light.

"This is a sight for sore eyes," Chris says.

"A little horse therapy never hurt anyone." Pearce tips his cowboy hat with his finger.

I could swear that I see his eyes are damp.

He wouldn't be the only one.

Sabin brings Mia from the water and rides toward us, trying very hard to contain a smile. When they are a few yards from us, he dismounts, keeping the reins in his hand.

He throws a hand over his chest and lets out a laugh. "Did you see that? She did it! I didn't want to freak out when we were in the water, but oh my God! She did it!" His joy is infectious.

Chris and I hug Sabin at the same time.

Then, I go to Mia and pat the side of her face and her nose. *Thank you*, I mouth silently over and over. *He needed that.*

I turn around just as Pearce says, "That was a big deal, son. Very nice job. Mia has a huge amount of trust in you, and you should be proud. It took a lot of bravery to do what you did. I could see that. There's a reason I rescued her, and now, I know why. It was to get you two to this day."

In a move that surprises me, Sabin immediately steps forward and hugs Pearce. I can see how firmly his arms are holding on and how tightly he squeezes his eyes. So overwhelmed with emotion, he can barely get out a thank-you.

Pearce chuckles and softly pats Sabin's back. "You're a good kid. You hear me? You're a good kid. You earned this."

If only Sabin had grown up with a father who treated him like this, so much would be different. Pearce is the kind of father Sabin deserved, but I am uplifted by the thought that maybe my friend can capture a little of that now. Maybe some of the past can be made up for.

Sabin finally steps back and goes to Mia. He puts his cheek against hers. "We're gonna do great things, you and me. I promise."

I lead Chris away and give Sabin some time alone with Pearce and Mia. Even though it's chilly, we head to the wet sand and take off our socks and shoes. I want to put my feet into the exact waters that Mia just faced, as if I could absorb some of Sabin's victory. The cold waves splash onto the shore and crawl up the sand, running up over our feet, and the jolting temperature makes us both gasp, but we don't back away.

My hand slips across Christopher's waist, and we both face the horizon.

"You were wonderful with Sabin the other day. And with me. No one else could have done what you did for us. I love you for that and for so many things," I say.

Chris hadn't slept at all the night he came home, I confirmed, and his intervention with us took a toll that was not insignificant. After, he spent hours either collapsed from exhaustion or in tears with worry that he hadn't done enough, that his words had not broken through Sabin's turmoil.

Over the next few days, I found my strength regenerating. I was able to find secure footing on which to stand, and I gave him the praise and confirmation that he needed. As strong as Chris was, he'd reached his limit, and his collapse into me was more of a relief than a concern. It meant that he'd processed how serious Sabin's fall had been. It just took some time after the initial events for it to set in.

Christopher's solidity is always mitigated by a real-world reaction to stress, and I actually find that a reflection of his character. To react, and crumble even, under severe stress is expected. So, it was with ease that I caught him, as he had caught me so many times.

"It was not easy to see either of you so upset," he tells me now. "I'm just glad I was able to help you sort through some of it. Sabin's got an appointment with a really good psychologist next week. It's a step, and I didn't even have to force him to call. He actually came to me with a list of therapists and asked me to help him research them."

I am enormously relieved that Sabin is determined to take control of his life. "I'm going to miss San Diego. Only a few more days here."

"I will, too. I like it here. And I like being with Sabin," Chris says. "Maine does seem very far away."

"It's probably unbearably hot here in the summer," I point out. "There's something not to miss."

"Sure. It's got to be miserable," he says unconvincingly. "The winters are nice here though. And you got a lot of writing done. Your editor seems happy, huh?"

"She is." I inhale salt air. "The parks out here stay busy over the winter, don't they?"

He looks at me and smiles. "They do."

"So, you might enjoy…"

"Being out here for part of the year?" he finishes.

I nod. "It's something we might want to consider."

"It is." His arm goes over my shoulder. "It's a beautiful life. Despite everything, all the shit we've been through, it's a beautiful life we have."

22
RUNNING THROUGH PAIN

OUT OF THE SHADOWS, I'LL FIGHT THIS FIGHT.

WHILE I LOVE MY RUNS AND I LOOK FORWARD TO ALL OF THEM—to the release, the energy, the mood, the restoration to my body and spirit—it's been a long time since I've needed a run the way I need this one. My arms rise above my head as I stretch, and I admire the Matthews College campus in front of me. I have missed this place. Next weekend, we'll be in Colorado for James's graduation, and I'm glad his didn't conflict with Eric's and Estelle's.

It's here where I nearly lost my fight with depression and self-sabotage, and it's here where I pulled myself from destruction with the help of the Shepherd siblings. It's also where I fell in love, in more ways than one.

We have a long day ahead of us with the twins' graduation in a matter of hours, and it seems a miracle that I managed to get Sabin out here with me. He somehow looks awake though, and we're going to run one of my old routes.

"Only three miles, right?" Sabin asks nervously as he bends to stretch his hamstrings. "I haven't run in over a year—or done much of anything, for that matter."

"I disagree. You've done a lot in a year."

He laughs. "I mean, exercise. My shrink is going to be impressed."

"So, you'll start now, and *you* are going to be impressed. I know this route. I know how to pace you and get you through it."

He blows out a long breath. "Okay."

"Have you asked out Mollie yet?"

"Are you trying to distract me by changing the subject from this dreadful running thing we're about to do?"

"Maybe. So, have you?"

He grins. "Maybe. And maybe she said yes."

"Of course she did. She's been nuts about you for months."

He shakes his head. "Or she's just nuts." But he looks happy.

"It's going to be a good year for you—and for you and me," I say. "I believe that."

"It can't be worse than this past year. That's for sure. I wish things hadn't gotten so messy between us, but I'm glad we made it through."

I face him and set my hands on his shoulders. "We made it through beautifully. Look how strong we are now."

"We're solid. I know that now." He gives me a hint of a smile. "You know, there is one thing that's been bothering me."

"What's that?"

He looks aside for a moment and then clears his throat. He speaks slowly, "We've had two *really* bad kisses, you and me. Thanksgiving and then on the beach."

I smile back. "And we can't go out like that."

"We're better than that," he says.

"We need one good one."

"We need one good one," he agrees.

I step in. "I am madly and platonically in love with you, Sabin Shepherd."

"And I am madly and platonically in love with you, Blythe McGuire." His expression is tender and caring. "I do adore you. This friendship…it gives me strength."

I put a hand on his face and look into his eyes. "This kiss will stay between us. It's just ours." I lift up and press my mouth against his.

It's a soft kiss but one with feeling and gratitude, and it's one that speaks to the reciprocity of our friendship. We kiss long enough to undo our other kisses and long enough to make this one hold us forever. His lips move over mine, gently and sweetly, and I feel his hand move to my lower back as he dips me backward.

Sabin lifts from me now and smiles. "That was much better." For the last time, he kisses me again, just for a few seconds. "Now, I've kissed a girl I feel something for. And it was beautiful."

"It was beautiful. I love you, Sabe." When he rights me to a stand, I face us in the direction of our run. "Definitely much better."

"Did you notice there was no tongue?" he asks proudly.

I laugh. "I did. Congratulations to us. You ready to do this?"

"Chris is still going to meet us for the last mile, right?"

"He'll be there."

He looks to me and sighs. "Run through the pain, huh?"

"Yes. Run through the pain. It works."

"It'd better." He takes his earbuds that are hooked to his music player and hands them to me. "We have the playlist Chris made for us, but first...I wrote another song for you. For us. Maybe for me. I don't know. It's a rough recording, but..."

"It's a really good place to start." I put in the earbuds, and then I clamp my hand into his while his music begins to play. "Here we go."

"I'm ready, love."

The terrain under my feet is all too familiar, and it brings back the same healing energy I used to get when I was a senior at Matthews. I hope that I can pass this on to Sabin.

We run, taking it slowly and steadily, and I listen to his words about his past, about reclaiming what he's lost, and about how he's going to fight like all hell for a future.

I SUPPOSE I SHOULD LET YOU GO.
FEAR IS ALL I'VE EVER KNOWN,
A FEVER OF A HIDDEN MAN.

CAN YOU TELL I'M A HURTING MAN?
CAN'T YOU SEE I WANNA BE YOUR MAN?
THIS IS ALL UNFAIR.

OH, THIS IS MY CALL.
I KNOW THAT YOU KNOW
BECAUSE YOU'VE SEEN MY SOUL.
I WAS A LONELY ONE,
IN THE SHADOWS.

So, I put it all in this song.
So, you'll know once and for all,
I was never home
Before you.

Courage, I need it,
And guilt, I feel it,
With my hands
And heart.

I'm not a coward, but I did not fight.
Been in the shadows all my goddamn life.
Time to hear my call.
Do you really know me?
Now, it's time for me to shed some light.
Out of the shadows, I'll fight this fight.
I can no longer live a lie.

How could I fight for you?
My own flesh and blood is tied up, too.
But I'll keep holding on.
It's too familiar.

So, take from me what you will.
You're the one that I lean on,
And I'm leaning still.

Though I'd never call me brave,
I'll never run away from you, no.

I've been late to the fight,
But, darling, not tonight.
I'll come running, running for you.

Courage, I need it.
And guilt, I feel it
With my hands
And heart.

RESTLESS
WATERS

THIS WORLD SEEMS TO OFFER ME NOTHING.
SUPPOSE I SHOULD FADE AWAY,
BUT YOU KNOW I'M NOT RUNNING, RUNNING AWAY.

CAN YOU HEAR MY CALL? IT'S SO LOUD.
CALL ME A COWARD IF YOU LIKE. I'M NOT PROUD.
CAN YOU FEEL MY HEART? IT'S SO COLD.
CALL ME A COWARD IF YOU LIKE. I WON'T FOLD.

CAN YOU HEAR MY CALL? IT'S SO LOUD.
CALL ME A COWARD IF YOU LIKE. I'M NOT PROUD.
CAN YOU FEEL MY HEART? IT'S SO COLD.
CALL ME A COWARD IF YOU LIKE. I WON'T FOLD.

CAN YOU HEAR MY CALL? IT'S SO LOUD.
CALL ME A COWARD IF YOU LIKE. I'M NOT PROUD.
CAN YOU FEEL MY HEART? IT'S SO COLD.
CALL ME A COWARD IF YOU LIKE. I WON'T FOLD.

CAN YOU HEAR MY CALL? IT'S SO LOUD.
CALL ME A COWARD IF YOU LIKE. I'M NOT PROUD.
CAN YOU FEEL MY HEART? IT'S SO COLD.
CALL ME A COWARD IF YOU LIKE. I WON'T FOLD.

So, together, we run through the pain, as we have before and as we might need to do again and again.

We will run as many days as we need to because we have strength and love and a friendship that will never drown.

ACKNOWLEDGMENTS

As always, I am deeply grateful to the people who have helped me get through writing a book.

Michele Scott shared her vast equine expertise and talked me through so much. Autumn Hull gave professional support, but more importantly, she gave me her friendship and love. Katie Pruitt Miller trudged her way through a very rough and unedited version of *Restless Waters*, and she gave beautiful feedback and advice.

And there is, as always, Andrew Kaufman, who is unfailingly there for me, no matter what else is going on. As usual, he did everything. He listened, cheered, edited scenes, strategized, and remained a true friend, even when I got to the stressed-out, manic stage of writing and should have irritated him beyond reason. But that's Andrew—patient, wonderful, and the best friend a girl could ever ask for.

The Park Side street team? Really? Those guys rock, hard. I adore my team and all the massive love that they throw my way.

The astounding fans on my Facebook author page routinely overwhelm me with love, support, and incredible heart. Together, we've built something wonderful on that page. It's more than a professional author page. It's become an important community made up of fabulous people who give and give. We share intensely personal stuff, we are brazenly honest and raw, and we cheer for each other all the time. I adore my readers, and they are the reason I write and push myself, challenge myself, and take risks. Writing can be frightening and emotional, but they give me a place to fall. My readers catch me time and time again. There are no words to say what this means.

Jovana Shirley can seemingly do it all, and I could not ask for a more professional, talented, creative, and lovely all-in-one copyeditor, proofer, and formatter. Knowing that my book will end up in her hands makes the writing process significantly easier.

I've always written to music, and finding the perfect song and tone to write alongside has been such a significant part of my work process. When I got stuck with how to continue with Blythe, Chris, and Sabin, I turned to music. And I found heart and feeling in so many artists. I dived into Matt Nathanson, John Mayer, The Low Anthem, Ed Sheeran, Christopher Jak, X Ambassadors, Peter Bradley Adams, and more.

Then, there was Troy. Troy is such a talent, and I've been a fan of his music for years. We have been trying to work together on a project for what feels like forever, and we finally got the opportunity with this book. He is brave and powerful and tireless with his music, and I'm not sure he has a bigger fan than me. The richly layered emotional quality in his voice has always affected me so deeply, and I remember when I finally made the connection that his voice is also Sabin's. It seems so obvious to me now, and I was thrilled when Troy agreed to let me use his music and lyrics. He and I connect so well, and in part, it's because we often channel our creative energies to write about pain, hurt, loss, understanding, and survival. His lyrics are emotional, his sound unforgettable, and I cannot thank him enough for giving me this opportunity. Please check out his links, and throw him the support and love he deserves! Also, huge thanks out to Dante Lattanzi from Caelum Music Production for the work he's done to produce and finalize Troy's music.

Thank you is not enough to convey what it's meant to me to get letters from people all over the world who connected profoundly with *Left Drowning*. The bravery so many have had to show in this life astounds me. I have been repeatedly moved by stories of surviving unspeakable tragedies and horrific abuse. I am unspeakably pained by what you all have endured, but it's an honor that *Left Drowning* managed to give comfort and hope to some readers. I have an overflowing email folder with every message I've received. That is what this whole writing gig is all about—affecting people, helping people, making even one person feel less alone. Your willingness to reach out and connect with me will never be forgotten.

To all of you: Keep fighting, and run through the heartbreak.

TROY

TROY GENEROUSLY ALLOWED HIS LYRICS TO BE USED IN *Restless Waters*, and he even more generously wrote an original song for this book, "Coward," that is available for purchase on iTunes and for steaming on Spotify. Keep an eye on his artist page there, and click that Follow button! It's a gorgeous track, and I'm so honored that he wrote this specifically for me and my readers. Troy and I send out huge thanks to Dante Lattanzi from Caelum Music Production for his gorgeous work on these tracks.

"Sheets" and "Honey" are from his time with a band called In Like Lions, so search them out, too.

Troy is busy recording final versions of some of the other songs featured in the book. Check out his SoundCloud page to listen to tracks, and sign up for his mailing list at www.troy-music.com/email-signup.html to stay updated on new releases!

To follow Troy on social networking and to listen to and purchase his music, please visit the following sites:

iTunes:
http://itunes.apple.com/us/artist/troy/id1027160940

Spotify:
http://open.spotify.com/artist/1LqB6e0Om0kR9q9CxxZ3ns

Facebook:
www.facebook.com/TroyRameyMusicPage

Twitter (@iamtroymusic)
http://twitter.com/iamtroymusic

Instagram (@iamtroymusic)
http://instagram.com/iamtroymusic

SoundCloud
http://soundcloud.com/troy-ramey

Website
http://troy-music.com

LYRICS

ALL SONGS ARE WRITTEN BY TROY,
AND "SHEETS" IS COWRITTEN WITH JAMES BRIDGES.

DAISY

So long, my love.
You know you were the one.
You ripped my heart in two,
But I'll still save half for you.

If you walked into this room right now,
I'd tell you how I feel for you still.
You're the one I love,
But now I'm going away.
So, if I am lonely,
I guess I'll have to be,
For a while anyway.

[Chorus]
The one I love,
Always on my mind.
You're still with me
All of the time.

So long, my love.
Daisy, you were my one,
But you ripped my heart in two,
And now it bleeds for you.

Take care of yourself.
I'll hold on hope.
You know it's always
Here to claim.

So long, my love.
You know you were the one,
But you ripped my heart in two,
And now my half is blue.

RESTLESS
WATERS

I'M SWELL,
BUT I'M SAD, MY LOVE,
SAD AS HELL.

HONEY

OH, LAST NIGHT, I TRIED NOT TO DRINK,
BUT I WAS SCARED I MIGHT NOT GET MY SLEEP.
MID AFTERNOON, STUCK IN A BAR SEAT,
AND SHE SAID, "BABY, WHAT CAN I GET FOR YOU
TODAY?"

OH, BUT SHE GOT
MORE HONEY,
MORE HONEY,
MORE HONEY THAN I CARE FOR.
OH, AND SHE GOT
MORE HONEY,
MORE HONEY,
MORE HONEY THAN I NEED.

[CHORUS]
OH, SHE BLEW MY HAIR BACK.
MY MIND SAID LOOK AWAY.
I DON'T WANT NOTHING TO DO WITH THIS PLACE.
IT AIN'T MY SOUND,
AIN'T MY SCENE,
AIN'T MY TASTE.
BUT SHE SAID, "OH, IF I HAD MY WAY."

AND SHE DON'T KNOW ME.
SHE DON'T KNOW ME AT ALL.

[CHORUS]
OH, SHE BLEW MY HAIR BACK.
MY MIND SAID LOOK AWAY.
I DON'T WANT NOTHING TO DO WITH THIS PLACE.
IT AIN'T MY SOUND,
AIN'T MY SCENE,
AIN'T MY TASTE.
BUT SHE SAID, "OH, IF I HAD MY WAY."

CITY LIGHTS

THESE CITY LIGHTS
SHINE SO BRIGHT,
BUT ONCE A YEAR,
WE PUT 'EM IN OUR MIRROR.

DIRT ROAD ON TIRES,
FIREWOOD ON FIRE,
SNOW-COVERED HILLS,
OUR COUNTRYSIDE HILLS.

[CHORUS]
NO, I WON'T CATCH A WINK,
NOT ON THIS CHRISTMAS EVE,
'CAUSE MY LOVE SHINES SO BRIGHT
IN THIS COUNTRYSIDE,
BRIGHTER THAN YOUR CITY LIGHTS.

THESE COUNTRY NIGHTS
FEEL SO RIGHT,
BUT ALL THE YEAR
WE PUT 'EM IN OUR MIRROR.

DIRT ROAD ON TIRES,
FIREWOOD ON FIRE,
SNOW-COVERED HILLS,
OUR COUNTRYSIDE HILLS.

[CHORUS]
NO, I WON'T CATCH A WINK,
NOT ON THIS CHRISTMAS EVE,
'CAUSE MY LOVE SHINES SO BRIGHT
IN THIS COUNTRYSIDE,
BRIGHTER THAN YOUR CITY LIGHTS.

FOLLOW ME BACK HOME

ALL THE WEIGHT I FOUND
IN MY HOME, THIS TIME AROUND.
ON MY KNEES, I WOULD FALL WITH EASE,
FOLLOW ME BACK TO MY HOME.

I DON'T KNOW WHAT'S RIGHT.
YOU COULD HOLD ME TIGHT,
BUT I STILL DON'T FEEL I FIT INSIDE THIS LIFE.

I DON'T KNOW THE LIGHT,
THE KIND OF LIGHT YOU LIKE,
BUT I'LL TRY TO SHINE IT ON YOU IN THE NIGHT.

WIND BLOWS THE LEAVES,
FALLING FROM THE TREES,
I COULD JUST BE HOME WITH YOU FOR LIFE.

'CAUSE I COULD SEE THEM HILLS,
MY MEMORY IS FILLED
WITH A LIGHT HEART IN THIS MOUNTAINSIDE.

I WANNA KISS YOUR SKIN,
JUST LIKE THE BIG SUN DID,
BUT I DON'T WANNA GO
WHERE EVERYBODY GOES.

FOLLOW ME BACK TO MY HOME.
FOLLOW ME BACK TO MY HOME.

[CHORUS]
FOLLOW ME, FOLLOW ME BACK HOME.
FOLLOW ME, FOLLOW ME BACK HOME.
FOLLOW ME, FOLLOW ME BACK HOME.
FOLLOW ME, FOLLOW ME BACK HOME.

RESTLESS
WATERS

I'D GIVE ALL OF ME
AND EVERYTHING I OWN,
IF YOU'D JUST FOLLOW ME BACK HOME.

I PUT ON A FACE,
FACE IT TILL THE END.
I CANNOT CONTINUE TO PRETEND.
THIS LIFE AIN'T ME.
OH NO, THIS AIN'T LIKE ME.
I DON'T KNOW WHAT WE'RE MOVING TOWARD.

I WANNA KISS YOUR SKIN,
JUST LIKE THE BIG SUN DID.
BUT I DON'T WANNA GO
WHERE EVERYBODY GOES.

FOLLOW ME BACK TO MY HOME.
FOLLOW ME BACK TO MY HOME.
FOLLOW ME BACK TO MY HOME.
FOLLOW ME BACK TO MY HOME.

[CHORUS]
FOLLOW ME, FOLLOW ME BACK HOME.
FOLLOW ME, FOLLOW ME BACK HOME.
FOLLOW ME, FOLLOW ME BACK HOME.
FOLLOW ME, FOLLOW ME BACK HOME.

VIRGINIA SKY

Cold, cold Virginia sky.
And tonight, tonight, we drive
Through them hills,
Black as all night.

We ain't running, no.
We're just staying alive.

Oh, and the moon
Was the only light that guides.

'Cause that Virginia sky,
It was on my mind.
You could never take my hand
'Cause you'd never understand
Why we ride
Through that cold Virginia night,
And we ain't running, no.
We're just staying alive.

[Chorus]
Oh, I said,
All I want,
All I need,
All I want,
All I want is you.

Oh, I said,
All I want,
All I need,
All I want,
I'm in love with you.

RESTLESS WATERS

COLD, COLD VIRGINIA NIGHT.
AND WE RIDE
IN THE CORNER OF MY ENTIRE LIFE,
ON DOWN SOUTH NOW
WITH DRAGONS AND MOONSHINE.
OH, AND THE WIND
WATERED MY EYES.

'CAUSE THAT VIRGINIA SKY,
IT WAS ON MY MIND.
YOU COULD NEVER TAKE MY HAND
'CAUSE YOU'D NEVER UNDERSTAND.

WHY WE RIDE
THROUGH THAT COLD VIRGINIA NIGHT.
AND WE AIN'T RUNNING, NO.
WE'RE JUST STAYING ALIVE

[CHORUS]
OH, I SAID,
ALL I WANT,
ALL I NEED,
ALL I WANT,
ALL I WANT IS YOU.

SONG MAN

MY DADDY WAS A SONG MAN.
OH, HE WAS A STRONG MAN,
REACHING OUT FOR MY HAND.
CAN'T YOU SEE?

OH, SHE WAS MY SHADOW. SHE HAD STRONG LOVE,
HOLDING IT OUT THERE,
ALL FOR ME.

OH, SHE RAN HER OWN LINE,
TOGETHER FOR A LONG TIME,
HEAVY LOVING FIGHTERS,
BUT PEOPLE ONLY SEE THE END.

ENDED UP A SAD LOVE.
MAKING LOVE WAS STARVED UP,
HOLDING LOVE WAS SILENT,
BUT STILL IN LOVE.

[CHORUS]
WE WERE ON FIRE TILL LONELIER DAYS.
LET IT RAIN ON ME BULLETS. I DON'T CARE.
'CAUSE WE WERE LOVESICK,
SO LOVESICK ON THE FLOOR.
YEAH, WE WERE LOVESICK, SO LOVESICK.
I WANT MORE.

HOLDING ON TO SAD LOVE,
IN AND OUT OF MADNESS,
HOLDING ON TO SAVE IT.
YOU DON'T SEE.
I HAVEN'T KNOWN FAITH, FAITH.
YOU KNOW I'M NOT—
HOW DO YOU SAY?—
A HOLY MAN,
SO YOU WON'T KNOW MY CONFESSION.

RESTLESS
WATERS

CAN YOU SEE ME FALLING NOW
WITHOUT MY SHADOW?
YOU SAW ME WITH SOMEONE.
THEN, YOU SAW ME SUFFER.
WITHOUT YOU, I'M ALONE.

[CHORUS]
WE WERE ON FIRE TILL LONELIER DAYS.
LET IT RAIN ON ME BULLETS. I DON'T CARE.
'CAUSE WE WERE LOVESICK,
SO LOVESICK ON THE FLOOR.
YEAH, WE WERE LOVESICK, SO LOVESICK.
I WANT MORE.

LET IT RAIN ON ME BULLETS,
RAIN ON ME BULLETS.

YOUR LOVER IS A SONG MAN.
OH, HE IS A STRONG MAN,
REACHING OUT FOR YOUR HAND.
CAN'T YOU SEE?

211

LUCKY ONES

AGED LIKE WINE,
YOU OWN MY TIME. HEY, YOU SORTED OUT
MY OWN HEAD.
YOU CALLED IT TIME FOR A WOMAN.

YOU STARTED TO KNOW, KNOW ME.
I STARTED TO KNOW YOU, KNOW YOU.
YOU SHUDDERED MY BONES,
HOLDING ON TO MY HAND.

[CHORUS]
HERE WE GO AGAIN.
I'M NOT THE LUCKY ONE YOU NEED.
HERE WE GO AGAIN, LOVE.
HERE WE GO AGAIN,
NOT THE LUCKY ONE YOU NEED.
HERE WE GO AGAIN, LOVE.

WAS IT ALL IN MY HEAD?
YOU FELL INTO MY CELL PHONE AND MY BED.
MY THOUGHTS STILL SILENT WITH
MY HEAD ON LOCK.

I WANNA FOLLOW YOU AND SEW MY TEARS.
FELL INTO MY HEAD, GIRL, MY MIND.
I WANNA FIND A LOVE THAT'S ALL MINE.
SO, SO.

[CHORUS]
HERE WE GO AGAIN.
I'M NOT THE LUCKY ONE YOU NEED.
HERE WE GO AGAIN, LOVE.
HERE WE GO AGAIN,
NOT THE LUCKY ONE YOU NEED.
HERE WE GO AGAIN, LOVE.

RESTLESS
WATERS

AND WE LET IT FALL,
AND WE LET IT FALL.
AND WE LET IT BURN,
AND WE LET IT BURN.

YOU WILL LOVE ME ALL,
OR YOU WON'T LOVE ME AT ALL.
I WILL NOT BE
PIECES OF YOUR FAVORITE SONG.

[CHORUS]
HERE WE GO AGAIN.
I'M NOT THE LUCKY ONE YOU NEED.
HERE WE GO AGAIN, LOVE.
HERE WE GO AGAIN,
NOT THE LUCKY ONE YOU NEED.
HERE WE GO AGAIN, LOVE.

RESTLESS LADY

"HEY, LOVE," SHE CRIES
ON HER KNEES AT HIS EMPTY BEDSIDE.
SHE CAN'T BELIEVE HER OWN LIES
SHE TELLS HERSELF ANYMORE,
LIKE IT'LL BE JUST FINE TO STAY IN THIS PLACE.
IN EVERY ROOM, SHE SEES HIS FACE,
AND SHE TRIES TO KEEP IT UP,
BUT MONEY AIN'T FALLING FROM TREES.
IF SHE COULD PAY WITH BLOOD,
SHE'D BLEED.

[CHORUS]
AND SHE'S HOLDING ON
AS HARD AS SHE CAN.
HOLDING ON BY THE SKIN OF HER HANDS,
HOLDING ON FOR HER BABIES,
HOLDING ON, RESTLESS LADY,
HOLDING ON, RESTLESS LADY,
HOLDING ON, RESTLESS LADY.

"HEY, LOVE," HE CRIES
AS HE SEES HER AT HIS BEDSIDE.
I'LL NEVER LEAVE YOU BEHIND.
YOU'LL ALWAYS BE BY MY SIDE.
DON'T CRY, DON'T CRY.
WE AIN'T GOT MUCH TIME BEFORE I SAY GOOD-BYE.

[CHORUS]
AND SHE'S HOLDING ON
AS HARD AS SHE CAN.
HOLDING ON BY THE SKIN OF HER HANDS,
HOLDING ON FOR HER BABIES,
HOLDING ON, RESTLESS LADY,
HOLDING ON, RESTLESS LADY,
HOLDING ON, RESTLESS LADY.

214

RESTLESS WATERS

You gotta move on
As hard as you can.
Move on by the skin of your hands.
Move on for your babies.
Move on, restless lady.
Move on, restless lady.
Move on, restless lady.

And she buries herself inside
A great big bottle of wine
To see if
Her love is hiding inside.
Hiding inside love, hiding inside,
Hiding inside love,
Hiding inside love.
"Hey, love, good-bye."

WHEN THE LIGHTS CAME

THE LIGHTS CAME.
NEW FIRE, NEW HOPE
WAS AN OVERLOAD.
HEAVY AIR THINNED,
BUT IT'S STILL THE SAME.
FED THE FIRE TOO LONG.
MY NEW HOPE WAS MY MOVE ALONG.
LONELY HEARTS WILL FIND A HOME.

THE KIND OF LIGHT YOU WANNA HOLD,
KIND OF LIGHT YOU WANNA SHOW,
KIND OF LOVE THAT BRINGS YOU HOME.

[CHORUS]
I WANT THE LIGHT, WANT THE LIGHT,
WANT THE LIGHT ON.
I WANT THE LIGHT, WANT THE LIGHT,
WANT THE LIGHT FOR THE TWO OF US.
I WANT THE LIGHT, WANT THE LIGHT,
WANT THE LIGHT ON.
I WANT THE LIGHT, WANT THE LIGHT,
WANT THE LIGHT FOR THE TWO OF US.
I WANT THE LIGHT, WANT THE LIGHT,
WANT THE LIGHT ON.
I WANT THE LIGHT, WANT THE LIGHT,
WANT THE LIGHT FOR THE TWO OF US.
LIGHTS CAME COMING,
SO I WENT RUNNING.

ALL LIFE LONG,
I JUST NEED A LITTLE HOPE SOMETIMES.
A GOOD FRIEND I HAD
ONCE GAVE ADVICE.
THE THINGS THAT YOU LOVE ARE THE THINGS THAT
WILL MAKE YOU CRY.
NEVER HAVE TO TELL ME TWICE.

RESTLESS
WATERS

THE KIND OF LIGHT YOU WANNA HOLD,
KIND OF LIGHT YOU WANNA SHOW,
KIND OF LOVE THAT BRINGS YOU HOME.

[CHORUS]
I WANT THE LIGHT, WANT THE LIGHT,
WANT THE LIGHT ON.
I WANT THE LIGHT, WANT THE LIGHT,
WANT THE LIGHT FOR THE TWO OF US.
I WANT THE LIGHT, WANT THE LIGHT,
WANT THE LIGHT ON.
I WANT THE LIGHT, WANT THE LIGHT,
WANT THE LIGHT FOR THE TWO OF US.
I WANT THE LIGHT, WANT THE LIGHT,
WANT THE LIGHT ON.
I WANT THE LIGHT, WANT THE LIGHT,
WANT THE LIGHT FOR THE TWO OF US.
LIGHTS CAME COMING,
SO I WENT RUNNING.

ROSARY

ALL OF IT WAS HIS PLAN,
THE HOPE OF A DYING MAN.
AND AS YOU SIT NEXT TO ME,
YOU REACH FOR YOUR ROSARY.
AND I ASKED, "DO YOU BELIEVE?"
YOU SAID, "LOVE'S THE ONLY CERTAINTY."
YOU SAID, "HOLD ON TO YOUR FAMILY TREE
'CAUSE YOUR MOTHER WILL CRY FOR ME."

WHY DID YOU RUN?
YOU WERE SO COLORFUL.
YOU WERE SO BEAUTIFUL.

[CHORUS]
IF YOU'RE BORN IN THE FIRE,
YOU WILL BURN.
WE AIN'T BORN ANY WISER.
YOU WILL LEARN.
IT'S GETTING COLD IN THE WATER, MY LOVE,
COLD IN THE WATER.

I WAS BESIDE MYSELF
WHEN YOUR SOUL LEFT THE ROOM
'CAUSE YOU TALKED OF MISTAKES YOU MADE
AND HOW YOU DIDN'T WANT THE SAME FOR ME, NO.
HOLD ON, LOVE.
BE STRONG
'CAUSE THE TEARS ALL STILL FALL AT WILL.

AND HOLD ON TO YOUR FAMILY
'CAUSE THEY ARE SO COLORFUL.

WHY DID YOU RUN?
YOU WERE SO COLORFUL,
YOU WERE SO BEAUTIFUL.

RESTLESS
WATERS

[CHORUS]
IF YOU'RE BORN IN THE FIRE,
YOU WILL BURN.
WE AIN'T BORN ANY WISER.
YOU WILL LEARN.
IT'S GETTING COLD IN THE WATER, MY LOVE,
COLD IN THE WATER.

COLORFUL, COLORFUL, COLORFUL, COLORFUL.

COWARD

I SUPPOSE I SHOULD LET YOU GO.
FEAR IS ALL I'VE EVER KNOWN,
A FEVER OF A HIDDEN MAN.

CAN YOU TELL I'M A HURTING MAN?
CAN'T YOU SEE I WANNA BE YOUR MAN?
THIS IS ALL UNFAIR.

OH, THIS IS MY CALL.
I KNOW THAT YOU KNOW
BECAUSE YOU'VE SEEN MY SOUL.
I WAS A LONELY ONE
IN THE SHADOWS.

SO, I PUT IT ALL IN THIS SONG.
SO, YOU'LL KNOW ONCE AND FOR ALL,
I WAS NEVER HOME
BEFORE YOU.

COURAGE, I NEED IT.
AND GUILT, I FEEL IT
WITH MY HANDS
AND HEART.

[CHORUS]
I'M NOT A COWARD, BUT I DID NOT FIGHT.
BEEN IN THE SHADOWS ALL MY GODDAMN LIFE.
TIME TO HEAR MY CALL.
DO YOU REALLY KNOW ME?
NOW, IT'S TIME FOR ME TO SHED SOME LIGHT.
OUT OF THE SHADOWS, I'LL FIGHT THIS FIGHT.
I CAN NO LONGER LIVE A LIE.

RESTLESS WATERS

HOW COULD I FIGHT FOR YOU?
MY OWN FLESH AND BLOOD IS TIED UP, TOO.
BUT I'LL KEEP HOLDING ON.
IT'S TOO FAMILIAR.

SO, TAKE FROM ME WHAT YOU WILL.
YOU'RE THE ONE THAT I LEAN ON,
AND I'M LEANING STILL.

THOUGH I'D NEVER CALL ME BRAVE,
I'LL NEVER RUN AWAY FROM YOU, NO.

I'VE BEEN LATE TO THE FIGHT,
BUT, DARLING, NOT TONIGHT.
I'LL COME RUNNING, RUNNING FOR YOU.

COURAGE, I NEED IT.
AND GUILT, I FEEL IT
WITH MY HANDS
AND HEART.

[CHORUS]
I'M NOT A COWARD, BUT I DID NOT FIGHT.
BEEN IN THE SHADOWS ALL MY GODDAMN LIFE.
TIME TO HEAR MY CALL.
DO YOU REALLY KNOW ME?
NOW, IT'S TIME FOR ME TO SHED SOME LIGHT.
OUT OF THE SHADOWS, I'LL FIGHT THIS FIGHT.
I CAN NO LONGER LIVE A LIE.

THIS WORLD SEEMS TO OFFER ME NOTHING.
SUPPOSE I SHOULD FADE AWAY,
BUT YOU KNOW I'M NOT RUNNING, RUNNING AWAY.

CAN YOU HEAR MY CALL? IT'S SO LOUD.
CALL ME A COWARD IF YOU LIKE. I'M NOT PROUD.
CAN YOU FEEL MY HEART? IT'S SO COLD.
CALL ME A COWARD IF YOU LIKE. I WON'T FOLD.

CAN YOU HEAR MY CALL? IT'S SO LOUD.
CALL ME A COWARD IF YOU LIKE. I'M NOT PROUD.
CAN YOU FEEL MY HEART? IT'S SO COLD.
CALL ME A COWARD IF YOU LIKE. I WON'T FOLD.

CAN YOU HEAR MY CALL? IT'S SO LOUD.
CALL ME A COWARD IF YOU LIKE. I'M NOT PROUD.
CAN YOU FEEL MY HEART? IT'S SO COLD.
CALL ME A COWARD IF YOU LIKE. I WON'T FOLD.

CAN YOU HEAR MY CALL? IT'S SO LOUD.
CALL ME A COWARD IF YOU LIKE. I'M NOT PROUD.
CAN YOU FEEL MY HEART? IT'S SO COLD.
CALL ME A COWARD IF YOU LIKE. I WON'T FOLD.

SHEETS

SHE DRIVES ME CRAZY. SHE GOES DOWN,
AND FROM THERE, WE HIT THE GROUND.
I WANT THE SHEETS TO MAKE THE SOUND.
OH MY, OH MY.

AND IT'S A PLEASURE TO BE DOWN.
BLOOD BOILED MOVE UPTOWN.
HEAR MY CALL, HEAR MY CALL, YEAH.

ALL MY LOVE IS WAITING.
ALL MY LOVE IS WATCHING.
ALL MY LOVE IS...

WATCHING YOUR BODY MOVE
TO SEE YOU IF YOU APPROVE.
I FEEL THE SWEAT OF YOUR SKIN,
THE TANGLE WITHIN.
YOUR ACTIONS ARE MY DREAMS.

HER AIR BREATHES INTO ME.
MY HEART SYNCS TO THE BEAT.
OUR LUST NOW CONTAINED,
THE BLISSFUL WAR REMAINS.

ALL MY LOVE IS WAITING.
ALL MY LOVE IS WATCHING.
ALL MY LOVE IS...
I'M BREAKING DOWN YOUR WALL.

[CHORUS]
YOU GOT ME WALKING ON WATER, BABY,
BUT DON'T HOLD IT AGAINST ME NOW.
YOU GOT ME BURNING ON FIRE, BABY.
I JUST SIT BACK AND WATCH YOU GO.
FALL AGAINST ME NOW.
FALL,
FALL AGAINST ME NOW.

AM I ALONE?
AM I ALONE?
AM I ALONE?

SHE GOES, "OH, OH."
I HEAR HER, "OH, OH."
SHE SAID, "OH,
AH."

[CHORUS]
YOU GOT ME WALKING ON WATER, BABY,
BUT DON'T HOLD IT AGAINST ME NOW.
YOU GOT ME BURNING ON FIRE, BABY.
I JUST SIT BACK AND WATCH YOU GO.
FALL AGAINST ME NOW.
FALL,
FALL AGAINST ME NOW.

Made in the USA
Coppell, TX
17 April 2020

20203405R00128